T0357998

William McInnes is one of Australia's most popular writers and actors. His books include the bestselling memoirs *A Man's Got to Have a Hobby* and *That'd Be Right*. In 2012 his book *Worse Things Happen at Sea*, co-written with his wife, Sarah Watt, was named the best non-fiction title in the ABIA and Indie Awards.

Also an award-winning actor and best known for his leading roles in *Blue Heelers* and *SeaChange*, William has won two Logies and an AFI Award for Best Actor in the film *Unfinished Sky*. He recently starred in the TV dramas *Deep Water* and *Rake*.

William grew up in Queensland and lives in Melbourne with his two children.

WILLIAM McINNES

the laughing clowns

hachette
AUSTRALIA

First published in Australia and New Zealand in 2012
by Hachette Australia
(an imprint of Hachette Australia Pty Limited)
Level 17, 207 Kent Street, Sydney NSW 2000
www.hachette.com.au

This edition published in 2013

10 9 8 7 6 5 4 3 2 1

A catalogue record for this
book is available from the
National Library of Australia

ISBN: 978 0 7336 3027 9 (pbk.)

Cover design by Christabella Designs
Front cover photograph: Getty Images
Author photograph: Lorrie Graham
Text design and typesetting by Bookhouse, Sydney
Printed and bound in Australia by McPherson's Printing Group

For Anna, Fiona and Maryjeanne

Acknowledgments

A thank you to all at Hachette who helped to get this story out, especially Bernadette 'Batman' Foley, Kate Ballard, Jessica Luca, Karen Ward, designer Christa Moffitt, and the typesetters Simon Paterson and Samantha Collins. Also thanks to Peter Bolton and Clem and Stella.

William McInnes

Preface

This book is a story. In part it's inspired by a peninsula in Moreton Bay called Redcliffe, a place of which I am inordinately fond, a place where I grew up in a family I loved and a place where my wife and I would later take our own family and, in so doing, it became a place that they loved, too.

But this story isn't about Redcliffe Peninsula or the people who live there. It is a story about something that could happen to anybody, a story about losing contact with the people who matter most in your life. And in trying to tell this story I have made events up. So, Ken Kennedy fought in a battle in the Korean War at a place called Papoyong, where a number of his comrades died. There was a remarkable battle fought by Australians in the Korean War at Kapyong, where thirty-two

Australian soldiers died. Ken's battle is based around the real event but I felt that it would show a greater respect to the Australians who served to create a fictitious battle fought by fictitious characters.

This is a story that draws upon some of the places I have lived but it is above all simply a story, a work of fiction, which hopefully will bring a bit of enjoyment to those who read it.

Chapter One

Peter Kennedy was a large man who was remarkably content with himself for somebody who probably shouldn't have been. Not that he was a bad person or a man who didn't care. He was just a middle-aged man who had, in the wider sense, quite a good life. A successful business, a long marriage, three healthy children and a lovely house complete with a friendly dog. He had no real reason to question his life and maybe that was the thing.

Then one night he fell asleep and began to dream. While he dreamed he thought, I hardly ever dream. He wasn't sure what went on in dreams, but he was pretty certain that you shouldn't be able to smell in dreams. And even if you could, then you shouldn't smell what he smelled. Luncheon meat, manufactured meat. A food substance described as being made of meat, including pork. It was actually made from several cuts of pork, lots of salt and a product known as a binder. If he had grown up in New South Wales or Victoria he would have called it 'devon', or 'polony' had he grown up in Western Australia. But he had grown up in Queensland and so it was called luncheon meat. He'd eaten countless school lunches made from this – slices of beige meat dipped in tomato sauce then stuck between two buttered bits of white bread. Tip Top bread.

In his dream he also smelled talcum powder. Yardley's English lavender talcum powder. This, he knew, meant only one thing – that he should wake up. But he didn't – he kept dreaming, and then he was at the little delicatessen section at the Cut-Price store in Margate with his nose pressed against the glass and before him was the display of manufactured meats, the orange smoked cod for Friday's dinner, some bacon and the red kabana sausage that nobody except the neighbours ate with XXXX beer and great Stonehenge-sized slabs of Coon cheese.

He saw a stack of creamy white slices and he knew he would ask, 'Why can't we have chicken loaf for lunch?'

He knew, too, that in the dream he was out with his nanna, who picked him up from primary school every second Friday to say hello and take him shopping. And that included her hand cuffing the back of his head.

'Chicken loaf is too expensive. Don't want to waste it on a little boy like you. Luncheon's the go.'

And English lavender. His nanna always smelled of that, even when she was working on her farm at Caboolture. It was a different smell from Johnson & Johnson's talcum powder in the bathroom cabinet at home; that came in a white plastic container, Yardley's English lavender came in a tin one. He knew that because when he stayed at his nanna's farm he would sometimes be 'Jet Man'. He would strip to his undies, knot a red towel around his neck, put on his nanna's bright yellow bathing cap and sunglasses and, with fists bunched tight in pink washing-up gloves from the sink, he'd fly across the sky with his talcum-powder jet-pack, leaving a trail of smoky talcum powder plumes behind him. He would chase his nanna's chickens. Space chooks.

But in this luncheon dream he wasn't a four-year-old boy but a man nearing fifty, with a hairy belly and bad knees. And he wheezed a lot as he chased the space chooks. But he chased them anyway, until his right knee began to buckle and get the familiar tight feeling and, as he started to fall, his nanna caught him by the back of his head. She actually held him by the yellow bathing cap and swung him.

It may have been a dream but Peter was surprised by how strong his nanna was as she gave him more than just a cuff on the back of his head.

He remembered his nanna saying to her youngest daughter, Peter's mother Mary, that a child like her boy Peter was what happened when you married someone from Pickersgill.

All the while Peter Kennedy smelled devon sausage, and the only thing he saw in his dream was the manufactured meat, sliced up before him. All that meat, including pork and binder and spices, made bleary on account of his nose leaving a smudge on the glass. And he could see that the luncheon meat waiting there hadn't been cut properly, the plastic wrap was still stuck around the slices. He'd have to pull the strands of plastic from his teeth because that's where they always ended up, caught there like old fishing line on a rock.

He realised then that he was grown-up Peter, that big man nearing fifty, puffing in his Jet-Man outfit in the Cut-Price store delicatessen.

And then he woke up, wheezing, flicking his tongue around his mouth. He was lying on his back in bed. And he could still smell luncheon meat.

I'm glad I don't dream that much, he decided.

He turned his head towards his wife next to him. It wasn't often that he lay next to her these days. Last night he had started off on the lounge in the children's old rumpus room and then moved to the bed in the spare room before coming in here to the big bedroom. Sometimes he could stay for a while and then leave before she woke, or he woke her first; he had a tendency to do that.

Occasionally when he woke before her, he would watch her while she slept. Sometimes she would be bunched up in a tangle of hair and bedclothes. This morning he saw her face, cradled by her hair and her hand.

Peter liked looking at Kate like this. They'd been married for twenty-five years. She was a few years younger than him. She had a strong face that could look a bit grumpy when she was thinking, and she was a woman who liked to think a lot. Sometimes he knew she thought long and hard about him. He always found her lovely, but never told her that. He used to. So she knew. He didn't tell her that much any more. Never, really. He'd hold her hand or give her a kiss or a hug, but he should tell her more often.

He kept looking at her. He'd tried to kiss her once when she was asleep, after he'd been watching her, as he was now. But as he leant forward, moving his lips to hers, an odd sound had come from his throat that he later put down to the fact that they had been to her sister's for dinner the night before. Kate's sister had made a runny lamb curry full of spice and oil and yoghurt and served a dessert of tiramisu. It all seemed to congregate in his throat like an Anzac Day parade getting caught in the bends of a street, all the brass bands, bagpipes and trucks of old diggers swirling together in a gargle and then emitting a sudden bang.

Kate had woken up with a fright and yelled.

'I love you,' Peter Kennedy had tried to say, but halfway through the words, the Anzac Day parade got snagged and the noise started up again.

Then she seemed angry and told him never to do that again.

Now he wanted to tell her about his dream, but he didn't. It could wait until later, he didn't want to wake her.

He couldn't quite figure out why he could still smell luncheon meat. He tried to get out of bed as quietly as possible but as he rolled on his side, away from his wife, his stomach rolled and pulled the rest of him with it.

Then he saw Bingo.

The dog looked up at 'the big one'. He knew 'the big one' would give him food sometimes if he barked.

Peter Kennedy smelled dog breath. He smelled luncheon meat and polony and devon. Who would have imagined that dog breath and manufactured meat smelled the same? Maybe he shouldn't have been surprised. He remembered all the times he had eaten luncheon-meat sandwiches. All that meat, including pork. And binder. What *is* binder?

He stared at Bingo and the big labrador panted back at him. The dog seemed to be weighing something up. How long had he been there? Peter realised that he had never spent so much time staring into the eyes of a dog. This was an odd morning.

Bingo let his tongue and his breath reach out and he licked 'the big one's' face.

Peter screamed, 'Bingo!'

He woke his wife; this was worse than the Anzac Day parade. She screamed. And the dog ran. Downstairs his daughter screamed and the two boys yelled. Peter tried to say sorry but he knew that somehow something wasn't quite right. For one thing, he could still smell devon. And talcum powder. Then he remembered. He looked up at Kate, who had got out of bed and was staring at him. She was thinking about him, he could tell by the expression on her face. He thought her so lovely and wanted to say so, but instead he half-smiled and said, 'I have to go to Pickersgill Peninsula.'

•

Peter hadn't been planning on going to Pickersgill until he was interrupted from enjoying his third Alabama cheese dog from the World of Hot Dogs, run by an ex-footballer and his much younger wife in the arcade around the corner, by a phone call.

He was going to let it ring out until he saw that it was Greer Harvson from Titan Developments on the line.

He swapped the hot dog for the phone. 'Greer.'

He wiped his lips, then fed a titbit of onion that had fallen on his desk into his mouth. It was a deft piece of finger-work by a large man and the voice at the other end of the line belonged to a person who had often been surprised by such abilities.

'Are you eating? You're eating, aren't you? Eating on the phone.'

'Yes. I'm eating a . . . salad.'

There was a laugh. 'Yeah, right. What part of the world are you shoving down your throat, Peter?'

'Alabama. Alabama cheese dog.' He could imagine her shaking her head.

'Oh, Peter. Do you think you could stave off a heart attack to do me a favour?'

Greer Harvson was in charge of the Future Implementation section at Titan Developments, one of the largest residential development interests in Australia. Even though she had known Peter Kennedy since university, she could never quite understand the architect who had such a fondness for Alabama cheese dogs, or any food that came from the family of junk.

'Peter, most architects I encounter are very neat – mostly always thin, but if not thin then they are nearly always neat.'

'I'm neat.'

'Peter, architects – the whole *idea* of them is neat.'

He took another bite. 'I'm neat.'

'Utzon; neat Danish purist. Albert Speer; well, he was obviously too neat.'

'Speer was German; he'd love a sausage.'

'Frank Lloyd Wright; total oddity but undeniably neat and ordered. Walter Burley Griffin; anybody who's spent any time in Canberra would know that the man who designed it would be neat.'

'You know there's a World of Hot Dogs in Canberra?'

Greer carried on. 'Even make-believe architects; neat. Mike Brady, he was neat. Even after he had his perm and started wearing the moustache he was neat.'

'Mike Brady liked sausages. What about Charles Bronson?'

'Who? Who does he work for? Is he the guy who designed the supermarket with the pool on the coast?'

'He was an actor – *Death Wish*. He played an architect who became a vigilante after his wife was murdered by street punks. Then he went around shooting people.'

'I bet you any money he was neat. Was he neat?'

Peter Kennedy had to admit that he couldn't remember. 'He wore a scarf a lot when he shot people.'

'There you go. Stylish, like the guy with the horse.'

'Sorry?'

'The guy with the talking horse.'

'*Mister Ed?*'

'No, that *was* the horse.'

'Wilbur. Wilbur Post wasn't a vigilante. And he didn't wear scarves, Greer.'

Greer didn't care. 'That's him, Wilbur with the horse. He was an architect, he was neat. Slicked hair and buttoned shirts. Neat. And he had a bag. All architects like bags – satchels – leather things and pens and accessories. You are the only architect I know who turns up to meetings with a plastic shopping bag and plastic pens.'

'Are you trying to be nice?'

'Not particularly. You're not like Howard Roark.'

'I think that's a good thing.'

'Come on! *Fountainhead*. He was tall and thin and had a hard body from a life of labour.'

'You're on Google, are you?'

'No, Peter, I always remember tall, thin hard-bodied architects.'

'With orange hair and a perm?'

'Howard Roark didn't have a perm.'

'Mike Brady did.'

'Peter, I'm just saying you don't strike me as the sort of person I usually associate with architects. But then you don't really design any more, do you?'

That was true.

'Greer, what do you want?'

'I want a favour.'

'Aren't you supposed to say "need"?'

'No, not really; that's only for neat architects. I want something.'

Something. He could guess what that might be and it wouldn't be anything to do with what he could offer as an architect. More likely his role as a conceptual development consultant. He didn't really design for Titan Developments, he conceptualised. He had given them a concept for the efficient use of space some years back and they had dubbed it 'The Kennedy Effect'.

Peter had come up with a clever way to squeeze more usable space from some tight building sites. It didn't work everywhere, but when height restrictions were the sole issue in medium- to high-density buildings it worked perfectly. If you managed to trim, say, fifteen centimetres off the floor to ceiling height of each level in a high-rise development with a set height, and then corkscrewed the apartments on top of each other, with each apartment slightly larger in area than the one below it, a pleasing result could be obtained with an increase in the individual unit capacity. Or, in other words, more rooms could be squeezed into a fixed space. The revolving design was a particular and pleasing shape that won some acclaim for the company.

Somebody in Marketing had called it dynamic. Peter's father had called it a dried dog turd. Whether or not it was pleasing was another thing, but it was dynamic enough to win a few awards.

So that was how Peter worked these days, offering his services as Development Consultant and Conceptualist. He hadn't come up with that title, the marketing adviser had. A thin man with a tight ponytail, a narrow, trimmed moustache, Buddy Holly glasses and a mole on his chin that Peter was pretty sure was a stuck-on beauty spot. Peter had noticed how it moved occasionally. He had listened to Moving Mole Man and accepted his suggestion to become a Conceptualist Consultant. In reality, though, he was a fixer; someone who found potential problems that might get in the way of a development and then made them go away. 'Circumnavigating them,' as Moving Mole Man had put it. A fixer.

He had been very successful. His friend was usually asbestos; the number of heritage buildings that had been razed on his recommendation because of asbestos was quite embarrassing. He wasn't necessarily proud of what he did but he wasn't ashamed either. He was reasonably successful and liked it when his work took his mind off home.

'Okay,' he said to Greer, and had another bite of his Alabama.

'I want you to do this favour for us. That town you grew up in –'

'Pickersgill Peninsula.'

'Jesus, stop eating. Yes, Pickersgill Peninsula. There's a very strong development possibility there, very strong.'

'You've been to Pickersgill, Greer. Did you like it?'

There was a pause.

'There's a very strong development possibility there.'

'You didn't like it, did you?'

'Peter . . .'

'Did you?'

'Peter, I always wanted to know where Toranas go to die.'

He laughed, and nearly choked on his Alabama.

Greer ploughed on. 'It's Crown land but with municipal amalgamation on the cards up there, there's a good chance it could swing open.'

'Where is it?'

'It's the showgrounds. Thirty hectares of under-developed land, forty k's from the country's third-largest city in the biggest growth corridor on the east coast.'

Peter stopped chewing. 'Why would I go up there?' He knew very well why he *wouldn't*.

'Peter, you know what we think of you; we know what we can do with this opportunity. We want you to go there and see if it's possible to use this place as a layered development.' She paused. 'Peter?'

'Yes.'

'We want to pay you a large amount of money to do this. We want you to go to the Torana graveyard and see if there is any possible reason why this can't happen.'

'When?'

'This week. Just for the rest of the week. Four days . . . Maybe you can take the family?'

Peter said nothing.

'And Peter, nobody knows why you're there, okay?'

'Why can't I tell anyone?'

'Because we don't want to complicate things. It's just sounding things out, having a look-see, and you're almost a local. Visit your mum and dad. Go to the show. There'll be lots of hot dogs and your sort of food there.'

He didn't say anything. Greer's people had done their work.

'Peter?'

He said nothing.

'Peter.'

He didn't need the money. But the money would be a large sum. Her voice was harder now, and he was glad that she had decided to ring him and hadn't asked to meet instead.

'Yes,' he said. 'Yes, that'll be all right.'

'Good. Good, Peter.' And she hung up.

He put his phone down, closed his eyes for a moment and then opened them to stare at his desk and what was left of his chewed Alabama cheese dog.

•

'Pickersgill Peninsula.'

'Pickersgill Peninsula?' repeated Kate Kennedy. 'You're going to Pickersgill?'

Peter could see she was thinking about him.

'When were you going to tell me?'

Peter said nothing. He could see Bingo in the back-yard, sitting on his hind legs. It must be cold out there, he thought. But Bingo seemed oblivious and stared through the drizzle at him.

'When were you going to tell me you were going away?' Kate asked again.

'I only found out yesterday.'

'Why didn't you tell me? We were going to talk, Peter. Try to sort things out.'

The talk. His wife had wanted to talk about things. About them. The two of them. Kate and Peter. He'd known this, and he hadn't forgotten and he knew that Kate knew he hadn't forgotten. But he didn't want to talk about the marriage. Relationship. Whatever it was she had wanted to talk about. They'd had friends who'd had counselling. All that had happened was that the husband had grown a ponytail and started wearing clothes that a teenager might wear. No, Peter didn't want to talk.

They lived in a lovely house in a lovely suburb of Melbourne and had three lovely children. The twin boys, Matthew and Philip, were at university and Eleanor was in her last year of high school. Their life was . . . lovely.

But Kate still wanted to talk. Of course Peter had said he wanted to talk to her, too; he *would* say that. But he knew as soon as Greer had asked him to visit Pickersgill that he would go.

'Who's going to Pickersgill Peninsula?' said Eleanor. She was sitting at the big table eating breakfast.

'Your father is, apparently.'

'Why?'

'Work. Development assessment.'

'Good one, Dad,' Matthew called out from the other room.

Eleanor stopped eating her cereal and asked, 'Did he forget about the father–daughter night at school?'

'Yes, he forgot,' said Kate.

They talked about him as if he wasn't there.

'It's work.'

'Hurry up and get your bags, Ellie. Do you boys want a lift?' Kate asked.

Matthew said he'd walk and the other twin, Philip, yelled from down the hall something that nobody understood.

Maybe Peter should tell Kate that he didn't really want to go, but that it seemed easier to be away.

'It's work,' he said again.

'Yes, Peter,' Kate said, looking as if she couldn't be bothered talking to him any more. 'I know.'

Philip appeared in the doorway. He wasn't yelling now, but smiling. 'Yeah, I'd love a lift.'

'Ellie has to go now so you'd better be quick.' And, almost as an afterthought, Kate said, 'You'd better say goodbye to your father, too. He's going to Queensland for a week.'

'What? Going where, Dad?' asked Philip.

Ellie picked up her bag and pulled at her hair. 'He's going to Pickersgill.'

'Planet Pickersgill! Okay.'

Matthew walked in and stood with his brother and sister. 'Don't worry, Ellie, it's not only you; he didn't make our father–son night either.'

'It's work!' Philip said. 'What are you going to pull down this time, Dad?'

'"The Kennedy Effect",' Matthew said, and laughed.

Ellie turned to her father. 'Can you do my collar, please?'

She stood with her back to him and he bent down and pulled out her school uniform collar gently and then neatly folded it over her blazer. She smiled and gave him a quick kiss. 'Say hello to Nanna and Pop Ken.'

With that, Peter's children walked out together and his wife came back and sighed, then gave a shrug of her shoulders. 'Call us. The kids will like it. Ellie can tell you about the father–daughter night.'

Peter sat down as his family disappeared down the hall and out of the house. Alone at the big table, he looked out into the backyard and at his dog, who sat watching him with unblinking brown eyes.

'It's work.'

Bingo lifted himself off his haunches and stood up.

'You'll miss me, won't you, mate?'

But by then Bingo had turned away and was busy licking his balls.

Chapter Two

Peter Kennedy was in the Qantas lounge waiting for his flight to be called. He had come here many times and, as was his habit, had walked in, put his bag down by a table and gone straight over to the food bar.

He scanned the selection of cold-cut meats and cheese, wanting to make sure he couldn't see any luncheon meat or devon or polony. Not that he'd ever seen any here before, but he wanted to be sure. Then he heaped a mixture of as much as he could fit on the small plate.

The food reminded him of Boxing Day at his nanna's place in Caboolture, with its heavy brown sideboard that usually held the adult drinks and the family photos. On Boxing Day it would be covered with bits and pieces of food served on her good crockery. Slices of cheese and ham, tomatoes, celery, lettuce, sliced beetroot on platters and two bowls of food he always found quite odd together – one bowl was filled with chocolates called TV Mix and the other with green and red pickled onions. 'Scallions', that's what his nanna had called them.

'Go easy on the scallions,' she'd say, then she would turn and say to his parents, 'He's scoffing all the scallions *and* he's got the TV Mix!'

This accusation, accompanied by a pointed finger, made Peter think of Madame Defarge. He'd taken some TV Mix and a handful of scallions and Nanna would tug at his collar. 'Don't scoff the scallions.'

Madame Defarge was the revolutionary from *A Tale of Two Cities*, who'd knit in the shadow of the guillotine and who had it in for the Marquis St Evrémonde. In the book and film she was tall and strong and scary. The first time Peter saw the film was, of all days, on Boxing Day. He sat with his family watching it on the television. They drank sweet Golden Circle orange cordial and helped themselves to TV Mix and the odd scallion on the side. Like his nanna, Madame Defarge would eat scallions by the handful on the sly. His nanna took a few and then wanted to know why anyone thought it would be a good idea to show a film on Boxing Day about a lot of French people getting their heads chopped off.

'Maybe they didn't get the presents they wanted,' somebody muttered.

Peter worked out it was his father, because all his uncles, his mum's brothers, laughed.

Nanna stiffened and Peter heard his father's voice: 'Very happy with my business socks.'

'Walking socks, Kenny, walking socks,' said his nanna, and a scallion dropped from her fingers onto the carpet near her dog, Errol, a mongrel she had named after Errol Flynn.

Peter had seen the scallion drop and watched it from the corner of his eye without turning his head. Was it a scallion or perhaps a chocolate sultana from the TV Mix? He wasn't sure. His hand was about to move but then, on the screen, Madame Defarge pointed towards him. 'Tell the wind and fire where to stop – but not me!' She pointed out with a fury that froze his hand and then he heard Nanna.

'Leave the scallion for Errol, it's been on the ground too long.'

His nanna was standing there above him as he sat on the floor; she was tall and strong. And scary.

Not that his nanna was a revolutionary. She said she voted for the Country Party long after they became the Nationals, and she would never wear trousers out in public. But she was tall and strong and had a thing about scallions. And talcum powder and her chooks. She didn't need the guillotine, she was scary as. 'Scary as'? Why think like that? 'Scary as.' Kids' talk.

In the Qantas lounge Peter poked his fork at the pickled onions on his plate. They rested on a bed of some sort of salami. The salami reminded him a little of lino flooring. But it was the pickled onions that caught Peter's attention. The scallions. Nanna.

'Silly old cow,' he muttered.

And from somewhere he smelled the faintest trace of talcum powder. He shook himself then heaved down onto a seat that was in a small nest of table and chairs.

Near him sat three people. A woman texting on her iPhone and two fellows in crumpled suits. Their plane must have been delayed because the two crumpled suits had made use of the bar. The four of them all waited, texted, sipped and ate. And cast a glance or two towards the TV.

Suddenly, a politician, a ten-gallon-hat-wearing Bob Katter, materialised like some character from an episode of *I Dream of Jeannie*.

Now there was a show, thought Peter. An astronaut finds a bottle on a deserted island and it contains a genie that grants him any wish. He would only watch it on the odd afternoon after school, but he was always slightly taken aback by it. A man in a military uniform would rub a bottle furiously and out from a stream of white smoke would pop a semi-naked woman, who bowed and called him 'Master'. Talk about classic comedy.

Here in the airport lounge, though, somebody had rubbed the wrong bottle, for instead of a half-naked woman out popped Ten-gallon Bob; all that was missing was a *boing* sound effect.

Bob's voice blared out about 'new paradigms'. He said it several times.

They all watched the talking ten-gallon hat. Another 'paradigm'.

'It's like an ad for a pain reliever: take two paradigms and a glass of water to soothe your headache. If pain persists see your local independent,' said Crumpled Suit One.

'God,' said Crumpled Suit Two. 'We're the laughing stock of the world.'

The other man nodded and said as he finished his drink, 'Bloody Queenslanders.'

Crumpled Suit Two got up to get fresh drinks.

Then somebody somewhere must have rubbed another bottle, for Ten-gallon disappeared from the screen and was replaced by, of all things, half-naked contestants from the Miss Universe quest.

'That's more like it,' said Crumpled Suit One.

At first, Peter thought the crumpled suit was saying it to himself, thinking out loud. But then he realised that the man was speaking to him, was nodding at him with a half-smile.

Peter looked up at the screen. Young women wearing more make-up than a badly bogged-up Torana stalked awkwardly around on high heels, smiling and grimacing in the manner beauty quests demand.

'Very nice,' said Crumpled Suit One, glancing across at the woman on the iPhone. She didn't do anything except look down at it, but she paused in her texting just long enough for Peter to suspect she knew what the crumpled suit had said.

Peter put a scallion, a piece of salami and something crunchy in his mouth. On the screen contestants posed, almost like store mannequins with Riddler-esque smiles. He suddenly realised he should tell his daughter that under no circumstances should she ever wear the combination of bikini and stilettos. Never, at any time in her life. And, just to be sure, he thought he should tell his sons, too. Then he looked back at the crumpled suits, who were transfixed by the smiling Toranas on the screen.

'Yeah,' said Crumpled Suit One, 'that mouth will make her a lot of money.'

And the other suit giggled.

Peter ate and wondered what it was the two men did for a living. He could see they both wore wedding rings. It didn't really matter. But they laughed a little too loudly when some American voice from the screen said that a contestant had 'an interest in health; in fact the health section is the first thing she reads in a newspaper'.

'Love that; she reads a newspaper – beautiful *and* smart.'

'Yeah, that mouth . . .'

The woman with the phone let out a sigh.

Peter stopped chewing. He thought of his wife and his daughter and his sons and these men. And the women on the screen in the shoes by Chinese Laundry and bikinis. He thought of Toranas and Madame Defarge. He felt odd. Odd because he suddenly felt he should say something. Like how those two crumpled suits had made four people sitting in a lounge together strangers. Marginalised. How they had let him join their little gang, but excluded the woman with the iPhone.

I should tell them, he decided, to pull their heads in. But then they were just being crumpled suits in a lounge waiting to go back to their homes, their families. One was balding and had pockmarks on his face, the other had a square sort of head, a ginger beard and a very large nose. They were a couple of blokes, two nondescript men who could sit and pass the time of day in an airport lounge, talking about the physical appearance of young women in bathing suits.

Four people sat together in the lounge, but they had stopped being four people waiting for a plane. Instead, in a few seconds, one of them had become eye candy. And maybe not even good eye candy. Not with a mouth that could make money.

Peter didn't necessarily mind girls wandering around in togs with bad hair and Torana make-up. Well, he hadn't up until then. He glanced at the woman with the iPhone; she had gone back to texting. She was going about her business and the women on the screen had turned into the mines of Western Australia.

Big trucks on the TV carried vast amounts of dirt away and, as they did, Peter started to doze off and remembered that he'd forgotten to book a rental car. He thought of Toranas again. And Pickersgill. And for no reason he could think of he saw Madame Defarge, standing in the Qantas lounge, looming over the crumpled suits and the iPhone woman. On her heaving breast, instead of the revolutionary tricolour was a rosette with 'Vote One, The Country Party' and a photo of a scowling Jack McEwen. Her finger stretched out towards him as she held a bowl before her with her other strong arm. The bowl was filled with scallions, TV Mix and the heads of a few run-of-the-mill aristocrats. And thin slices of luncheon meat.

'You, Jacques!' she boomed. 'What is "binder"?'

Peter woke with a start and coughed. Madame Defarge had disappeared.

The two crumpled suits and the woman with the iPhone turned to him.

'Luncheon meat,' he croaked.

•

Airports in big cities are a little like Kmarts; they are the same the world over. Wherever you may find yourself, if you apply the Kmart blueprint of floor layout, somehow, through instinct and shared experience, you'll know exactly where to go and how to navigate your way around.

Brisbane airport is like that; shuffle off the plane and into the terminal and you know exactly where you're headed. The difference, of course, is with the locals who inhabit the city in which the terminal squats.

If you had blindfolded someone so the whole flight had been a dark nothing, then let them loose at the mouth of the passenger arm that opens into the terminal, Peter thought, they would know they were in Brisbane.

He couldn't quite put his finger on it, but it felt almost like being in an emergency evacuation centre during some sort of natural disaster. Groups of people lounged or slumped in seats wearing clothes that they had thrown on before they escaped from whatever calamity had befallen them. Nobody, he decided, would ever have considered wearing these sorts of clothes if they had had time to dress properly. T-shirts with brewer's names across them and back-to-front baseball caps and shorts. Loose-fitting shifts or clinging leggings, and clothes that seemed to render their wearers shapeless.

It was July, the air was warm. Peter could never get over that first sweep of warm air closing in around him when he arrived in Brisbane. It wasn't a bad thing, just something he felt he should have grown used to. He saw a few people wearing jumpers or hoodies here and there, but most people were happy to dress in their evacuation-centre gear. The only difference from an evacuation-centre crowd was that nobody appeared concerned in any way. There were no hapless individuals in tears or shock; this crowd couldn't have given a stuff about whatever had happened to delay them, they were content to sit. And stare. There were some who were mesmerised by the monitors, the flickering arrivals and departures screens blinking back at them, but you'd see them in any airport.

Not everybody, to be fair, was dressed in the evacuation-centre style, but Peter Kennedy still felt that he stood out like a sore thumb as he loped along in his chinos and loafers and heavy winter clothes.

I used to be one of you, he thought, one of you.

He saw one man; a man standing near the car rental desk wearing sandals and a striped cotton shirt tucked into a pair of Ruggers. Ruggers: elastic-waisted cotton drill shorts with shallow pockets on either side. The Stubbies of the new millennium, Peter had once heard them described by his father.

The man wore steel-rimmed glasses and a part ploughed through the middle of his freckled head. He was holding a mobile phone, which seemed a bit out of place as he wasn't favouring the evacuation-centre gear but had instead gone for a 1950s church-fete stall volunteer's outfit. He held the phone out and studied it like a botanist looking at some unknown flora. He was mumbling, half-attempting to read a text. 'Plane . . . Plane . . . What does that say? "Plane late leaving, check –" Oh dear! How, dear? And I've just gone and parked the car.'

Peter Kennedy ignored him and asked the large woman behind the desk if any cars were available.

'Oh, yeah; you'll be lucky, champ,' said the man with the phone. He drew out 'you'll' like it had forty syllables in it.

Peter Kennedy turned to Church Fete '57. 'Sorry?'

'Yoooooouuu'll be lucky, champ! Won't he? Hmm?' he repeated, turning to the woman behind the counter.

The woman giggled, then bit her lip. 'We'll see. Been a rush on.' Her voice rose at the end of each sentence. 'Are you a Valued Customer member?'

Peter Kennedy said he was.

'Let's see . . .'

'Oh, then you might be right then. Not like that German bloke,' said Church Fete '57.

Peter passed over his Valued Customer membership card and the woman smiled. Not far from them, a grumpy looking blond man in brand-new hiking gear was frowning at him.

Peter Kennedy took this to be the German man. He wondered if the man had travelled in that outfit, a patchwork of green-and-khaki material connected with zips. Zips everywhere. He looked like something out of Frankenstein's surgery; the monster in a blond wig goes cross-country.

The woman smiled at Peter. 'You're in luck – we do have a Valued Customer vehicle for you. It's a Getz; I'm afraid that's the best we can do.'

'A Getz. A tiny little car.'

'Yes. And it's red.'

'A red Getz.'

'That's it. Won't make it any bigger but red ones always go faster.'

Peter Kennedy smiled and nodded his thanks.

'Well done, champ. Valued Customer, eh?' Church Fete '57 whistled, before going back to his phone. 'Arriving . . . late. I could have told you that. Oh, hello, helloooooo . . .'

Peter Kennedy glanced up from signing the rental papers to see the German man striding up to the counter. He towered over them, and as he loomed there, staring down, he began to unzip various pockets, all the while shifting his gaze between Peter and the woman behind the desk.

'Somebody's not happy,' said Church Fete '57.

'G'day,' said Peter Kennedy.

The big German man zipped and unzipped until he found what he was looking for – a wallet.

The woman behind the desk smiled pleasantly. 'Yes, sir?'

Von Zip stared at Peter and Church Fete '57 again and then spoke to the woman in the highest voice Peter had ever heard coming from a human being that size. He sounded like he'd inhaled a hundred helium balloons and spoke in the broadest Yorkshire accent he'd heard since *All Creatures Great and Small* was last screened.

'And woy doooose he git it?' he said with such intensity that Peter couldn't help but laugh.

Church Fete '57 coughed a little.

'You see, sir, this gentleman is a Valued Customer member and so, according to our company policy, he has access to additional vehicles.'

'Really,' said the former Von Zip, now named by Peter *All Creatures Great and Small*.

The woman smiled and Peter half-shrugged his shoulders in apology.

'Wull then, Mr Valued Customer, have a fooking great trip in your little car.' And he picked up his wallet, zipped and unzipped some pockets and stalked off.

The large woman behind the desk sighed. 'Shame.'

'Well, he wasn't a German. Didn't he look like one? What a funny thing. His voice,' babbled Church Fete Man.

Peter Kennedy looked back at Mr '57 and suddenly realised that he would have been the same age, or maybe even younger than himself.

'What a funny old day,' said Church Fete '57.

Peter half-smiled and walked off to find his car. It was the only one left in the waiting bays and it was certainly red. And very small.

He squeezed himself in and his knees bunched up, pushing his stomach into his chest. He felt for the slide bar underneath his seat, fiddled a bit, shot back all of a couple of inches and let out a noise.

There are many ways to remind yourself that you are getting on in years, of prompting a gentle realisation that time's passing. There are seemingly random bodily noises corresponding to movement; when rising from a chair or getting out of a car you might hear a sigh, a grunt or an *Ooooo* sound, only to look around to see who is making the sound and realise it's you.

The sound Peter emitted now was on the more energetic side of the involuntary-noise ledger, a prolonged *Oh* with a hump in the middle and a sharp end that could not be mistaken for anything conversational, as in, 'Oh, really?' It was the sound of a man being caught unawares. He sat and panted with effort. He looked down at the gearstick; a manual. It had been years since he'd driven a manual. Well, it would only be for a few days.

He started the car and kangaroo-hopped over a series of speed bumps, scraping the bottom of his Getz. As he turned onto the arterial road that led away from the terminal, he crunched the gears and half-stalled, in front of Mr *All Creatures Great and Small*, standing there zipping and unzipping his pockets for no apparent reason.

'What a funny old day,' he said to himself, and he nearly laughed.

•

It was late afternoon and Peter was familiar enough with Brisbane to know that the traffic would be beginning to congeal on the motorway to the north and he knew that somewhere along the route there would be road works or maybe even a new road that would lead nowhere. The problem was the signage. Roads would be built with no accompanying directions, or with signs that were helpfully hidden from obvious view.

As a result of this, Peter found himself shouting quite a lot when in Brisbane – not at other drivers but at the gods of bad signage. More involuntary howling moments. Once, haring along Breakfast Creek Road, he had followed a merge sign and disappeared down a tunnel, screaming all the way into its depths, like some pilot diving in to attack the guns in a bad war film. Plummeting into the dark he saw a woman out of the corner of his eye convulsing in laughter at him from the passenger seat of a car in the next lane.

Speeding along with the tunnel side lights blurring into what seemed like the opening titles of an old *Dr Who* episode he emerged not on some intergalactic bad set, but somewhere infinitely more worrying – the other side of the bay. Attempting to find his way back, he came across his very favourite piece of road signage-cum-life advice, the ubiquitous 'Wrong Way Go Back'. Peter saw more of those signs in Queensland than anywhere else; big green luminescent hoardings blaring at people about the mistakes they had made.

Concrete flyovers and ramps shot this way and that from the airport like some mini version of a scene from a *Looney Tunes* cartoon, but he knew the way to Pickersgill Peninsula well enough. Sort of; there were a few odd moments when the roadway inexplicably narrowed and lanes disappeared, making the infrastructure here about as generous as a scrape of butter on boarding-house toast.

He settled into crunching the gears and slotting into the long line of traffic that was driving through the wetlands that surrounded the airport. Here, you always had the sense that it wouldn't take long for the vegetation to take over from the concrete, for the dark green grass and plants to creep along and then over, around and under the road.

The big man in the little red Getz rolled along. Red Getz; it sounded like a spokesman for the Pentagon or some international expert you might see via satellite on a late-night current affairs show. All lantern-jawed and buzz-cut, bristling with American certainty.

Peter smiled and made poor Red squeal as he went from fourth to second a little too quickly. He considered turning on the radio, but even though Red was simple enough, trying to work out which amongst the little black buttons was the tuner, on/off button and volume control soon made the exercise beyond him; all Peter could manage was a half-tuned FM station. So he was marooned without the distraction of noise from the tiny radio.

He scanned the other cars and their drivers. None of us is going anywhere in a hurry, he realised, so it's a chance for us to get acquainted with each other. He saw that the guy in the high-sitting tradie ute behind him wasn't happy, wasn't happy at all. He, Peter Kennedy, and a couple of thousand other people in his way, were heading north towards the Sunshine

Coast on a Tuesday afternoon. Very slowly. Peter was sorry he'd made the guy in the ute unhappy; he'd meant to indicate a lane change but had turned on the windscreen wipers instead – a dead giveaway about his usual driving preference. He was a Volvo driver undercover in a Pentagon Spokesman. He was doing a good job of blowing Red's cover. He had no idea why European cars have the indicator and windscreen wipers reversed. He supposed to some it's European styling; to others it's an annoyance. One of Greer's neat architects might be able to find a reason. Is there a preferred side on which to indicate? You only dwell on such fundamentally important matters when you are stuck in traffic.

Bearded Guy, with his tradie tools festooning his ute like decorations on a Christmas tree, was clearly a serious bloke and indeed a serious driver, who had to put up with the likes of Red.

Peter tried an apologetic wave and was greeted with a contemptuously dismissive shake of the head. This made him laugh. At least he'd *tried* to indicate; not like the P-plater in a shiny blue bubble car, who was on the phone and peering into the mirror to adjust her make-up and hair. She wore sunglasses the size of the Parkes radio telescope and the colour of her hair was as natural as polyester, Peter thought. She drifted in and out of lanes and then nearly ran into Red, but as everyone was going at a snail's pace it wasn't that much of a problem. Still, he gave what he hoped was a friendly warning toot, but a big middle-aged man in a little red car elicits a strange response. The P-plater was mouthing words at Peter, to the effect of him being most definitely in the wrong.

Never mind, Peter decided, as an imperious white Range Rover rolled past, filled with a lugubrious-looking family, who stared out like myopic fish watching the world from their aquarium. One of the kids gazed out the window and slowly picked his nose.

Not far away there was a friendly Commodore with a couple howling helplessly with laughter and a woman in a Peugeot belting out a song at the top of her lungs. Peter Kennedy couldn't hear her, but she was going for it, even adding a few head thrusts for good measure. A man in a Falcon was doing the same thing and banging his steering wheel. All reassuringly odd, all of them in their own little metal-and-glass bubbles, moving slowly along.

Peter sat and cast his eyes over the flowing south-bound traffic.

There're no Toranas, he thought. And he looked up at the Range Rover and the kid still picking his nose. Nobody seemed to be talking to anyone else in the aquarium so why *wouldn't* the boy pick his nose?

Peter was sure some marketing genius somewhere had an idea that the car you choose to drive says something about you. What do those big aquariums on wheels say about their drivers?

Once, Mr Don Dixon, father of Wayne Dixon, Peter's childhood friend, had given Peter a lift in the Dixon family Holden Premier to a footy game. Very clean, it smelled of air freshener, and the back seat was covered in a plastic-bubble seat-protector. Peter had asked why the seat was covered and the kindly, if rather fastidious, parent had said with a smile, 'We love our Holden and we don't want your footy dirt rubbing off on the seat.'

No, Peter Kennedy didn't know if the car you drive says anything about you, but as he considered the P-plater in front he decided that the stickers you choose to decorate it with most certainly do.

Across this bumper were two stickers: 'Bad Girl' and 'There's a hot bitch in here'.

There was a time in Peter's life when stickers had been a precious commodity and it didn't matter if they were freebies – he had considered them gold. He could never quite fathom why his father had yelled at him to get that bloody crap off his truck when, as a Father's Day gift when he was about ten, Peter had placed an 'I like Swipe' cleaning-liquid sticker on his father's truck window. He was more embarrassed than upset and to be fair, Peter had only given his father the sticker because he hadn't bought him a present. He knew that his sister Pearl had made a cake, but not leaving it there she had gone and knitted a maroon-and-white Pickersgill team beanie for their dad. His mother had given Peter the 'I like Swipe' sticker after a visit from the loud woman from down the road who flogged Swipe cleaning products.

Peter had stood there, staring up at his father in his new beanie as he pointed at the sticker. He heard his mother's voice calling softly to her husband, 'Ken! Kenny, have a look at it, will you?'

His father had scowled and loitered at the truck window with his wife. Peter heard his mother read what was printed on the sticker. '"I like Swipe",' and then she read what was written in Texta, in Peter's ten-year-old hand, '"But I love my Dad".'

His father walked back to him and put his hand gently down on his son's head. 'Well, maybe we can keep it on for a bit.'

And then Peter had turned to his sister. She yelled with a mixture of indignation and outrage, 'It's only Texta! It's only Texta!'

Their mother told her to shush, that that wasn't the point, and after his mum had walked away Peter had smiled sweetly back at his sister.

Chapter Three

Now, in the traffic, Peter checked in his rear-view mirror and saw the tradie with the beard. He imagined putting an 'I like Swipe' sticker on his window. He laughed and Tradie Beard shook his head. That's what his sister had done.

These days, car stickers are usually trying to be humorous: 'Watch out for the idiot behind me!' The tapping man in the Falcon had that one. Or, 'All men are idiots, I married their King', like the one on the Peugeot. But there's nothing like political stickers; bumper democracy: 'I Vote Green because I care' was attached to a nondescript white Toyota Camry two lanes over.

Nothing self-righteous about that, is there? Of course only Green voters care; the rest of us are selfish unthinking buffoons, thought Peter Kennedy. Then he remembered the 'I hunt, I fish, I vote' sticker he'd seen; the modern man's equivalent to Descartes' 'I think therefore I am.' He had seen that the other day on a freeway in Melbourne.

Then, before him now, a beauty; a little beige car, whose driver had entered from a side bay with a friendly wave of thanks to Peter and Red. 'If you can read this, thank a teacher. If you can read it in English, thank a solider.'

He read it twice. He could have read it again if he'd wanted to – the traffic moved so slowly – but he didn't.

On a station wagon was the classic 'Baby on Board' sticker. Why does the baby get a sticker? What about the rest of us? Peter wondered. 'Vaguely happy, a few disappointments but nonetheless a sort of content middle-aged man on board.' Alongside that declaration was one with a school emblem: 'We're a Grammar Family'.

Aspirational bragging or school spirit at work? It made Peter pine for 'I like Swipe'. 'I Like Swipe High.' There's an idea. His sons and daughter had gone to schools that delivered such stickers as a reward for the payment of fees. First his sons had put one from their school on his car, then Ellie had covered it with her school emblem and then, somebody – Peter never knew who – had stuck a black square of cloth tape on top of both. When the car had been traded in for a newer model the salesperson, noticing the rear-window sticker, had said in all seriousness, 'Nice to see a little North Fitzroy inner-city mystique on an Eastern Suburbs beast.'

The Range Rover had crept on and there was a school sticker on its bumper, but more noticeable were the six little 'My Family' figures that adorned the back window, showing the make up of the car's occupants.

This sticker struck Peter as creepy and a bit naff. He saw a smiling dad with glasses and a fishing rod, a smiling mum with a saucepan and a computer, a smiling son with a tennis racquet, a smiling daughter with a hockey stick, another smiling son with a skateboard, and a dog with a bone. Nobody picking his or her nose. Nobody staring out, mouth open, not talking.

Maybe honesty wasn't the point of the stickers. But what *was* the point? Peter wondered. To let the world know the occupants were a happy family unit? Six figures with no correlation to what he had seen in the aquarium.

The car in front had the same make up as his family. He thought back to that morning around the table, their talking about him as if he hadn't been there. He thought of his wife, the expression on her face. And then he thought of his daughter. He knew he'd run away by coming here, but it would only be for a few days, and it was work. There'd be time enough for talk when he got back.

He saw a shadow of himself reflected in the window. He hadn't forgotten about the father–daughter night, he had wanted to get away. So it wasn't really the same as with the twins; he'd simply forgotten about their father–son nights. Well, no; he'd only forgotten one of their nights, the Little Twin's.

The twins. Big Twin and Little Twin. They were as close to being identical without being identical; two large young men, but one an inch shorter than the other. So, instead of being called Matthew and Philip, they were referred to as Big Twin and Little Twin, even at school.

Both the schools his children attended organised a 'retreat' night, where father and child would listen to a few people speak and then sit down together and exchange letters they had written about what they meant to each other. It was, in the words of a flyer that Peter had found on the table at home, 'An affirmation of love between parent and child.'

He'd asked his sons if it was important and they had both said, 'No, not really. Two days off school and a night with you.' Then they had burst out laughing, wanting to know what he would write.

'Will you get someone from the office to do it?' And 'Don't download a template from the internet like Marco's dad did. How weak was that? He couldn't even come up with something original to say about Marco!'

Peter laughed a little. He felt a twinge of sympathy for Marco's father; it was not easy to know what to write for such an occasion.

'The poor sod probably wanted to do the right thing. The internet, boys; it can be a trap for young players.'

'Oh, come on, Dad; he could have tried – it's like writing a birthday card or something.'

'But if a bloke treats it like that and just dashes something off, then he's the world's worst.'

'Yeah, but the *internet*!'

'Well, I'll tell you this for nothing –'

'I love it when you talk like a Queenslander, Dad.'

'Yeah, like Pop.'

'Look, I'll tell you this: not much is original and almost all is derivative. So if this guy Mark's dad –'

'Marco.'

'Marco's dad. If this guy had found some other words that could communicate the way he felt then what's wrong with that?'

'You're going to get it off the net, aren't you?'

'No!'

'He is.'

'No, I'm not!'

'Dad, he didn't even change the way it was written.'

'What do you mean?'

'Some guy from New York wrote it and so it was all about "rootin' for the Yankees" and hot dogs and Central Park. And *"Mom"*! *"Mom!"* *"Mom* really *luurves* you".'

Peter Kennedy winced a little. That *was* weak.

'Don't forget,' said the Big Twin.

And he hadn't. He hadn't forgotten Big Twin's meeting. Little Twin hadn't been as fortunate. His meeting had been on another night. This was so it would be a more individual experience. Apparently the school's Head of Faith had suggested it and Kate had agreed. She must have told him – she told Peter most things – but . . . But what?

Peter couldn't remember, he thought he must have been at work or the Little Twin had been sick or had football training. Or something. When Kate had phoned to remind him it was too late, his meeting was just beginning. He had said he was sorry and then heard something that is known to most men like Peter Kennedy, something that sends a shiver of alarm along the spine to that tiny part of the brain that instigates total meaningless action. It was The Pause. Nothing quite like it for putting the wind up a man. It would usually come about in response to a run-of-the-mill apology. 'Sorry, the meeting's started and I can't get out.'

The Pause.

Weigh the pause. Was she collecting her thoughts, trying to register what he'd said, maybe waiting for him to say something else? Maybe she just hadn't heard. The worst thing you could do was to jump in too soon with an admission that you'd stuffed up. No urgent blurting of, 'Kate, oh Kate, I'm so sorry,' would lessen the strength of the pause. But Peter hadn't let the pause continue into a silence; he had gone in with, 'Are you there? Hello?'

That jaunty business-bloke question, meaning, *Oh, must have had a drop-out but now I can hear you, so let's sort out your problem.* That 'Are you there? Hello?'

All guns blazed. He was hit amidships and began to take on water. 'Listen, I'll shoot something off to the school and he'll get my letter and he can bring it home and I'll read it with him tonight.'

'Peter, we've talked about this,' said Kate.

And they had. The twins were fifteen. That 'special' age, that age when things begin happening.

Kate had been given some reference material by the school and had passed it on to Peter. He had read it one Saturday while they had been having coffee and biscuits together, and he'd recognised one of the names on a list of suggested reading. A learned man with a smiling manner, like a friendly doctor in a TV show. He was described on the back cover of the book as an 'expert' on teenagers – particularly about 'how to manage and improve a young man's self-esteem and confidence during this tumultuous and momentous time in their lives'.

Peter hadn't paid much attention, though. He'd got by fine in his 'tumultuous time' and felt the best thing to do would be to let the boys come to him or Kate if they had any questions.

'The school handles most of that stuff,' he had said, quite conversationally, as he popped the last of the Tim Tams into his mouth.

'Really?' said Kate.

The next week he had seen a copy of the resident expert's book next to their bed. Peter had picked it up one night when Kate was in the shower. He'd flicked through a few pages, stopping at the ones that had been marked. 'Always give the man/child a private space to discover and understand the changes that are beginning.'

The resident expert sounded more like Tarzan than a trained clinician. Who calls a kid a 'man/child'?

'The man/child's appearance will change. This can cause a question within him. You should encourage him to celebrate the change.'

'Oh, Jesus wept,' Peter said softly to himself.

The resident expert had hit the jackpot with Tarzan-speak. 'Man/child finds hair in places not seen before . . . Must not put him off when he fights lion. Man/child starts to think at night. Get thoughts of Jane, make do with cheetah.'

Peter turned the page to find the next rather startling piece of advice from Dr Tarzan. 'Some of the changes that a parent can praise are the more obvious physical ones; the growth in height, the new physical strength and the growth and change in the genital area.'

Peter Kennedy read the last phrase again. 'Growth and change in the genital area.'

Hair? *Okay, Tarzan, that's obvious.* The next sentence did it.

'A casual remark about the change in size of the man/child's penis is encouraged. Here, humour is a good tool.'

Peter snorted. What a choice of words and what a dud thing to be telling a kid. He said to himself in his best Tarzan voice, 'Oh, by the way, Tarzan say man/child has whopping cock.'

'What was that?' he heard Kate say. As she appeared from the bathroom Peter quickly put the book back on her bedside table.

'Nothing,' he said.

'Were you reading that book?'

He could go two ways: say no and leave it at that or say yes and talk about what he'd found. She might like that.

'Yeah, had a bit of a look.'

'That's good; good to see you taking an interest.'

He didn't like the sound of that.

'What?' she had said. 'You want to talk about what you read?'

He didn't answer.

'Peter?'

He spoke. Sort of. 'That book, you know . . . You don't want to actually be too . . . literal . . .'

Kate was nonplussed. Then she seemed to start thinking hard about her husband. 'Do you want to talk about something, Peter?'

He let out a sigh, half-began a sentence and then waved with his right hand. 'No, no. No. It'll be all right.'

And that's where he left it.

Until the Little Twin's father–son night and that pause on the other end of the phone. That's why he had said quickly to his wife, 'Look, Katie, it'll be okay; I will shoot something through to the school.'

And so he did. He wrote a page in fairly legible writing, which was for him an achievement in itself, saying much the same as he had to the Big Twin but, just for good measure, adding an afterthought. Or two. And a joke. He emailed it to the school, texted Kate to tell her and went off to his meeting where, as nearly always happens, nothing was sorted save for the organising of a new meeting.

He arrived home later that night, after stopping on the way for the last Hot Kaiser Kransky from World of Hot Dogs, to find his wife and the Little Twin waiting for him. He heard the Big Twin laugh from his upstairs bedroom.

'Matthew!' Kate yelled.

The Big Twin was silent.

Ellie looked at her father before giving him a hug good-night. The look wasn't encouraging. He felt like Bingo after being caught crapping in the laundry; it was the sort of look she gave the labrador before he was dragged outside.

'Go to bed, Ellie.'

'Yes, Mum.'

The Little Twin started to giggle.

'Philip!'

This made the Big Twin upstairs laugh too.

'Matthew!'

This made the dog bark.

'Bingo!' yelled Kate.

'Hello,' said Peter and if he had had a tail he would have wagged it.

Kate said slowly, 'Why did you write this?'

Peter saw his emailed letter on the small table in the living room.

Little Twin was trying not to laugh.

'I wrote it because it was . . . Well, I said I'd shoot some-thing through to the school for Phil.'

'Thanks, Dad,' said Philip, looking down so he wouldn't laugh.

'What's happened?' asked Peter.

He saw his wife was thinking very hard. 'What happened . . . ?' she repeated very slowly.

What had happened was that Kate had taken the Little Twin to the Grand Hall at the Brother Whiting Centre at St Mark's College. It was, as its name suggests, a Catholic boys' school and the twins had attended it since their last year at primary level. They seemed to be very happy there and the school seemed to Kate to dispense large helpings of good old-fashioned values blended with a refreshing focus on social justice rather than privilege.

'Like to think of ourselves as more Father Bob than Cardinal Pell,' a very affable enrolment officer had said with a wink, when the boys had started there.

Still, it was a boys' school and Kate had no idea of the protocol of a father–son night without the father. The mother–daughter nights were designed along the same lines, but you never knew with boys, so she had gone to the assisting teacher and explained her son's situation.

The teacher had smiled. 'Ah, those work commitments, eh? Why don't you let the Little Twin sit in on the lectures and the film on his own and you come back for the letter-reading?'

Kate had given the Little Twin a hug and spent an hour at her parents' home, sitting with her mother over a cup of tea and that weekend's crossword. Her father was out at a Rotary meeting and so mother and daughter had the house to themselves. Her mother said nothing specifically about her son-in-law's absence from the father–son night, but she ·

did passively in answer to 24-down, 7 letters – 'American leader who met his end in a motorcade' – scribbled rather pointedly as 'Kennedy'. She added, before sipping her tea, 'I wouldn't take a pistol to him but a good clip around the ears might help.'

Kate didn't say anything, instead looking to her mum and giving the answer to 22-across.

When she returned to the school, the assisting teacher pointed her to an area where some boys sat at tables with their mothers or grandparents or uncles. 'This is the "significant others" section and Brother Regis Dooley will sort you out.'

Kate sat with Philip and passed the time chatting with another mother, whose husband was also stuck at work.

'Did yours manage to write anything down?' asked the other mother.

'Yes, I think he did,' said Kate with a smile.

'Well, that's something. Doug is going to call and say a few words over the phone. I don't know.' And she half-laughed as much as sighed.

An old man with a large head marched up to them and smiled pleasantly at Philip. 'Hello, there. Now I believe your father has left you somewhat in the lurch tonight, hasn't he? It's good to be busy, though, isn't it? I'm Brother Regis Dooley and I'm here tonight to lend a hand, assisting, if you will.'

Brother Regis explained that he had been a teacher for longer than he cared to remember and was really quite happy when 'his kind', as he liked to refer to himself, had been eased out of the Catholic education system in the mid-1980s.

He had been invited to be a part of the faith and mission program here at St Mark's, and had even been quite happy to pop in occasionally and give a little talk on things that the boys may find interesting.

Brother Regis didn't often talk on matters that had an obvious connection to faith and mission. Instead, he had always been the sort to cast a wide net. So it was that he had passed into St Mark's legend by giving an annual chat at the commencement of Lent about the great trotters of Australia. One memorable year it was the 'Paleface, Adios' chat.

'Dear old Paleface was the St Peter of the pacers. The rock of the gravel track. The rock upon which you could build just about anything if you'd had the courage to drop your packet on his nose. Never needed the whip but always gave his all. There's a lesson in that. Yes, very nice.'

And as he grew older, he had a tendency to grab hold of that phrase, 'Yes, very nice.' He also had a habit of elongating vowels in his mellifluous voice, so 'yes' became 'yeeerz' and 'very nice' became 'veeery niiize'.

But it all came to a head when Brother Regis sat down with Philip and held forth the emailed letter from his father.

Now it was customary for the old Brother to ask the young man before him if he would like him, Brother Regis, to read out his father's letter, in case that would be preferred. Thankfully, it never was.

So Brother Regis was quite taken aback when the Little Twin had said that he would like the letter read, but nonetheless he rose to the occasion. 'Oh, yeeerz, veeery niiize.'

Then he coughed, put on his glasses and went into Brother-Regis mode, which, as most of the older teachers there will tell you, was loud so the ones at the back can hear.

Kate sat there, not knowing whether to go or to stay.

Philip sat there and tried not to smile.

'"Dear Phil,"' boomed the old Brother. It was all much the same as the letter the Big Twin had received and only slightly excruciating for Kate to hear.

'"You've made me very proud and I have learned a lot from you, Phil. You may be a twin but you are your own man."' Brother Regis stopped and smiled. 'Yeeerz, veeery niiize.'

There was a bit of 'keeping your head down' and 'doing well', but 'always remembering to watch out for others less fortunate'. And that should have been it, but then came the afterthought, the bit Peter had tacked on. '"Your mother is a wonderful woman and you should respect her as much as you love her." Oh, yeeerz, veeery niiize.'

Obviously Brother Regis had liked that bit and so repeated it and went on with oratorical enthusiasm. '"Respect. Respect as much as you love her,"' he boomed away. '"But if she tells you you have a big penis, she's only trying to be nice. There's nothing wrong with the equipment you've got; more than enough to keep you happy at night."'

To be fair, Brother Regis did try to put the handbrake on, but 'penis' came out in elongated vowels as 'peaaaaaanuuursss'. It sounded as if he was varying his delivery for dramatic effect.

'"But there's no point in pretending you've got a Hummer stretch limo when what you're tooling around in is a nice compact sedan. You know what they say to the question, *What's worn under a Scotsman's kilt?* Well, *Nothing; it's all in perfect working order.* And that, Phil, is the main thing." Yeeerz, veeery niiize. "Remember, your mum just read a book. Love, Dad".'

There was a long silence, then Kate got up and stood still. The other mother she had chatted with gave a little shrug of her shoulders. Brother Regis didn't move and then said slowly, almost to himself, 'Yeeerz, a little bit unexpected, that bit, but I suppose there's a truth in there somewhere. Yeeerz.' And he smiled at Kate. '"Read a book." I take it you like to read those help-yourself books? Veeery niiize.'

So that was what happened. Peter Kennedy was about to say something but was beaten to it by the Little Twin. 'At least you didn't get a template off the internet.'

'I didn't want him thinking that, you know . . .'

'What? That I tried to tell him he was hung like a donkey?' said Kate. 'Christ, Peter.'

Philip snorted.

'Did you think I told Matthew that, too?' she asked.

'Well, you read that book – you marked those pages.'

'Yes, I did,' said Kate. 'I marked them because I thought they were ludicrous. Funny. And after all, what the cretin was trying to say wasn't anything to do with the size of a dick. It was all about paying attention and noticing things, letting the kids know they're not alone.'

'Oh,' said Peter.

Upstairs the Big Twin growled, 'Yeeerz, veeery niiize.'

There was a silence and then Kate's face broke into the most beautiful smile, the smile she let rip when she had no guard up, a wide cracking smile. And she laughed. Her laughter was like a call to joy.

The twins erupted, the dog barked and Ellie came down from her room, smiling because her father hadn't been given the Bingo treatment.

Kate walked over to her husband, trying to stop her hysterics long enough to speak. 'You must talk to me, you must talk.' And she laughed again.

•

Now, Peter sat in the red Getz looking up at the back of the big white aquarium and the stickers of the happy family. He heard his wife's laughter, but also the look that she had given him that morning.

Her laughter died. *You should talk more.*

He stopped watching the other cars, their drivers. He followed the Range Rover all the way along the Gateway, past the turn-off for the Sunshine Coast and over the long thin bridge that led to the Peninsula. His family had driven over it many times when they had visited his parents and had always counted the pelicans that rested on top of the tall light poles. Ten was the sign of a good holiday. And they never saw fewer than ten.

Peter couldn't see any pelicans today. A councillor had demanded small spikes be fixed on top of the poles to stop the birds perching there and shitting over the cars below.

No pelicans. No happy family in the car with him. Only stick figures stuck to the back window of the car in front. He tortured Red into fifth and passed the white aquarium on the inside lane. As he did so, he saw the kid had fallen asleep against the window with his finger in his nose. And still nobody seemed to be talking inside the Range Rover. Peter sped past and crossed into his old home town and felt suddenly very alone.

Chapter Four

At the end of the long bridge across the inlet, the lane splits into three turn-offs, which become the main arterial roads leading to the various parts of Pickersgill Peninsula.

If Peter headed left he could go to the golf course, the botanical gardens and the industrial areas. If you weren't familiar with the Peninsula, though, it was actually quite hard to spot where they each began; they sort of bled into one another. A council had once cared enough about this to put up signs directing drivers to each spot. But, sadly, despite the best of intentions, civic planning had always been a little haphazard in the area, to say the least. This had resulted in the unique placement of the golf course's 'Lucky Seventh' green.

It was situated across from the rear entrance to the town's brothel, which was owned by a man called Nev Bracewell and so was given the name of Nev's. Most people had forgotten the brothel's real name – 'The Lotus Flower'. This was probably for the best, because a Chinese takeaway at the other end of town had taken the same name some years ago. Occasionally a few bad jokes were made by old-timers who couldn't resist ordering a combination chow mein with a wink and a nudge.

The rear entrance was supposed to give those visiting Nev's some discretion, but in a town like Pickersgill Peninsula it was used so much that it became more like the front door. Golfers would often lean on putters at the lip of the green to have a look-see at who was 'popping out Nev's rear'. This led to the naming of the hole the 'Lucky Seventh' back at the clubhouse, because it was always a bit of a lucky dip as to who or what you might witness from the green. Men had to be extremely careful on the Ladies' Day competition, which was held every Wednesday morning, and not for the obvious reasons.

In the record books the Lucky Seventh was known as the Percy Sorenson Seventh Hole. This was in honour of former alderman and long-time Pickersgill Golf Club member, Percival – aka Percy – Sorenson, who gave his all as an officiating steward for the mid-week Ladies' comp.

It had been on the 'Lucky Seventh' that Percy, just checking a drop from the bunker, had glanced over the green to see his wife Margaret – aka Madge – Sorenson leaving 'Nev's rear', laughing and with a decided skip in her step.

After a pause, one of the members of the Ladies' mid-week comp was heard to say, 'She's had her hair done as well, Percy. Looks nice.'

All eyes shifted from Madge's hair to a gasping Percy Sorenson, who promptly collapsed on top of the green and, as the Ladies' mid-week comp members gathered around, spoke his last words: 'Penalty . . . shot. Ball not dropped correctly.'

And then he died.

Whether it had been Madge's new hairdo, the skip in her step or the incorrect drop shot, nobody ever really knew, but the least they could do, it was decided, was to name the hole after him.

Still, it paid to be careful on the Lucky Seventh.

•

The road straight ahead was called Flinders Avenue, according to the Main Roads Department and Google Maps, but to those who lived there it was known as 'The Guts', as in 'up the guts', the very middle or spine of the Peninsula, and it ran from this point up to some canal developments and a small harbour that catered for trawlers and yachts at the other end of the town.

But Peter didn't take The Guts; he drifted round to the left, past a little collection of shops and the new high-rise residential towers that had begun to dot the town. To his right was the first of the beaches and bays that ringed the Peninsula, and the shallow water was glistening as the sun began to set in the late-afternoon sky.

It was quite a picture but Peter didn't really notice, he was looking over at the other side of the road. He pulled to the right and wove around, following the drive-through instructions, and stopped at a microphone in the smiling mouth of an upturned fibreglass hot dog. White-gloved, it gave a friendly thumbs up with one hand and held a world globe in the extended palm of the other. The hot dog's little spat-covered feet were crossed elegantly in the insouciant style that befitted the Hot Dog King, mascot of the World of Hot Dogs chain. Peter didn't know what it was about them, but the outlets were nearly always run by ex-footballers of note.

This one was run by Bevan Krunt, an ex-front-row forward for the local rugby team, the Marlins. A thin teenage voice piped from the hot dog's mouth, saying something unintelligible.

'Hello?' Peter said to the hot dog after a while.

The hot dog started to cough. A real hacking, wet, sick cough.

Peter sat in his little red car and waited for the coughing to stop. After a while he said, 'You right?'

The hot dog, responding cheerfully, sniffed and said, 'Oh, sorry, I'm just so –' before it coughed again and sniffed. Then a shrieking sound, like a show-bag kazoo being blown too hard, and another sniff before finally, in perky drive-through tones, the voice said, 'Hello, welcome to Krunt's World of Hot Dogs. May I take your order, please?'

For a moment, Peter debated the wisdom of ordering food over a microphone – especially one in a winking, white-spatted hot dog – but it was only for a moment. He went for a Malaysian Satay Super Dog with cheese and drove around to the next window, as instructed by the hot dog.

There, a teenage boy in a purple-and-yellow uniform, hairnet and King Dog cap and with more pimples on his face than there was cheese on the Malaysian Super Dog, sniffed at the window with Peter's order.

'Not feeling too well?'

'Sick as a dog,' said the boy; Tyson according to his nametag.

'Ah, that's no good,' said Peter. 'Cheers.'

Tyson sniffed. 'Thank you and enjoy your meal.'

As Peter rolled away he heard the kid cough again.

Almost instant gratification. That is why you go to World of Hot Dogs. You order and less than a minute later, with the touch of a microwave button, your packet of food is waiting for you.

Peter unwrapped the hot dog with his left hand and steered the car back onto the crescent road running along the bay with his right. Eating while driving was easier when he was in his Swedish silver tank, which was a feather-touch automatic. Red Getz was more of a challenge, and as he flicked between the gearstick, the hot dog and his mouth, he drifted across the road like a runner who has popped a hamstring. I haven't stalled yet and I am eating, driving and changing gears. Pretty good. You should see me with a mobile in my hand, Peter thought proudly.

Kate didn't like the way he drove. Not that he usually did any of those things while she was in the car with him. It was just that one afternoon when he was driving along the Tulla in Melbourne and had picked up a few dim sims to keep him company. He had taken the precaution of asking for a fork and all was going relatively well until his phone started to bleep. He managed to balance everything between his hands, thighs and stomach so he could open the message and read that he should 'Look to the left when you come to a stop.'

The telecommunications universe will send obscure messages sometimes, but as the traffic slowed ahead at an on-ramp Peter knew that this one was meant for him.

He turned, chewing a dim sim and holding a soy-sauce-covered plastic fork and phone in his hands, to see, not more than a metre and a half away, his family. His three children laughing and his wife staring. Thinking hard about him.

He tried to smile but panicked and bit down on the dim sim, which was very hot. A spurt of soy sauce, like a jet of squid ink, shot out of the window. Nobody had cared later that he had burned his lips.

'If you lie about stuffing junk in your mouth while you drive, what else do you lie about, Peter? Do you understand?' Kate had asked afterwards.

No, he didn't. It wasn't like he was being unfaithful, it was only a steamed dim sim. A nice one, but still just a dim sim. So he had stared at her and then said, 'I love you.'

And she had got mad, and he had promised not to eat in the car again. And he hadn't, however nice dim sims might be.

Malaysian Super Dogs were different, though, so he carried on hopping along in Red and weighed up the merits of said Super Dog until he felt a warm splodge of something runny on his shirt. It had a hint of onion and peanut about it. And something else. He turned at the first of the town's three CWA halls and became so involved in trying to determine that other taste that he didn't see the police car as he went past the croquet club and headed on up the hill that led to his parents' home.

There were two hotels in this part of town. The Savannah, right on the water by the jetty, once a bare-knuckle fighting pit, was now a breezy family beer hall. Its renovation had signalled the beginning of the rebirth of Pickersgill Peninsula as Brisbane's 'Riviera', in the words of its mayor, Edwyn Hume.

Peter passed this and drove uphill to the Crown Hotel, which stood on the crown of the hill, giving rise to its name, overlooking the bay.

There was a vacant lot to its left and then a large wooden house ringed with a verandah. His parents' home.

He came to an abrupt halt outside it and sat running his tongue around his mouth. He knew the taste. He could smell it now, too. He frowned. Manufactured meat. He still hadn't noticed the police car pull up behind him or the officer walking slowly towards his window.

Peter sat there, opening and shutting his mouth like a person tasting bad wine, and said slowly, 'Luncheon meat.'

Then he opened the door onto something very large and blue. A very large police officer.

Peter Kennedy started and the officer jumped back. 'Sorry, sorry!' Peter yelled. And, for good measure, 'Sorry!'

The police officer stood in a practised pose and pointed towards Peter as another apology wobbled and then died on his lips.

'Dux Doublies double runner!' he exclaimed. 'Peter? Peter bloody Kennedy, I thought it was you!'

Peter bloody Kennedy didn't say a thing.

'Peter!' said the copper in an exasperated tone.

Peter looked into the face of Wayne Dixon. He was Sergeant Wayne Dixon now. Wayne Dixon. The son of Mr Dixon, he of the pristine Holden Premier. Wayne Dixon. One of Peter's oldest friends. Well, from Pickersgill, at least. They had gone to primary school together and there they were quite unremarkable in all respects. Neither was exceptional at anything. Wayne could run very fast and even though obvious physical prowess carried a certain amount of cachet in primary-school land, the fact that he always wore his shirts, be they button-ups or tees, tucked into pants that were invariably pulled high, pegged him as pretty ordinary. He also wore a hanky pinned to his pants that never had pockets, and believed if he hitched them even higher with a mighty ritualistic tug before he ran, he'd go faster – all this adding to the impression of a speeding choco Charlie.

Peter was quick but not fast, clever but not the smartest, could draw a bit and make a pretty good underarm fart sound but there were faster, smarter and better underarm farters about.

So Peter and Wayne were just a couple of also-rans and although not close at first were bound together by an incident in fourth grade in Mrs Thompson's class when Wayne was showing flashes of his football skills with a small piece of Dux eraser, no bigger than a large frozen pea.

Peter sat next to him as Wayne repeatedly placed first one and then another piece of eraser in his nostrils and then blew them into his pencil case. Wayne had taken time to colour the bits of eraser green with a felt-tipped pen, adding a brightness to the little missiles ejected from each nostril.

It was pretty impressive until Wayne uttered the foolish declaration that he could go 'Doublies'.

Peter Kennedy was sceptical. 'No way.'

'Yeah.'

'No.'

'Yeah.'

'Better not.'

'Yeah, well, I coulda.'

There was a pause, then Peter Kennedy spoke. Why not call this kid with the pinned-on hanky's bluff? 'Do it then.'

'What?'

'Do it then. Do it: go "Doublies".'

Wayne Dixon didn't seem sure but he couldn't back down in front of Peter; he didn't want to slip any further in the playground pecking order than he had since his mother, not being able to find a hanky, had pinned a shred of a Currumbin Bird Sanctuary tea towel to her son's pants that morning.

He placed the eraser peas up each nostril and for a minute Peter Kennedy thought he had lost his nerve, but with an intake of breath and a rush of trembling fingers he pulled off two more corners from the rubber.

Mrs Thompson was speaking about the role of a flower's stamen. 'Now sticky bits stick to bees and other insects as they rest and nibble on other bits of the flower. And these greedy bees go and carry the pollen to other plants and a new flower will grow . . .'

As Peter Kennedy stood remembering this in front of his parents' house he was sure that he had heard Mrs Thompson say under her breath, as another eraser pea was pushed up Wayne's nostril, 'That's really all you have to do, girls: feed them, keep them happy, let them do their business and you can go on spreading life. Slightly depressing, but I'm sure you girls who want to, will find ways to mitigate it.'

Wayne's eyes had blazed in triumph, and Peter had had to give him credit. It was impressive.

'Doublies!' cried Wayne and then he tried to expel the peas with a blast of air.

That was when it went pear-shaped or, as the headmaster later put it to Mrs Dixon with a heavy handed attempt at headmaster humour, 'Pea-shaped'.

Wayne couldn't rid his nostrils of the Dux Doublies and he began to panic. Peter sort of laughed and turned away. Nothing to do with him if the kid with the high pants and the pinned-on hanky wanted to stick stuff up his nose, but then Wayne began to cry. He began to panic and strike out.

Very hard. Not only was he fast but it seemed he was pretty strong, too. He tried to extract the Dux Doublies with a compass, but the point got stuck and he began to cry harder. To stop Wayne from belting his arm Peter had grabbed hold of his hand and held it. And the longer he held it, the calmer Wayne became.

Mrs Thompson left stamens behind and strode over to the boy with the high-waisted pants – Wayne's sartorial tendencies had made an impact in the staffroom – saw a compass hanging from his swollen nose and made a quick assessment that stunned even Wayne. Perhaps it was the talk about greedy bees, but Mrs Thompson boomed, 'Have you been stung by a bee?'

Wayne eyeballed her and almost yodelled in adenoidal outrage, 'No! I did Doublies!'

Peter stepped in. 'He went Doublies with the Dux rubber bits and they stuck and so he tried to get them out with his compass.'

Wayne pointed to Peter and the parrot on his hanky flapped. 'He dared me to go Doublies. He dared me!'

Mrs Thompson had been a teacher for a long time, and not much fazed her. She was accustomed to the fact that young boys have a tendency to try to fill holes in their bodies with all sorts of odd things. She probably thought this was somehow fitting in the light of the lesson she was trying to teach, but she dealt with the situation as she did with most matters. 'To the headmaster's office!' She sounded a little like Batman talking to Robin when he says, 'To the Bat Cave!'

Wayne Dixon rose obediently, still holding Peter's hand.

Peter looked at Wayne and then at Mrs Thompson; he didn't like the idea of going to the headmaster's office.

'Quickly, go with your friend,' said Mrs Thompson, addressing Peter, then she went back to talking about flowers.

From that moment on, Peter and Wayne had sort of been friends; it had been declared by a teacher, after all, and anyway, their stocks had bounced up. Wayne Dixon had done a Doublies on stuff up his nose and by way of association Peter had got a look-in on the limelight too.

It's hard to underestimate the impact of seeing a boy walking along with a compass dangling from his swollen nose, even if his pants are high and he has a flapping parrot pinned to his hip. Peter even threw in a little nod to the onlookers now and then as they went on their way to the headmaster's office. Then, as they reached the the hallway that led to the cave, Wayne had stopped. He had stopped and shaken his hand a little and said softly to Peter, 'Thank you. Thank you for holding my hand.'

'You're right, Wayne,' said Peter.

Over the years that followed, they played sport together and later, after Wayne had gone through a 'tennis stage', they had both packed down in the second row for various lower grades in the local rugby team. What distinguished their football careers was almost exactly the same as what had distinguished their school careers. Wayne still ran fast with pants hitched very high and did incredibly stupid things with his hands – not as stupid as sticking bits of Dux eraser up his nose, but throwing dummies to nobody and poking himself in the eyes when he ran or tackled.

Peter did just enough to stay on the team and his involvement gave birth to the Dux Doublies, a call made by players in possession of the ball when they wanted teammates to run together; the first being a decoy runner and the second being the receiver. Dux Doublies caught on for a while, in the lower grades, at least.

And then the boys had gone to high school and afterwards they went their separate ways; Peter to university and Wayne into the police force. And they hadn't seen each other since.

Now, here Peter was, confronted by a face from the past, striking a pose and whispering, 'Dux Doublies.'

'*Wayne?*'

They both laughed.

'Jesus, Wayne. Sorry.'

'No, you're right.'

'You're still a copper.'

'I certainly am. And you're nicked, mate.'

Peter Kennedy frowned.

Wayne laughed. 'No you're not, you silly tool. God, your face!'

'When did you come back?'

'A couple of months ago; I'd been in Rocky before that.'

'How long were you following me?'

'I saw you pull out of the old Krunt's. The way you handled that hot dog; mate, you're an artist.'

Peter smiled a little.

'You're wearing some on you shirt, though, mate. Peter . . .' Wayne took an appraising breath. 'You've been in a very good paddock, haven't you?'

'Well, yes.'

'You shouldn't try and do too many things when you're driving a vehicle.'

'Yes, well . . .'

'You're right?'

'Well, yes.'

'You up for the show?'

Peter paused before responding. 'That's right, yes, and a bit of work.'

'You brought the family?'

'No.'

'They good?'

'Yes, all good.'

Wayne laughed. He had a nice laugh and did so often, apart from when he had Dux frozen-pea erasers up his nose.

'Saw your mum down by the jetty, walking those dogs of hers. Always give her a wave. She's looking well.'

'That's good.'

'Your dad?'

'He's good, I think.'

Wayne nodded.

'Yeah. Think about him a lot.'

Peter stood there, breathing heavily. You have had a fright, haven't you, Peter? he thought.

Wayne was about to say something else but stopped for a moment, and then laughed. 'Mate, we should catch up – you around for that?'

Peter breathed a bit more and thought, why not? It wouldn't take long to do the showgrounds. And depending how his parents were, it might be good to get out. 'Yeah, maybe.'

'I'll give you a ring tomorrow, then – or will you be at the bingo?'

'Bingo?'

'Yeah, Big Valley Bingo up at Wharton Hall at the showgrounds. Pearl's running it, still, but you'd know that. Gary's going to be there, I think.'

Gary, the youngest of the Kennedy children. Peter looked back at Wayne, who suddenly seemed a little concerned.

'Yeah, I suppose I'll be there. But give us a ring, yeah? Be good to catch up.'

'On my word. Very good.' And Wayne smiled his nice smile. 'Do you see anyone from the old days?'

'No.'

'Know who I bumped into the other week?'

'No.'

'Debbie Spillman.'

'Debbie Spillman?' Peter had no idea who Debbie Spillman was.

'Yeah, you know Debbie Spillman. She won the Fastest Check-out Chick in Queensland back in Year Ten?'

'Year Ten?'

'Yeah, 1979. She got interviewed by Mike Higgins. She didn't make it onto the telly, though; she was at some stand at the Brisbane Show.'

Peter stared at the policeman.

'Yeah, got her for speeding, just off the bridge. She's looking okay, sort of okay.' Then, after a moment of consideration, he said, 'She's been doing something to herself.'

Peter stood still. He could feel some peanut sauce seeping through his shirt onto his stomach.

'And I caught up with Neville Mason down by the gardens. He's a tradie – a painter.'

There was a pause.

'Although his apprentice will be doing the driving for a while; old Neville blew over.'

Peter nodded slowly.

'And Lisa Sykes. Had a chat with her when she didn't indicate. She was good, looked amazing. Doing very well for herself, had a Lexus. Latest model, too.'

Peter nodded. 'You've been busy since you've been back.'

Wayne Dixon laughed and agreed. 'You know, catch up on me social life and top up me quota. I'll give you a bell tomorrow.'

He seemed very fit and very strong as he stood there, smiling back at Peter. 'Good to see you again.' And then he pointed up at the home behind him. 'This house; I remember your old man building it.' He paused and then nodded. 'Say hello to him for me. And your mum. And Pearl,' before adding, 'and Gary, too!'

He swung himself quickly into the police car and pulled away, winding down the window as he went, and calling out, 'Dux Doublies!'

Peter watched him go. Wayne Dixon. Then he touched the peanut sauce on his shirt and realised he hadn't even told his parents he was coming. The sun, about to sink from view, filled the bay with the glowing blood-orange of early evening. And Peter realised it didn't matter about not telling his parents, they never locked the back door.

He turned away just as the sunlight shone at its richest, took his bag from Red and walked slowly to the back of the house.

Chapter Five

Peter hadn't been to his parents' house for nearly a year, but he could walk the path to the back door with his eyes closed. He'd grown up in this house, lived here for nearly nineteen years, until he left the Peninsula for a share house in Milton when he was at uni.

This house on the crown of the hill had never had a fence, even when his family had had the mad dog that used to bark like the end of the world was coming. His name was Cider because he seemed sweet but had a nasty bite. Peter Kennedy's mum had given him that name, changing it from Tippy.

It was Peter who had given the dog the name Tippy; he'd read a book about a boy on a farm who had all sorts of adventures with his dog called Tippy. They went camping and swimming and foiled a gang of sheep rustlers and even ended up winning a prize at the local show from the mayor, who didn't really like the boy or his dog but had to say that they had certainly saved the day.

The only adventure Peter had had with his Tippy was getting half his arse bitten off once when he came back from swimming club. Pearl had laughed later that night at the dinner table at how Peter's own dog had bitten him.

''S'not my dog. Never said it was my dog. I just chose the name.'

'Your dog bit your bum,' said his sister, laughing.

His mother smiled at him. 'He certainly took a nice little nip out of you, Peter.'

Peter stared down at his plate.

'Sook,' whispered his sister. 'Sooky, sooky sook.'

Cider never went beyond the point known as Kirk's Place in the front yard, which was marked by a big concrete lump. It was supposed to be a dugong and had been created by Peter's father and one of his mates, who fancied himself as a bit of a sculptor.

Howard Whittaker was a plasterer by trade and Ken Kennedy had used him for quite a while to do finishing work in the houses he built. Howie was a bloke with a dream, eager and self-taught with, in his words, a 'natural eye' and a vision.

His vision was garden sculpture.

'Ken, it's the way of the future. Outdoors will be the place where we'll all be living in the seventies and the eighties.

You want more than just a couple of rubber-tyre swans. You want something that says "I'm here".'

Ken thought Howard Whittaker was half mad but he was a good worker, had four kids to feed and had always been a fellow who was 'up for a crack at things, even though he's nearly as blind as a bat'.

It was true; close work was all right for Howie but anything more than a metre away was where the trouble began. He wore thick, horn-rimmed spectacles and when he wanted to look at something with, as he put it, 'a bit of perspective', he would whip off his glasses and squint through one eye.

One Friday night, after Ken had said goodbye to Mary and the kids as they left to spend the long weekend out at her mum's farm at Caboolture, he had stood in the Royal Bar at the Crown and slapped Howard Whittaker on the shoulder.

'Right then, you silly coot, we'll give you your first commission. Let's whack something up.'

Ken initially had ideas of helping Howie put something up in his own backyard but Howie lived in a flat down in the middle of town and so it was decided, after another few beers, that Ken and Mary Kennedy's front yard, with a view to Moreton Bay, would be the site of Howie's first effort.

'It'll be something for Mary, for when she gets back. Something that says "I'm here". A lovely surprise,' said Howie, whipping his spectacles off and squinting at Ken.

Howie's vision for the sculpture was of a dugong swimming at the feet of the first Europeans who had seen these waters. Why he chose a dugong was anyone's guess but an explorer-cum-coloniser – well, one of the first English-speaking ones that anyone could think of – hit the 'I'm here' button well and truly.

Howie was torn between a statue of Captain Cook and the man who had given the Peninsula its name, Richard Pickersgill, a young sailor and one of the two master's mates on board the *Endeavour*. According to legend, it was he who had sighted the second peninsula in Moreton Bay as the ship made its way up the eastern coast of this great southern land. James Cook had statues, towns, parks, highways and even a cottage named after him – while to most people's knowledge Dick Pickersgill had none, only a plaque that the lantana had grown over in the Rotary park down by one of the beaches.

As fate would have it, both men met rather sticky ends, although Pickersgill's was more in keeping with the atmosphere of the peninsula that bore his name. Cook came to grief at the end of a spear in Hawaii while Pickersgill rose through the ranks and circumnavigated the world three times before attaining a command of his own. Unfortunately, just as greatness beckoned, he arrived at his vessel after a night on the town and attempted to board it while it was moored on a rising tide in the Thames. It had been a little too much of a good night because a rat-arsed Richard Pickersgill slipped and fell from a ladder as he sang a popular music-hall ditty, drowning in the fast-flowing river before he could finish the second verse. The last words he was heard to utter were those of the chorus of 'Mary's the Lass with the Tasty Tarts'.

And away we go
Though winds will blow
For the rum warms your blood
Mary's the lass with the tasty tarts.

'Sort of suits, doesn't it?' Ken had said when hearing the story.

•

Young Peter was hanging around his father at a family barbecue when Ken said to him, as he occasionally did, 'Well, tell your old man what you learned this week.'

So Peter had told his father what he had learned at school, starting with a riddle he had heard.

'Why do pirates wear big hats?'

'Don't know, son. Why do they wear big hats?'

'To keep their buccaneers warm.'

There was a pause that stretched on for too long and then Peter's grandmother's head popped out from the kitchen window and his mother said in a ferocious whisper, 'What was that? What did you say, Peter?'

He added quickly, in a whine, 'A boy – a big boy told me.'

His father nodded slightly. 'Just keep that one to yourself for a bit, old son. What else have you got to show for yourself?'

Peter panicked and later told himself he hadn't been thinking clearly that day. He crossed his arms, put his palms under each opposite armpit, underarm farted twice, palm-farted once, flipped down onto his back and, with his legs in the air, did a double behind-the-knee fart followed by a couple of solo efforts. Then he stood up and said, 'That was "Yankee Doodle Dandy".'

Ken poked a sausage on the barbecue and nodded his head slowly.

Peter's nanna's voice boomed out, 'It's easy to see whose son he is, Kenneth.'

Ken smiled a little and Peter's mother tried not to laugh.

Then Pearl appeared from nowhere and said that she had learned that Pickersgill Peninsula was named after a famous sailor who had served with Captain Cook. That early one morning as he stood on deck, he was sure he had seen a mermaid swimming below.

Peter listened, knowing this story off by heart, having learned it too. He hoped that Pearl would make a mistake so that he could correct it, but she didn't.

Pearl went on to explain it hadn't been a mermaid but a dugong and that as Richard Pickersgill had watched the creature swimming he had looked out to see a peninsula in the bay. So it was decided by Captain Cook that Pickersgill's name should be given to the land he had spotted.

'Well, that's the legend,' said their grandmother. 'He liked a drop a bit too much did, Mr Pickersgill, and that was his downfall.'

Ken had smiled. 'You're right there. And it sort of suits, doesn't it? Most of the blokes who sail out of the harbour here are as full as old boots.'

Peter remembered his nanna laughing. 'He'd probably had a rum ration and a half to mistake a dugong for a mermaid!'

'Long sea voyages can do all sorts of things to a fellow.'

'Oh, Kenneth.'

And Nanna had laughed some more.

•

After giving it some consideration Howie had whipped his glasses back on and decided to sculpt Richard Pickersgill. He would be standing, pointing, as a dugong frolicked in the water below him.

Howie was enthusiastic bordering on the frenetic and maybe because of this, even though Ken was there to help, the curse of Pickersgill struck.

The problems started with the dugong, a charmingly innocuous creature that continues to graze the vegetation in the shallow waters of Moreton Bay today. Although typically quite graceful in the sea, in Howie's frantic hands this pleasant marine herbivore became one elongated grey mass that Howie assured Ken, 'Will be right once it's set.' But it never looked like anything other than a dog turd.

Howie didn't give up and moved on to Richard Pickersgill who, although looking quite heroic at first with his thinly reinforced skeleton made from straightened wire coat hangers and chook wire pointing stoically out to the bay, started to lose his shape. Whether it was the rain that set in later that afternoon or the bottle of rum that Howie had bought in honour of the old sailor, things went spectacularly south. First, Pickersgill's arm collapsed, his finger now pointing down towards the blob that was the dugong. Howie and Ken tried to fix him up but the more the rum disappeared the more drastic poor Pickersgill's metamorphosis became.

In desperation Howie, his imagination fuelled by watching a rerun of the Kirk Douglas movie *The Vikings* at the Moonbeam Cinema, tried to turn Pickersgill into a Nordic warrior of the waves.

'It's a seal, a big seal, and he's hunting it with his sword,' explained Howard Whittaker as he stood squinting with one eye closed while the rain fell around him.

'Righto, Howie,' said Ken Kennedy as he wandered down to the Crown for some tallies of Carbine stout.

When he returned he found that Howie had added a long sword to a bearded and horn-helmeted Viking.

'I'm here!'

Whatever a Viking was doing in Moreton Bay pointing at a dugong that looked more like a giant dog turd was anybody's guess, but it was certainly a surprise for Mary Kennedy. Especially when she arrived home in the dark.

She always had a tendency to swing in fast from the street, and who could blame her; the block was deep enough. But when she saw a man with a pointy head, big knife and glowing eyes, courtesy of some fluorescent road-marking paint Howie had borrowed from his council worker brother-in-law, Mary was taken by surprise.

She had swung in with her usual gusto, chatting happily away to her children. 'Here we are, home ag – Jesus *Christ* all-shitting mighty!'

It was, Peter Kennedy realised, the first time he had ever heard his mother truly swear.

She was lucky the car didn't plough through the neighbour's fence and Ken Kennedy was lucky he was allowed to stay in the same hemisphere, let alone the marriage bed that night. He eventually won her over with his big lopsided grin and purred words, 'It'll grow on you.'

And so it did; Kirk the Viking was a fixture in the garden for years, always eliciting a few exclamations of alarm from the Crown's patrons and the garbos on rubbish-collection nights.

Kirk certainly kept Cider honest. Had the sculpture not been watching him the dog would have been off nipping at the first sight of flesh that passed the front of the house, but instead he had tried his canines out on Kirk and Cider had come off second best.

So, while Cider spent the next three years haring around the back and side yards and through the big house itself, he never crossed that magic line defended by the glowing Kirk.

There was no Cider to worry about now, though. He'd ended up keeping Peter's grandmother company at Caboolture, until he finished his days old and contentedly grumpy and was buried out the back somewhere, past the old chook house.

And Kirk had finally come to grief one wet summer in the nineties, collapsing in on himself. Peter remembered it clearly. He and Kate had arrived for the Christmas holidays to find the dugong sitting in the front yard all by itself.

'Where's Kirk?'

'Oh, he's quite happy in Valhalla,' was all Ken Kennedy had said.

'It doesn't really seem the same without him, the front yard, does it?' said Mary.

Ken had picked up one of his grandsons and nuzzled him close, rumbling to the boy, 'You know, young Phil, I *told* your nanna old Kirk would grow on her.'

'Yes, my old man, you certainly did.' Peter's mother had smiled and stroked her husband's cheek.

•

Now Peter Kennedy walked past the ivy-covered dog-turd dugong and down the side garden, encouraging a toad with a gentle nudge from his loafer to hop next door into the neighbours'.

As he turned he could smell the backyard. Even in July the scent of the deep green moistness of ferns and rubber trees was intense. The side of the house that was always in shade was still covered by the huge leaves of the *Monstera deliciosa*.

'Amazing things really, aren't they?' said Ken of the plants one afternoon when Peter was young, as the family all lay here and there in the backyard. He was holding some of its fruit, shaped like a big green cob of corn, covered in hexagonal scales. 'You could do somebody a bit of damage with this, couldn't you?'

'Or put a smile on somebody's face,' said Mary Kennedy.

Peter's father had laughed. 'Steady on, children present.'

His mother had said that some people called Aztecs believed that the plant was a magic food, Aztec magic food.

Peter had asked where the Aztecs lived and his father had said, very seriously, 'Well, they come from Kippa-Ring over in Redcliffe there.'

His mother had laughed.

Pearl had wanted to know why the food was magic.

'Apparently, if you close your eyes, eat a piece of the monstera and think of a food, then it will taste like that food. Magic,' Mary said.

Pearl stared.

Gary picked his nose.

Peter stared.

Ken patted him on the head. 'Like to try the magic, Peter?'

Peter wasn't sure he'd like to try anything from the big green thing.

'Nothing to be scared of, mate,' reassured his father.

Pearl jumped up. 'Me! Me! I'll try!'

So Pearl had stood, eyes closed tight and little fists bunched.

Ken Kennedy picked small pieces of the fruit from under the scales and gave them to his wife.

Mary spoke softly to her daughter. 'Now, remember to keep your eyes shut and think of a food.'

'Fish fingers.'

'Wait till it's in your gob, Pearlie,' Mary said.

Pearl chewed and squealed. 'Fish fingers! It tastes like fish fingers.'

Mary popped in another piece and Pearl jumped up and down. 'Chewy, it's sort of chewy.'

Peter's parents laughed.

Ken closed his eyes and chewed a piece, too. He jumped up and down. 'Four-X and mashed potato.'

Mary chewed and sang out, 'Turkish delight!'

Gary Kennedy, who'd just taken his finger from his nose, closed his eyes and chewed. 'Snot, boogie snot.'

His parents and his sister and Gary laughed. Peter stared.

'Peter?' his mother said.

He shook his head. He was sure they were making things up, just playing. He stood and went upstairs.

His father stopped laughing for a minute, then went back to the fun in the garden.

That garden was silent now, save for a screech from a bat or two in the big mango tree that loomed over the shed. Peter breathed in the sweetness in the air.

He never quite got over the fact that there were so many wild things here, things that you couldn't control. He looked at the Aztec magic food again, then he walked up the stairs and at the top he saw him.

Ken Kennedy was sitting in his big chair on the back verandah, asleep. Peter looked at his father. He seemed older, thinner, paler. He supposed that was what happened when you grew old.

His father had built this house, had shaped it and grown it with each passing year. Peter remembered coming home from school to see him adding the second level and then the verandah.

Walking up from the primary school that sat right on Nelsons Beach, you would follow the shoreline before heading up the hill, where the Greeks had their fish-and-chip shop, and then up the bluff and finally to the crown. Even halfway up the bluff you could see Peter's home, see the new beams and struts going up, and see his father standing there on the timber.

Sometimes Ken Kennedy would lean against a beam, resting on his shoulder or propped up by an outstretched arm. His carpentry belt would be slung across his hips and his other hand would sit on the head of his hammer.

Peter would look at his dad, standing there, so big against the blue sky, one of his funny floppy hats plonked on his head and wearing his Stubbies and work boots, and think his father was like a cowboy from the movies. He would walk closer to his home but his father would never change in size, he always seemed immense.

Once, when Peter was by himself looking up at the house from the top of the bluff, at his father standing high against the sky, he thought he saw his old man wave to him. He wasn't quite sure but a few paces on he definitely saw his dad wave. To him. He felt something deep inside, in his chest, a quickening of his heart, and he smiled. It was his dad's point wave, where he would brush the air with his falling hand. But then, from behind him, Peter heard some kids calling out, a whole party of five or six or maybe even more, all of them waving and jumping up and down. One was swirling a jumper above his head. It was this band his father was waving at, not him. He started to cry, and he cried all the way home, even when he was running, before going inside to his bedroom and crying some more.

Now, Peter looked at his father sitting in his comfy chair, at his tartan zip-up shoes and white socks. He was eighty-two and he looked so old, his shoes loose around his feet and a cardigan sailing around his arms. His hair was white and thin and his skin sunken at the temples. His breath was shallow. His father. Peter felt a stab in his chest.

And then his father opened one eye, then the other. He blinked and they stared at each other.

Ken held up his hand and, letting it fall, brushed the air with it. He smiled.

'Well, how'd you be, you big thing? How you'd be?'

And suddenly he didn't seem so old, and his eyes shone. He was happy.

Peter smiled and nodded slightly. 'Pretty good.'

'Good. That's a fine thing to be.'

Peter held his father's gaze and racing through his mind was one of the first things he had done when he had started at uni. He'd gone to Mayne Library and looked up 'monster delicio'. Its proper name was *Monstera deliciosa*, a plant that's native to the rainforests of Mexico. It had other names: cheese plant, Swiss cheese plant, monster fruit, Mexican breadfruit and delicious monster.

He wanted to tell his father that he knew all along that they had made up the story about the Aztec magic. He knew. All the times that his own children had visited their nanna and Pop here in the house where he grew up, and had sat in the backyard with their eyes closed tasting the magic Aztec food, he had wanted to say, 'I know you're making this up.'

And to top it off, his wife Kate had sat there laughing, her eyes closed, with their baby daughter on her lap, and yelling out, 'Turkish delight!'

'Your mum's got very good taste,' said Mary Kennedy.

I always knew you were making it up, he thought now. But he didn't say it out loud, he just thought, this, all this, is slightly odd.

There was a bark behind him and he turned to see a fat little fox terrier-cross at the bottom of the stairs, quickly joined by a barking, equally fat labrador. Then he heard his mother's voice.

'Omar, Pavvo, stop, now!'

The foxy was named after the actor Omar Sharif and the labrador's girth and howls were an obvious indication he was named after the tenor Luciano Pavarotti.

'Oh yeah, I'd be barking at him, too,' said his mother to Pavvo as she rounded the corner.

She said it with a smile, and Peter smiled back. She was nearly as old as her husband but she was still tall and strong. She started up the stairs, dressed in a bushed-cotton tracksuit, her shirt collar folded neatly over, a hanky popping out from the bottom of her sleeve and in her hand her stick. She didn't need the stick for support but her husband had found a nice bit of wood on the beach one morning and had shaped it into a hiking stick for her.

She looked at Peter with shrewd eyes and a smile. A gentler version of her mother.

'Well, don't just loom there on the stairs. Come on then, give me a hug.'

He bent down and his mother poked him in the stomach with her stick. 'And what's this, here?' she said, pointing at the satay-sauce stain on his shirt.

'You've got problems with your sump-oil rings, have you?' said his father.

Peter had never got over the way his parents worked as a type of double act. Sometimes good cop–bad cop, sometimes Morecambe and Wise.

'Just a bit of food,' he said.

'Bit of food? A bit! You've been eating in your car again, haven't you?'

Peter stood at the end of his mother's stick.

'I saw you, you know, in that little red car as you came between the Savannah and the jetty. All over the shop and a mouth full of food.'

'Oh, he's here now,' said Ken.

'Ran into your friend Wayne Dixon the other day; he's in the police now, you know,' continued Mary.

'I know, Mum. Said hello to him.'

'He pulled you over, didn't he? You were all over the place.'

'No, he just said hello.'

'That was nice. He was always a nice friend to you.'

Peter Kennedy thought that Wayne had been a bit over-enthusiastic. And he said, half to himself, 'Yeah, wanted to catch up tomorrow night, maybe . . .'

'Well, that'd be good.'

'Maybe.'

'What are you here for, son?'

'Yes, why are you here?' asked his mother.

'You brought your crew, have you, Peter?'

'No, they're all at home.' It's only me, he thought.

'They wouldn't fit in the car. *You* barely fit in it, like a swollen Noddy.'

'Well, there's a thing,' said his father.

Yes, just me. 'Only up for a few days. Bit of work.'

'Never really liked Noddy – bit too chummy with his mate. Did you like Noddy, Peter?' said his father.

'Big Ears,' said his wife.

'Big Ears, that's right,' said his father. 'Big Ears.'

'So you're here for work,' said Mary.

'Pulling down or putting up?' said Ken.

'Just a look-see at a few things. Mind if I camp here?' He heard himself and wondered why on earth he spoke like someone of his father's generation when he was back home.

Ken coughed up a small laugh. 'Camp here? Of course you can.'

'You can come down and have coffee with Pearl and us tomorrow,' said Mary. 'Before you go off to work –'

The labrador started to howl again.

'Oh, Pavvo.'

'Always got – Pavarotti, shush now – a room for you here. Stop it.'

Omar growled at Peter.

'Maybe they can smell that spill on your shirt, Peter?'

Pavarotti started up again.

'I'll take you out for tea at the Leagues Club if you like.'

'Oh, no time for that. Show week,' said his mother.

'Why didn't you say you were coming?' said his father.

'Didn't know until yesterday.'

'And your point being?' His mother turned to the dog. 'Now stop it.' And she banged the stick on the step and Pavarotti stopped howling and looked about with large apologetic eyes. 'Could have told us, you big thing,' she continued, putting down her stick and giving Peter a cuddle. And a kiss. 'It's lovely to see you, Peter.'

'Cracking,' said his father.

'How's Kate?'

'Good.'

'And the kids?'

'All good.'

His mother looked at him for a bit and then held his hand. 'Well, that's good.'

'You're in time for the show,' said his father. 'I've got a lovely stout and even better pilsener in this year. Should do very well.'

'Don't know if I can stay for the show.'

'Oh, come on Peter, you've got to stay –'

'Your mother's got a cracking chutney in and some top-shelf lemons plus all the usual –'

'Yes, lemons are very good this year and the tangelos are a lay-down.'

'Don't get ahead of yourself, my love.'

'Ken, the tangelos are a lay-down.'

'All right, just saying. Remember the grapefruit.'

'Well, you always want to bring up the grapefruit, don't you?'

Ken Kennedy slowly held his hands out in front of him like some kind of prophet. 'Just saying, Muz,' he said gently.

'Yes, well, I suppose Mrs Dunstan's were pretty spectacular so that was a bit of a turn-up, but there we have it.'

There was a slight pause and then Mary Kennedy winked at her husband before turning back to Peter.

'Come to the bingo night. Say hello to your brother and sister.' She tugged softly at her husband's hand. 'Let's go in and we'll see Gary now on the telly,' she said. 'Come on, my old man.'

Ken eased himself up from his comfy chair, straightened his cardigan, picked at his shorts and led them into the house.

Chapter Six

The dogs rolled in and headed straight into the kitchen, bouncing by the sink as Mary washed her hands then chatted to the dogs while she fed them.

In the living room Ken Kennedy stood over the table with a collection of remotes. 'These bloody things!' he rubbed his fingers and thumb together, hovering over which control he wanted to use, like a surgeon deciding which instrument to pick up. 'Pearl's fellow Len sorted all these out the other week. Said there was one – this one, I think – that was a universal control. Except the bloody thing isn't.'

'Ken, it's the one with the Band-Aid on the bottom,' Mary called out.

'Yes, love – got it.' He rolled his eyes. 'Ah, the Band-Aid. I mean, we used to manage all right, but the bugger comes in and changes it almost every bloody time they're over.'

'Ken, he means well and really he's quite handy. His shop is doing well.'

'Anybody can mean well, love. There's people who'll tell you Hitler meant well if you let them.'

'How is Len?' asked Peter, and he heard his mother laugh.

'Orlendo, if you please,' said his dad. He had his tongue jammed between his teeth in concentration. 'This should do, shouldn't it? Yes, Orlendo Lane. There you are.'

'Orlendo?'

The television hummed into life.

'That's what Len calls himself now. Orlendo Lane.'

Peter Kennedy stood quietly and then laughed.

'Yes, all right,' said his mother. 'God, Pavarotti eats like you, Peter. He's all over the shop.'

'He's changed his name?'

'Well, he thinks it sounds better than Len Lane. Or Leonard Lane, for that matter.'

'See if you can come for coffee with us and Pearl tomorrow, just see,' sang out his mother from the kitchen.

On top of the television was an old GI Joe doll of Peter's. One of the models with soft spongy hands that were heralded as 'Kung Fu Grip'. When he was about ten he was given one at the RSL Christmas party, and the scary Mr Sorenson was playing Santa and barking at each kid who was given a present, 'Now what do you say? What do you say?'

Peter had stood staring at the bellowing Santa, grabbing hold of what there was between his legs in fright. And Santa had told him, in his booming voice, 'Don't play with yourself, just say "Thank you".'

Peter remembered thinking, years later, when he heard that Mr Sorenson had died on the golf course, that it served him right. He was always yelling. Ken Kennedy had said it was because he was in the Navy but had never been to sea. 'He's a cranky old blowhard who never really did that much.'

Bob Boxal, the father of Peter's friend Gavin, had said not to worry about Percy Sorenson because he always liked to yell at the kids of fathers who had served. 'It's because your dad did his bit in Korea, young fella, that's all. The only action old Percy saw was what he dropped down the toilet. You'll be right. And you've got your dolly soldier.'

His dolly soldier.

Peter had never really played with it that much so it had been forgotten until some years ago when his mother had found it and made it a little maroon outfit, coloured its fuzzy buzz-cut blond hair ginger, sat it on a plastic toad that one of the twins had given her as a birthday present and rechristened the old GI Joe Darren, after Darren Lockyer, the Queensland Rugby League player. Then Darren had been placed on the television set. After every State of Origin series Darren either rode the toad with his Kung Fu Grip hands held high in triumph or cupping his bowed ginger head in misery. This year had been a good one for the Maroons so Darren rode the toad happily.

The wall behind the television was covered in family photos, and the effect could be disconcerting at times. At first sight the images were like a congealed mess, but whenever anybody stood before them for any length of time or sat watching television, an image would jump out and cease to be just a photo but turn into a memory. The photos stretched back to the childhood shots of Ken Kennedy and Mary Dauth, as she was known then.

There was a photo of the uncle that both his mother and father had said Peter would end up looking like, Donald Dauth. The picture depicted a tall man, shirt tucked tightly into his trousers, standing a little forlornly in a 1950s Brisbane park. He looked like the last remaining bowling pin waiting for the ball to come hurtling down the alley to clean him up. Alongside this was a photo of a shirtless man in army shorts and slouch hat tipped at a ridiculously jaunty angle, a 21-year-old Ken Kennedy. Next to this Mary Kennedy beamed out in a short white sixties-style dress patterned with large blue circles. She was impossibly young then.

The twins and Ellie were Ken and Mary's only grand-children and there were a number of photos of them – posed school portraits, sporting successes and the three of them sitting on the dugong dog turd. Not far from the dugong shot was a corresponding one of Peter with his brother and sister in the same pose. His three kids, he decided, all seemed happier than he and his siblings did in their photo.

Amongst the childhood photos were little histories of his time with Kate – her introduction to his parents when they had both made a fuss of the girl from Melbourne; Kate in high-waisted jeans, a lime-coloured jumper and white sports shoes; 1985. That photo had been taken a few minutes after the girl from Melbourne had met Peter's mother. And only half a minute after Ken Kennedy had said appreciatively to his son, 'Jesus, Peter, you must be using better berley to attract a catch like her. Well done, you.'

One of Kate and his mother spitting watermelon seeds into a bucket. Peter and Kate's wedding; he in a blue suit with a ruffled shirt and bow tie and Kate in a swirling dress with her hair cascading dowon in a mass of brown curls. Shots of his children mixed in with ones of him as a child. Kate's parents and his. And his best man, his brother, Gary, looking even slimmer than today and very handsome with a full head of hair. There were a few of Gary and his friends, all fit and tanned and smiling, all with lots of lovely hair.

Peter laughed a little. Where did all that hair go, Gary?

Then there were the photos of Pearl Kennedy, or Aunty Pearl, as Peter called her on the quiet to his kids, and Leonard Lane, now known as Orlendo Lane.

It's one thing to know someone all their life. Watching how their life flails about, stalls, takes a couple of bad turns then continues to limp along with the occasional but spectacular scraping against fate's speed bumps with sparks showering all those close to them. It's another thing for that person to be your sister.

The wall of photos was a record of of Pearl going from disaster to disaster. He had never known anybody to be in so many photos with eyes half-closed and grimacing in mid-smile, or simply to be caught in mid-rage, perplexed or in some operatic pose. Pearl's wedding, when it had poured with rain, set the benchmark for catastrophe very high. Her dripping hair had fallen down around her face like melted cheese from a burnt toasted sandwich. She was caught in the shot with one eye half-open, the other one shut and her mouth agape, like a landed fish. It was her cousin Millie who had later described the image as 'a homicide scene' when the photos were being passed around.

A little hard perhaps, but unfortunately very accurate. Gary had said it wasn't *that* bad and decided it was more like an image from one of those trashy magazines with their photo spreads of celebrity deaths.

'Oh, Pearl would love to hear that,' Peter had muttered at the time to his little brother.

The marriage itself hadn't been a success. Ed Bovaine, a tall man with no chin and bad skin, had been a financial planner who, although quite successful at advising people about what to do with their money, especially Pearl, had been less than reputable when it came to where his personal interests lay. He had fallen passionately in love with a woman who worked in a fish-and-chip shop, then with the receptionist in a real-estate office and then with an account manager at the bank before returning to the fish-and-chip shop woman. There had followed the fire services union representative, and the pattern continued. Pearl's marriage hadn't resulted in any offspring and hadn't lasted two years.

There was a cheerier series of photos showing Pearl with pets; dogs, usually. The dogs got smaller as Pearl got larger. A few cats, a lizard, an axolotl, a three-legged horse and Pearl with both of her eyes closed. She had been a volunteer at the animal shelter for a very long time now and had these photos to prove it. Sadly, in these shots even the dogs rescued from the floods appeared to be more enthusiastic about life than she did.

Pearl, oh Pearl. There were yet more pictures of her with various children, who stood beside her like strangers. They were some of the foster children she had cared for over the years. There was a photo of an angry-looking boy with a crew cut and red hair, who was always breaking windows at the big house at barbecues and who'd pick unripened lemons off the tree and throw them. When he was told off by Pearl, who demanded to know what he was throwing them at, he said, 'Nothing, just the sky.' His aim was slightly off, and his best effort was two bedroom windows and a set of louvre doors. Then there was the dark-haired girl who was always drew on whatever she could find. She was pictured biting her lower lip and holding a pen in her hand while Pearl half-blinked with the Diploma of Education she had received that night, holding it back to front and proudly to the camera, a collection of the girl's drawing efforts – random shapes and buildings in black Texta – plastered across the paper. Then there was the one of her dressed as Boy George standing next to Demis Roussos. Well, Len Lane, as he was known then.

It had been taken at Pickersgill's charity Big Valley Bingo Night, a fundraising event held during the show for the animal shelter and a foster-parent organisation. It was the first time that Boy George Pearl and Demis Len Lane had posed together in public. They had met through an introduction agency and been together now for over a decade. 'To think,' said Pearl, 'that we met through the internet and yet Len lived only two streets away in Mead Crescent. *And* he was a volunteer at the animal shelter. Life!' She had smiled, shrugged her shoulders, shook her head and eaten some chocolate.

Len ran a relatively successful leaf-blower outlet, a fact that said a lot about him and also this place that was home to the kind of people who would buy leaf blowers, thought Peter Kennedy.

But Len Lane also had ambitions to become a radio broadcaster and in particular a sport broadcaster. And very particularly, a football broadcaster. Len was encouraged by Pearl and had, on occasion, called the local Rugby League team's matches on the community radio station. He was a civil celebrant, presented the trivia night at the Leagues Club, did the trots, was the Pickersgill Show announcer and stuck his hand up for most community events where a microphone and a loudspeaker were involved.

All this was very generous, but Len had modelled himself on the rather hyperbolic and old-fashioned radio sound of Ray Warren. Most of the time he spoke as if he were commentating a football match, in preparation should his chance ever arrive. This made his work as a celebrant a little eccentric at times.

Berryl Ginzanti, an old friend of the Kennedy family, had died about five years ago and at her funeral service Len-now-Orlendo, on the microphone, worked his way through the long list of charity and community work Berryl had been involved in as if he were calling a length of the minute back-line movement. 'Red Cross work with tea; Ladies Auxiliary started it off and then onto CWA committee work, over to the Show Society cookery and floral arrangement, then came Meals on Wheels and Bush Children's Holiday Camp. Berryl Ginzanti, steaming onto the mid-years with great work at the library, the Pickersgill Little Theatre and the work of Ginzanti at Zonta, topped off a remarkable piece of life. Would love to see it again.'

Changing his name to Orlendo had been a part of this preparation for the assumption of League-calling duties and a decision that both he and Pearl agreed would work.

Orlendo Lane. There he was, his photo displayed, appropriately, on the wall directly behind Darren Lockyer. Standing smiling in the good blue suit he always wore for show announcing. Orlendo was also the owner of one of the worst toupees known to man, a thatch that was exactly like a Davy Crockett raccoon-style hat with its puff of hair that tapered down into a darker mullet.

'Yes, your brother said he should have changed his name to Vegas Lane,' explained Ken to Peter. 'Sad thing is, I think Len –'

'Orlendo,' corrected his mother from the kitchen.

'Orlendo, yes; Orlendo quite liked the idea.'

'How is changing his name going to do anything for him?'

Ken looked directly up at his eldest child. 'How in Christ's name am I supposed to know how the fellow thinks? I can't even turn on the television!'

Peter turned back to the bank of photos.

He was very slim in the blue suit. And Kate seemed so happy. He could see himself now, dimly reflected in the humming TV set. He was no longer slim and his father wasn't a laughing young man any more, either.

Peter Kennedy resembled a giant avocado while his father seemed to be all cardigan and skinny legs.

'It should be this one, Mary. This is the Band-Aid one.'

Maybe I do look like bowling-pin Uncle Don, Peter realised. And not far from the wedding photo he saw a figure of a little boy in green shorts and red top, clutching at his balls as a cranky Santa held out his present.

The TV made a sound at last and just before the screen lit up, he was struck again by the enormity of the avocado reflected back at him.

'Oh, Peter,' said his mother as she walked in. 'Sit yourself down. Here you go, just in time. Gary's mate's finishing off the sport.'

The six o'clock news was on and a bloated-looking sports presenter threw back to the tight-faced newsreader with a moustache and hair that reminded Peter of Orlendo's Davy Crockett mullet. 'And next up is Gary Kennedy with all the weather. How's it looking, Gary?' said the newsreader.

There was the youngest child of Ken and Mary Kennedy, smiling handsomely in a shiny grey suit with his hair combed across his head in a valiant attempt to ward off middle-aged sparseness. He had his father's wide smile.

'Should be a cracking day, Gavin. All the details after the break.'

There followed an advertisement for pools and spas, another for a hardware company, one for good behaviour on the rail services and one for Crime Stoppers.

'He's looking well, isn't he?' said his mother of her youngest.

Peter nodded. The weatherman on the television. He realised his brother bore a striking resemblance to the happy ginger-haired Darren Lockyer, although with less fuzz on top to work with.

Peter and his parents sat on the couch together and his mother reached across and touched him lightly on the knee.

'This is lovely, all my babies back for the show. Just lovely.'

'Yes, cracking,' agreed Ken.

Peter smiled slightly. The show. The showgrounds. Best not tell anyone why he would be heading up there tomorrow, that's what Greer had said. So he nodded back to his parents. His brother reappeared on the screen, smiling, and chatted away about highs, lows, 'ripping conditions for the yachties' and other such weatherman banter. Peter looked past his handsome young brother, to Kate, smiling beautifully there on the wall.

His wife, he knew, hadn't smiled like that for a long time.

Chapter Seven

Peter woke in his old room and lay in his childhood bed. He looked up at the tongue-and-groove ceiling that his father had built. Lying there was always slightly disconcerting because the timber ceiling mirrored the floorboards so it felt as though the world had been upturned and he was floating in mid-air, looking down.

This house was an ode to the home renovation fads of the 1970s. Peter had the pine room; in his brother Gary's old room he could see an homage to dark wood panelling, and then if he cared to wander into Pearl's former bedroom he could have borne witness to the world of burnt orange and mission brown.

He sat up and scratched himself here and there. The room smelled of lavender and the past. He yawned and worked out that two days should do it as far as the showgrounds were concerned.

A trip to the land registry office and the relevant council department would be fine. And perhaps the local library for the title archives. Yes, two days and then he could go home, he decided, standing up to look out at Moreton Bay and a plane taking off slowly from Brisbane airport.

He should ring home at some time, but not now. They'd all be getting ready for the day. He reminded himself to dash something off for the father–daughter night.

Peter watched the plane climbing higher, up above the dock cranes and out over the bay. Where are you off to? he wondered, just as he always did when he saw a plane, even as a child.

It was the sense of possibility that attracted him. He flew often enough to know that most passengers were probably travelling for work. But the idea of heading somewhere different had always struck him as exciting.

As a kid he used to wave to the people in the plane but not now; some things should only be done when you're young. But then suddenly he changed his mind and gave a wave. Just a little one.

'Bye,' he said, before turning to get ready for his day.

•

A little later on Peter and his parents sat on the footpath outside the Galleon, a coffee shop down the road from the Kennedys' home. It was one of those cafes that played music to help you enjoy your coffee. A slightly dodgy practice at the best of times, but this morning even more so, with a song from a band called Racey straining out from the speakers in all its late-seventies glory, 'Lay Your Love on Me'.

It was a warm clear morning, not much after eight o'clock.

In the daylight his father seemed younger and stronger than he had the previous night, and he waved a long finger towards his son. 'Now you must come and see the beer section this year. Maybe you can give us a hand setting some of it up if you have to scoot off before the show starts.'

'Well, that'd be nice, wouldn't it?' said his mother.

Peter didn't respond, staring instead at men his own age exploding from tight Lycra cycling outfits, some trundling past, others on foot, leaning their bicycles against the cafe wall before clacking inside for a coffee.

They teetered clumsily like men in drag at some football prize night, wearing high heels and giggling to each other. They were practically skating on their riding cleats; most of them wearing wraparound sunglasses and sponsors' names plastered across their podgy bodies.

Why they would think it a good idea to stop for a coffee in their riding gear, Peter thought, was anyone's guess.

'I'll tell you this much for nothing,' said Ken Kennedy. 'If I'd worn that sort of gear when I was their age I would have been bloody locked up.'

'Yes, doesn't leave much to the imagination, but there you have it,' agreed Mary.

'Have what?' said Ken.

'Well, what do you think you have?'

'I don't know – you didn't tell me. Did she?'

'Oh, Ken, do you really need to know?'

'It'd be nice.'

'Well, there they are in their tight wrapping with not much to show for themselves.'

'Oh, steady on, love, children present.'

Peter wondered if his parents would ever stop speaking like this or whether it would get worse as they grew older.

A car pulled up at the side of the road. A police car. It was Wayne Dixon.

He wound down the passenger-side window and sang out, 'How are we this morning, Mr and Mrs Kennedy? Big Fella, how are we?'

He called me Big Fella, thought Peter. That's odd.

Both his mother and father waved back.

Why did he call me Big Fella? Why did he shout it out?

Wayne whooped his police siren and laughed, causing some of the goat-footed cyclists to turn their helmeted heads. One spilt his coffee over his Lycra-clad crotch.

Ken laughed.

Mary sang back, 'Not to worry, there's not much to scald there!'

Wayne gave a thumbs up. 'You right for tonight?' he shouted to Peter. 'Dinner? Couple of beers?'

Peter continued to stare. Then he heard his mother.

'Go on, Peter. He'd love to, Wayne. Like the old times!'

Wayne Dixon laughed his nice laugh and yelled, 'Well, we won't be getting any chips from here!'

Mary laughed.

The cafe used to be a fish-and-chip shop, the fancy one on the Peninsula.

'See you tonight!' And he drove off.

He was a little too eager was Wayne, decided Peter, and he looked at his mother. 'Thanks for that.'

'Oh, don't be a pain, Peter.'

'I've got to work.'

'Yes, what exactly are you doing?' asked his father.

'Just having a look-see.'

His father rolled his eyes and his mother said to her son, 'Well, if I could buy you a minimum of chips with 'mato sauce to make you feel better, I would.'

Peter found himself laughing.

The cafe was next to the site of the old ice works. The ice works had been a big building but it was the fish-and-chip shop that had stood out like a beacon. Above the door there'd been a sign with a top hat, gloves and a cane. It was called Top of the Town Fish and Chips, but almost everywhere on the Peninsula it was known as Astaire's or, more commonly, Fred's.

The fish they served was nearly always fine; the problem was with their chips. There were usually burnt bits in them that Peter Kennedy was convinced were fried beetles. As for their dim sims, they were the size of mines that could sink a ship. All yellow-blistered pastry, as thick as sheet iron and unique to Queensland.

It had been in this shop that Peter witnessed something he never believed could happen. One evening a man in red Stubbies, black thongs and a white T-shirt emblazoned with a Channel 0 iron-on transfer, ordered two crumbed mullet, a dim sim and 'the minimum' of chips.

How Peter loved that phrase: 'The minimum of chips.' It belonged to a special time and place. The era of Leo Muller Toyota, Wymps Tyre Service, Brisbane Bitter, Don Seccombe and Curtain Wonderland.

On top of the classic fish-and-chip order this daredevil went for something that placed him on the Mount Olympus of junk food – the only time Peter Kennedy had ever seen it happen. He ordered a jar of mussels from a shelf behind the frying vats. Even the dark-haired woman who ran the place seemed uneasy. 'You sure?'

Mister Channel Transfer T-shirt nodded. 'My word, let's get at them.' And then he paused, while Peter looked on. 'How much are these things?' he continued.

The woman smiled tightly and said, 'Haven't got enough?'

There was a silence. It was as if she was accusing him of using the cost of the jar as some sort of excuse not to eat them.

Channel 0 Transfer tilted his head back and then rummaged through his wallet, frowned and retrieved some coins from the front pocket of his Stubbies.

'There you go, it's a sheep's head, but that should do you.'

Peter Kennedy knew, even at the age of eight, that the sheep's head was an old style ten-cent piece. But he also knew it all depended on the person who the coin was given to, whether it would work or not. He had once taken a sheep's-head ten-cent piece on the sly from the ashtray in one of his father's utes and tried to spend it at the corner shop by the draper's on the walk home from school one afternoon.

He had stood by the lolly case and gone through the painstaking process of choosing between Cobbers, Fags or Black Cat chewing gum while the man behind the case tapped his fat knuckles on the glass top with increasing irritation. 'Come on, come on.'

Peter had settled on two packets of Fags and had handed over the ten-cent piece with the sheep's head.

The man stopped tapping his fat knuckles and loomed over Peter. 'This is a shilling – not legal tender, champ. You can't buy anything with this.'

Peter Kennedy had stared as the man took the sheep's-head coin and put it into the till. 'I'll keep that for the government.'

Peter knew it was a lie but the man was a grown-up. There were times, even now, when suddenly he would think of that man and his lie. Looking after it for the government. Sure.

The expression on the woman's face at Fred's made him think she might be like Fat Knuckles, but as she took the sheep's-head coin she smiled like a gypsy selling some potion in an old midday movie. 'Here are your mussels.'

Channel 0 Transfer took them with a nod, went outside and, while waiting for his mullet and the minimum of chips, he gave a defiant look to the gypsy woman inside and cracked the jar open.

He picked out a couple of mussels.

'F--k a duck.' He grimaced. 'They taste like snot!'

Peter's mother had roared.

'You reckon I should?' Channel 0 Transfer asked her.

'Come on, you.'

'Fair enough.' And with that he finished them off.

'Well done!' Peter's mum yelled before starting to applaud. She turned to her two children, standing there in their slippers and pyjamas. 'Come on! How about that?'

And taking her cue first Pearl and then Peter began to applaud in appreciation.

Channel 0 Transfer gave a little nod, like an old-time cricketer saluting the crowd after a half century, as if to say, 'Thanks, but it's really not that much.'

A jar of mussels from a shelf above the frying vats. Actually, Peter thought, that was better than a half century, it was like a hundred before lunch.

Now, all these years later, Peter noticed that the shop was missing its sign with the top hat and gloves. He was pretty sure that the table where they now sat was the same spot where he had stood and applauded Channel 0 Transfer's mussel feat.

'You thinking of mussel man?' said his mother.

'Oh, that's something I'd have liked to see,' said his father.

Peter smiled.

'A jar of mussels from on top of the fryers. On this very spot. Mighty effort, that.'

'Where do people like him go?' asked Peter softly.

'Well, where do you think they go?' said his father. 'They just go home.'

'Get on with their lives,' agreed his mother.

'He probably would have gone straight to the toilet though.'

'Ken!'

'Well, a whole jar of mussels!'

Peter glanced around. There weren't any red Stubbies about; just Lycra, cleats and a few crying babies and three-wheeled prams.

'Oh my giddy aunt,' said his mother.

'Holy Christ,' said his father.

There was the ding of a bell and Peter turned back to the road.

And there she was, his twin sister, Pearl, with Len-now-Orlendo Lane. The two of them on bikes. Although, on reflection, Peter decided, he couldn't really say they were *on* bikes. Orlendo was long, very thin, very tall and sort of draped over his bicycle like a passionfruit vine over a trellis. And as for Pearl. Oh, Pearl. She wobbled on her bike. And it wasn't as though she was that big, but she seemed unbalanced in her Lycra. Indeed, her close-fitting outfit was really a variation on a theme, because along with racing-team names and logos were some hand-crafted touches – on the left front was a Hobbytex labrador with a patch, which was the symbol of the Pickersgill Peninsula Animal Shelter, and on the back there was a stencilled figure in a glittered jumpsuit. This was a tracing of Frank Ifield, a popular Australian singer from the early 1960s. Peter looked at Frank Ifield as his sister turned after stepping off her bike. Who would use his image on anything? Oh well, his nanna and his father had liked him well enough, and somehow it was just like Pearl to do this.

Frank sang songs about yodelling, about being taught how to yodel, about yodelling when he was blue and yodelling when he was happy. And even when the song *didn't* involve yodelling, Frank would yodel anyway. 'I Remember You' was his big hit, and he yodelled in that too.

The stencilled figure was a tracing Pearl had done from the cover of a greatest hits album for which yodelling Frank had donned a sparkly jumpsuit. His slightly distorted figure became the symbol for Big Valley Bingo, which Pearl organised and called, with Orlendo as spotter. The Big Valley Bingo logo arced over yodelling Frank and also Pearl's rather broad bum.

Pearl tried to lean on her left foot but the cleats slipped on the bitumen. She grasped the hoarding that doubled as a windbreak to the cafe, and the whole thing trembled like a bed sheet on a washing line in the wind. She wasn't large, but she'd always been described by her nanna as 'a strong girl, that Pearl'.

Peter noticed that his sister now had an iron grip on the hoarding and she gave a low grunt as she steadied herself. He remembered when they were not yet ten, watching the Commonwealth Games one rainy Sunday from New Zealand. It wasn't anything that exciting like swimming or the running, but, of all things, shot-put. Nobody was really paying that much attention to the athletes hurling cannon balls with grunting effort. Although Peter Kennedy did think that of all the odd sports you watch on these Olympic or Commonwealth occasions, you never heard much grunting or obvious signs of effort. But the shot-putters, they did grunt. And shriek. 'She's loud,' he said to nobody in particular.

His father looked over the top of the *Sunday Mail* and peered at the television.

'Very hefty effort,' said a disembodied voice from the telly.

'You ever thought of shot-put, Pearlie?' Peter heard himself say.

Pearl lay on the floor colouring in a competition from the *Sunday Mail*'s 'Kids' Corner'. It was of a smiling princess and happy squirrels.

She looked up at the television.

Another grunt and a smattering of applause. 'Also a mighty heave there,' came the disembodied voice.

'You'd be good at it, Pearl.'

There was a silence, then Pearl burst into sobs and ran to her room.

His sister Pearl.

His father leant down and gave him a clip over his ears. 'Peter, if you meant that the way it sounded stop being such a smart-arse. Go and apologise to your sister. And if you didn't mean it the way it sounded then for a smart boy you're a bloody cabbage head. Go and apologise.'

And so he had. He sat there remembering what he had said. 'I'm sorry, Pearl. I didn't mean it like you might think. You're not big and noisy like those hefty girls. I just think you'd be good at it.' Although as he said it, he had wondered, What's wrong with being a strong and healthy girl? It wasn't much of an apology. He had stood and watched as she pushed her face further into the pillow.

His sister Pearl.

'And hello there to you. What a beautiful morning,' said Orlendo in a voice that seemed to have been borrowed from a 1966 *Four Corners* report.

Peter laughed and Pearl stared at her brother.

'We're out and about on pedal power,' said Orlendo.

'Yes, I can see that,' said Mary Kennedy. 'When did you take up riding a bike?'

'And wearing that gear?' added Ken.

'It's a recent look-see effort, if you will, but we've taken to it like . . . Well, like ducks to water!'

Pearl slipped again in her cleats, grabbing the hoarding and grunting some more.

Mary tried to not say anything. Peter Kennedy laughed again. Orlendo, meanwhile, was in full Ray Warren mode. 'Nice to see you, Big Fella. Perhaps you'd like to put your hoofs to the old Malvern Star?'

'Thanks, mate, but I think I'll be right.'

'That's not a Malvern Star though, Len – Orlendo – is it?' asked Ken.

'Well, no. No, you're right. Just some generic bike chat. Now, can I fetch you a coffee, tea or Bonox?'

'We're right thanks, Len-Orlendo,' said Mary Kennedy.

Pearl sat down, took off her helmet and a mess of dyed hair sprang out. Then she removed her wraparound sunglasses. 'Hello, Peter.'

'Pearl,' said her brother.

'What are you up here for?'

'A bit of a look-see,' said Ken.

Pearl tossed her head and shook her hair. There was a lot of it.

'How far did you ride?' asked Peter.

Pearl gave him her look. A look that said, 'I'm ready to be hurt and upset.'

It was the sort of look that actors in soap operas have. Peter Kennedy had sat in a departure lounge once at an airport somewhere staring at nothing really and then had found himself watching the television, which was tucked high in a corner almost as an afterthought.

It was playing a show with two women, one blonde, one dark-haired, and a man. The women had big hair and the man had not much and an eye patch. They paused a lot and stared.

Then the screen was filled with the woman with the big black curly hair. And big earrings and odd make-up. And then she opened her mouth and stared with wide brown eyes and the camera rolled steadily in.

Peter Kennedy had sat transfixed. She looked exactly like Pearl.

And then she spoke, 'Roark, you were my destiny and yet you stand before me with my own sister Revella, and tell me our love was tainted by my jealousy!'

And she stared. Then the man with not much hair and an eye patch walked towards Pearl's doppelganger and cupped her chin in his hand. 'Cassandra Denim, look into my eye!'

And then she had really stared. 'You have made good choices in your life.'

The show was called *All This and Tomorrow Too*.

Peter looked at Pearl now in her Lycra, giving her *All This and Tomorrow Too* look and he started to laugh.

'What's wrong?'

'Nothing. Just wondering how far you've ridden this morning.'

'Come on, now,' said their mother. Mary spoke to them like they were still children.

'Orlendo and I thought we might enjoy a new way of getting about.'

'That's lovely,' said Mary.

'And we've ridden to the bridge and back.'

Peter knew that Pearl would want to talk about the last conversation they'd had. Fight, he guessed she would call it. The last time he had mocked her. It had been Boxing Day two years ago.

They had been having lunch over at her and Len's house. Well, it had been Len back then. It had rained and so the barbecue was a bit of a trial. Pearl had made her creamy lasagne and salads with radish.

They were all sitting on the verandah. It was humid. Fetid even. Clothes stuck to skin. Then, as it does in the south-east of Queensland, it began to pour. Not with rain but with hail. From nowhere.

The hailstones pounded the corrugated-iron roof. As they fell the family, packed tight on the verandah, heard a cry.

'Was that Len?' asked Mary.

'Is he all right?' said Peter to his sister.

The sound intensified, the hail hammering so hard that it stopped being just a noise. The atmosphere seemed to vibrate with so much energy that nobody could hear anything except the golf ball–sized hailstones. Peter had turned to Ellie to see if she was okay and saw her standing wide-eyed and smiling, gripping her mother's hand. The backyard was a bubbling broth of hailstones.

Just as quickly as it had started, the hail stopped.

There were a few moments of silence, during which everyone seemed to hold their breath; the noise had been so deafening that afterwards all anyone could do was sit.

It's always exciting when nature throws a little bit of anarchy your way, but there on that verandah something was added in those few moments after the storm.

A little touch of Ray Warren, or a would-be Ray Warren.

Len had always had a habit of going relentlessly over his favourite passages of sports commentary, to keep his hand in and his whole being ready. Sometimes he'd call doing the dishes as he did the dishes or phantom race calls in his shed in the backyard. He would invariably turn the volume down on the television to call the football matches.

And then he hit upon the idea of calling any program that might be on, just to test his range.

Len's real party trick, though, was to let his guests, friends or whoever might be handy pick a program, DVD or even something off the internet and then he would proceed to call it for them.

His fall-back call was a mash-up of race caller Greg Miles bringing home Makybe Diva in her last Melbourne Cup win combined with his classic rendition of a last-minute State of Origin try to Queensland.

Earlier in the afternoon the kids had switched on the TV, turned the sound down on a randomly selected program, and dared Len to call the play. They had all gathered around and to Peter Kennedy's intense delight the program was, of all things, *All This and Tomorrow Too.*

'Siiixty out and a minute to play, Meningaaaaa to Langer and then a dummy runner, to the cunning hands of Walters, the Blues encroach onto Carne, the Blues defence is there. Not before he floats a pass to the grasping fingers of Renouf.' He loved to roll his Rs on Renouf. 'He gathers and he's off – away from Barnhill now Renouf into HanCOCK! Here comes Queensland, onto Darren Smith he draws the defence, to Langer, here's the big fella, Meningaaaaaaaaaa surging to the line now it's Coyne, it's to Coyne, a try. Try, Queensland. Try, try, a nation stands to its hero and a champion becomes a legend!'

There was no correlation between what Len Ray Warren-ed away at and what was occurring on TV. The fact that each time Pearl/Cassandra appeared on the State of Origin-cum-*All This and Tomorrow Too* Len was howling 'Meningaaaaaa! The Big Fella' was an added bonus.

That and the fact that every head looked at the screen and then back to Pearl, standing there in her cracker paper crown, big hair and earrings, and back to the television set and Cassandra, her big hair and her tiara.

Ken Kennedy was about to point out the similarity but was stopped by a poke in the arm from his wife. He took the hint, smiled absently and said, 'There you go.'

Len looked pleased with himself and nodded to Pearl and just for good measure had, using what he called his Mr Midnight voice, repeated softly, staring into Pearl's wide eyes, 'Meningaaaaaa!'

They had words in the kitchen. After that Len's trips to the drinks fridge downstairs became a little more regular. He was alway a very generous host, and after the chat in the kitchen with Pearl he became especially generous to himself.

There was nothing Len liked better than a storm on the roof, a wall of noise where he could just let rip, so the burst of thundering hail provided the perfect opportunity. Fumbling with the lemonade and Ken's home brew, he wasted no time and almost as soon as the first stones hit he began to bellow.

To Len's ears all was well as he happily collected a stout for himself while calling forth his favourite lines.

It was, however, a very strong stout and Len had been to the fridge quite a few times. So instead of the sweeping commentary of Queensland play his tone was more like a rolling cavalcade of some of his favourite sounds. Unfortunately, he never really got past Meninga.

'Meninga –, Meninnngga – a, Meninga – gaaaaaaaa, Meningaaa, a nation stands to its hero and a champion becomes a legend!' That's when he hit his head on a crossbeam.

The storm had muffled most of Len's howls and by the time the hail stopped he was taking another breath and a sip of stout.

The family's mass intake of breath after the storm was ended by the explosion of 'Meningaaaaaaaaaaaaa!'

'Holy Christ!' exclaimed Ken.

Mary dropped her cup of tea and Gary jumped.

After another 'Meninga!' there was a shuddering thump from below and Len staggered up holding his head, slipping on the hailstones.

'You've made good choices in your life, Pearl,' Peter said, smiling.

Nobody spoke, save for Len, who intoned 'Meninga' one more time.

Pearl had said nothing back then and she said nothing now, as they waited for their coffees outside the cafe.

'How's the teaching going?' Peter finally asked his sister.

'Three days a week. Very good, suits me.'

'You don't want to go full time?' he asked.

Pearl shook her head.

'Pearl's got more on her plate than most, Peter,' said their mother. 'She teaches Art and History.'

'You still doing the school plays?' he asked.

'Of course I am. Nobody else puts their hand up for them.'

'And she's organising the local play again, too,' said Ken.

Pearl looked at Peter.

He smiled. 'What are you up to there?'

'We're doing *Old Time Music Hall* and then another musical. Haven't decided on it yet, though. Maybe *The King and I*; we did that one at the school.' She shook out her hair.

'*The King and I*?'

'Yes, now that was good when you did it. A bit confusing but it was good,' said Ken.

'Dad!'

'I said it was good, Pearl.'

'What was so confusing?'

'Well, I just didn't know who was who. It was hard to tell who was Siamese, Taiwanese . . . No, they're Thai, aren't they?'

'Dad, racial considerations do not come into casting!'

'Or whatever "wanese" they might be, then, and who was English and who . . . I know we're made up of all sorts now and that's lovely –'

'Dad, the roles are not racially defined any more!'

'Yes, all right, but I don't know why the person playing Deborah Kerr was Chinese.'

'She was Vietnamese.'

'Ken, that girl is as Australian as you are,' said Mary.

'Yes, I know, and she had a lovely voice but why did she have the red wig on?'

'She decided on that herself, Dad.'

'It was a bridge too far for me, that one,' he said.

'But it was good and they all seemed to have had fun,' said Mary, smiling at Pearl.

'Which was good,' agreed Ken.

'Good, yes, good,' Mary and Ken said together.

Pearl turned back to her brother. 'Your friend Wayne Dixon has joined the Musical and Arts Society.'

'Has he?' said Peter.

'They're going out tonight,' said Mary.

'Really? Now he'd be good in a musical,' said Ken.

'Why's that?'

'Well, he's got that nice laugh.'

Jesus, thought Peter Kennedy.

And thankfully the coffees arrived with Orlendo.

The waiter was a young man in a black T-shirt and tight jeans. He put down the tray of drinks. 'Two lattés, a cappuccino, a strong flat white and a skinny latté. Enjoy.'

Enjoy. He said 'Enjoy' like 'Up yours'. Peter hated it when waiters – or anybody for that matter – said 'Enjoy' as they presented something and then left with a flourish.

I'll enjoy it if it's any good, he thought. He was going to say it out loud when a woman in a turban and a pink tracksuit appeared in the doorway and strode over to their table to say hello to Pearl.

The two women stood and went to air kiss each other, but Pearl skidded on her cleats and Orlendo moved to try to catch her. Sort of.

'This is Joanna Whiles,' said Orlendo, as if he were introducing Barack Obama. He introduced her as someone who didn't need an introduction.

Who was Joanna Whiles? Peter wondered.

'Oh, please don't get up. Enjoy your coffee,' said Joanna Whiles graciously. 'I've just had my morning fix – a wonderful latté, half-Arabica blend lightly roasted.' She patted Pearl on the shoulder. 'Afraid I'm too much of a coffee enthusiast.'

'Joanna works in the arts industry,' said Orlendo. 'A gallery owner.'

'Yes,' said Joanna Whiles. 'And we're all coffee enthusiasts.'

'She used to live in Melbourne,' added Orlendo.

'Now that's where everybody's a coffee enthusiast.'

'Peter's from Melbourne.'

Joanna Whiles turned her turbaned head to Peter. 'Really?'

Peter nodded.

'Moved up here or . . . ?'

'He's up for a look-see,' his parents said together with a laugh.

'Oh yes?' said Joanna.

Peter nodded again.

'Where in Melbourne?'

'Mont Albert.'

'Oh,' she said, touching her turban. 'Very nice – the leafy eastern suburbs.'

Peter stared at her.

'Yes, you do look like you come from Mont Albert. Nice and comfortable.'

'Well, he's originally from here,' said Pearl. 'He's my brother.'

Joanna Whiles continued to look at Peter. 'So *you're* the Melbourne brother.'

Peter didn't say anything, just held his cup of coffee.

'You know, there's one thing that's a surprise about Brisbane and that is the coffee.'

He wondered why she'd said this.

'Good coffee. Very good coffee in Brisbane. Who would have imagined?'

'There you go,' said Ken Kennedy.

'And a thriving art scene all over the town, too – very surprising. Who would have thought in Brisvegas!'

Joanna Whiles, Peter decided, was the sort of person who equated coffee shops with culture and couldn't conceive that Australia has changed and grown over the years and that different cities celebrate their culture in different ways. In other words, the worst sort of showboater.

Brisbane has always had a fine coffee tradition, thought Peter, indignantly. He remembered when coffee meant big glass jars of brown powder with a blue sombrero on the lid. Pablo. Now that was coffee. It was superseded in the Kennedy home by International Roast, because, according to Ken, 'They use this in the Café-Bar at the BP servo. Top-shelf stuff.'

And then one morning Ken had actually gone and bought a Café-Bar coffee maker. 'It's all automatic,' he'd said, gesturing to the plastic knobs of the machine with 'Café Break Café Bar' emblazoned across it. It was accompanied by plastic bottles filled with powdered coffee, evaporated milk and sugar.

'All automatic, and this one comes with another special coffee – Caterer's Blend.'

Photographs were taken of family members standing next to it, as if it were a new colour television.

We could tell you about coffee, Joanna Whiles, thought Peter now. We could tell you about the TV ad with coffee grown by villagers somewhere in South America, waiting for the coffee buyer–adventurer with aviator sunglasses, bushy blond moustache and poncy hair, in a safari suit. Like the bigger brother of the Construction Worker from the Village People. He jumped from a helicopter, sipped the coffee like a nanna who'd lost her false teeth and enjoyed it as happy villagers threw their sombreros in the air. Peter had forgotten the brand of coffee, but knew the ad was shot at the Glasshouse Mountains.

Whenever the Kennedys saw the ad they would all scream, 'Glasshouse Mountains, *óle!*' Mary would do the same when she saw the coffee on the supermarket shelves. And the first time his mother had taken Peter for an espresso he had pronounced it with a Spanish accent, '*Éxpresso.*'

'Authentic coffee,' his mum said.

Authentic coffee in the Chermside Kmart.

Mary had ordered a Vienna coffee, which was a tower of cream from a spray can that cascaded over her cup in the manner of one of Engelbert Humperdinck's frilly white shirts.

Now *that* was a coffee.

'Well, we all just love a cup of half-roast Humperdinck Glasshouse, *óle*,' said Peter now.

And to his surprise Pearl burst out laughing.

His mother joined in, and his father.

'So,' said Joanna Whiles, bristling. 'I'll leave you to it.'

And as she started to go, Peter said, 'Enjoy,' in an even less sincere tone than the waiter had used.

Pearl had stopped laughing and was looking at her brother.

And Peter Kennedy caught himself thinking, I just thought of these people and me as We. We.

'Now that's odd,' he said to himself.

Chapter Eight

When they finished their coffees Orlendo suggested breakfast. Peter would have liked nothing better than to eat, but he'd had enough of the company for one morning so, standing, he gave his apologies, saying that he really should get going.

Orlendo Ray Warren-ed, 'That's a disappointment, but we'll be seeing you tomorrow night, no doubt.'

Peter stopped a moment.

'It's the Big Valley Bingo fundraiser,' Orlendo reminded him.

'Oh yes, yes. I'll have to see what I can do.'

He looked at the four of them sitting at the table. One long thin man in Lycra, one large woman in Lycra, and two old people holding hands. His father gave him a wave. 'Well, we'll be seeing you then.'

Peter nodded then walked to Red Getz, parked by the corner. His stomach rumbled and he realised he really did want to eat. He squeezed into the car and wondered about stopping at the bakery on his way to the showgrounds and the land registry.

As he mulled this over, he couldn't quite believe the number of people he passed on bikes. He shared the road with more of the same as the Galleon crowd, and some school kids without helmets riding on the footpaths, acrobatically throwing their stubby stunt bikes this way and that.

A clutch of about six people, wearing their Lycra riding outfits like second skins, were bunched together at a set of traffic lights. Drawing closer, Peter could see some of them trying to balance themselves and their bikes as they waited for the lights to change.

As he sat squashed into his car, he could see that these people were very fit.

One man gave up trying to balance and lifted a cleated foot from one of the pedals to the ground. He didn't, Peter noticed, skate precariously the way Pearl and Orlendo had done when they scrabbled outside the coffee shop. This man's leg was rock solid, like a billiard table's.

The group laughed and the man with billiard-table legs put both cleated feet on the road and nodded. The other balancing cyclists followed suit, all except for one. The riders whooped a little and laughed as she, too, finally balanced her bike with unnerving ease and grace. She flashed a brilliant smile and he could see that she was, for want of a better word, very,

very fit. Peter then realised that a few of the Lycra-clad men were looking at him.

It can't be, he thought.

He glanced back almost involuntarily to see her again, but found he had missed the light, and the group had already pushed off and started to gather pace.

There came a beep from a ute behind him and Peter revved up his car and accelerated past the cyclists.

No, it can't be, he thought again. Or could it?

He remembered a phone conversation with his father last year and being told, 'Every bugger up here seems to have gone bike mad. It's as if we've turned Dutch overnight!'

Peter had never quite understood what that meant, but on Ken's one trip overseas with Mary – a three-week bus tour of Europe – he had been particularly amazed by how many pushbikes there were in Holland.

'Every bugger's on a bike in Holland, you've never seen such a thing,' Ken had said.

Peter passed another group of riders and realised his dad had been right; they certainly had turned Dutch up here.

When he was a boy the only grown-ups he'd see on bicycles were the postie, old people with trouser clips and big straw hats and the occasional person who wouldn't normally be riding a pushie were it not for the fact that they'd lost their licence.

Pickersgill Peninsula was a small town so if you started to get around by bike you couldn't hope to escape the resulting ignominy. Riding was a sure sign of having done your driver's licence.

Peter's mother had an uncanny knack of being able to spot a rider on their bike of shame. Even before they appeared in her line of vision, she somehow sensed them. Driving up The Guts one morning she had suddenly cried out, 'Oh, there goes Mr Lamb on a *bike*. Must have done his licence.'

Peter hadn't seen anyone and then, as his mother slowed, she gave a couple of sharp toots of the horn in greeting. There, as if she'd discovered him with some inbuilt bike-riding radar, hiding between a bus stop and the Cut-Price store was Mr Lamb from the little hardware shop. He was riding a pushie and gave a shamefaced nod of acknowledgement before looking away as he tried to hold onto the bag of cement balanced on a rickety tray above the back tyre.

'Lost his licence. Knew it! That bag of cement is a dead giveaway.'

Peter shook his head now as he slowed to find a park not far from the Cut-Price store, which was these days the offices of a financial planning company called Bernie Nunn Wealth Creation.

He remembered his dream and wondered what had become of the women who had cut the slices of luncheon meat with the plastic wrap still on them; they had probably just gone home.

At least the bakery was still there. And, he noticed, so were a few of the more recognisable members of the Pickersgill pushbike brigade. Some of the old school.

Peter knew that cycling keeps you fit, and it had been a while since anyone could have called him anywhere near fit. He was overweight, but he was also tall, so he carried his weight well as his aunt had said when he was a boy.

'Tall men always carry weight well.' That was what Aunty Eunice had said, and even though she was as mad as a cut snake and had been fuelled by half a bottle of Pimm's and some hefty buckets of Blue Nun wine one New Year's Eve when she'd said it, for some reason Peter had tucked this little piece of wisdom away for future use in justifying his lifestyle.

He knew it was nonsense, especially when he remembered his uncle Brian, who had been the subject of her observation.

Uncle Brian was a tall, florid man with Brylcreemed hair plastered to his forehead. And he wore his weight all right. He was one of those men who, for reasons never really defined and which have long since been lost in the mists of time, always belted their trousers tightly around the middle of their vast gut, leaving symmetrical balloons above and below the belt line. Uncle Brian worked the cheerio bowl like a machinist in a factory. He didn't discriminate and picked up and then dipped a succession of cheerios, the little red-skinned sausages that tasted like rolled luncheon meat, into a smaller glass bowl of tomato sauce with clockwork precision. He only paused once when he picked up a particularly violently split cheerio, dripping with sauce, and observed, 'What about this? It's almost indecent, isn't it?'

It was a rhetorical question, really, because he didn't wait for an answer, which was just as well because Peter didn't want Uncle Brian explaining why the pink flesh dripping with tomato sauce was indecent. Thankfully, the offending sausage disappeared down his throat.

Even though Peter knew that cycling emits no pollutants, is good exercise and that most cyclists are probably very reasonable people who aren't insane would-be Lance Armstrongs or kamikaze city couriers and must be careful and competent enough to put up with a lack of bike lanes and the intolerance and indifference of motorists, he still didn't understand the clothes.

The advertising logos that plastered the body-hugging Lycra, the teardrop helmets and little white socks of the modern-day cyclist made the big straw hats and bicycle clips of old look like sartorial elegance.

That's the last time I feel bad about going to the local shops in my pyjamas, he decided.

Like his father said, once you would have been locked up if you went into coffee shops wearing goblin costumes, yet today people sit down to breakfasts undisturbed in their bizarre riding outfits while their perspiration dries quickly.

That is what Peter had been told by his junior planner, Claire, an avid cyclist; Lycra clothes dry perspiration quicker, and give comfort where it's needed most.

'Peter,' she had said, 'you'd appreciate it if you were a part of it.'

I see, he thought, like the Latin mass or Zumba or World of Warcraft or Facebook.

Then he couldn't help but think of the woman balancing on the bicycle. She did look very familiar, but it couldn't be her . . . Perhaps it was her daughter?

Peter was in the bakery now, along with an old-school Pickersgill pushie rider, who wore an orange construction hard hat with 'Utah Mining Blackwater' stencilled on the brow; it must have dated back to the late seventies and come from the first generation of great open-cut coal mines of central Queensland.

How this bloke had managed to find it was anybody's guess. Christ, thought Peter, I'm even *thinking* like my father talks.

He was snapped back into the present by Utah Coal Mines' order: 'Give us a lime milk – large – two party pies and a large pastie, thanks.'

Glancing around, Peter could tell that the bakery had changed hands. This was new Pickersgill. No more neat white triangular sandwiches in GladWrap straitjackets, no more long doughnuts with Engelbert Humperdinck ruffles of cream and too-sweet crimson jam, no more glutinous custard tarts or cream buns on steroids. Instead, lots of 'organic' this and that and 'gourmet' bits and bobs.

There were two people behind the counter, a pretty woman with a pierced nose and a pretty man with a neatly styled beard.

Peter wondered why Utah had come here. 'What are the Cornish pasties like here, mate?' he asked him.

'Cornish' apparently signified to Utah that Peter was a fellow crusader for old-school bakeries. There was no way a place like this would have Cornish anything.

Utah turned to him and, as one aficionado to another, confided, 'Mate, it's a bit 'spensive but they taste good. Real good. I usually hit the Viet place up by the water tower but me gout's got me this morning.'

'Right,' said Peter.

'No way I'd make it up the hill with me gout; bloody ankles are like a pair of Plumrose Christmas hams.'

Utah was from an era when people would think nothing of passing their time in conversation with complete strangers, telling tales of various bodily ailments, from breathing complaints and mental disorders to skin conditions.

Of course to Utah, Peter wasn't a stranger, he was a Person from Pickersgill and even if he didn't know Peter's name, he wasn't a stranger because he was here talking to him in Pickersgill.

'Got no grunt in me legs, not like the flash mob with their bikes out there.'

Utah collected his cardboard tray of goods and the pretty man with the styled beard asked Peter, 'How can I help you?'

This took time to register; it was something a doctor or dentist might say, but a bloke in a bakery? No matter how organically gourmet the food might be or how neat the man's beard, the question just didn't sound right.

'I'll have a beef pie.'

'Wagyu, Angus or regular?' said Styled Beard.

'I'll go the Wagyu,' said Peter. 'And I'll have a vegie-and-feta pie.'

'Flash order, champ,' said Utah, sounding a little betrayed.

So, with a salute to the spirit of Pickersgill bakeries past, Peter added, 'And a Cornish pastie and a chocolate milk.'

It sounded like a lot of food, even coming from Peter, and Styled Beard shuddered a little with uncertainty.

'And a *pastie*,' he repeated back to Peter, accentuating 'pastie'. 'And that's as takeaway, for one?'

'Yes, for one. And a chocolate milk too, please.'

'Well, if you're big enough and your pockets are deep enough, good luck to you,' said Utah.

Peter was going to respond when he heard a clack, making both he and Utah turn to see her as she entered. And Peter knew; he knew it was her.

Wayne Dixon had said she looked amazing. And he wasn't wrong. She was the same age as Peter, but standing there in the bakery he couldn't quite believe it. He thought of Aunty Eunice and about carrying weight well and stood watching this woman as she came in. Behind her in the glass doors he saw his reflection, not quite the ten-pin uncle, but he still dwarfed her. Peter had to admit that although Aunty Eunice might have been a tipsy old soak she nevertheless had a point.

The woman clattered in on her cleats, wearing her sunglasses and helmet, yet she didn't look awkward, and moved gracefully in her riding gear of clinging Lycra. She had, Peter decided, a confidence and a surety about her.

The effect wasn't lost on anyone; both the girl with the stud and the boy with the beard lit up as she approached the counter.

Peter remembered the first time he had seen her, that morning, near his home and on a pushbike of all things. It must been nearly thirty years ago and really not that far away from where he stood now, listening to Utah. It had been exactly seven thirty-five and thirty-eight seconds. He remembered that because he had just checked his LED Omega digital watch that his nanna had bought him for his birthday.

It was silver and the size of Ayers Rock. It did a number of things if you pressed the stubby little buttons on the side, but Peter had never really worked out exactly what. Sometimes it would flash a display of zeros, sometimes it would become a stopwatch, and sometimes it would go into alarm mode and emit a series of sharp beeps. But for some reason on that day, as Peter made his way to the bus stop, the watch had simply told the time.

And as he looked up, he had seen her on a bike, an old-style one even then, white with a blue stripe and a basket on the front. She was pedalling very fast but not going anywhere; the chain must have come off. She was wearing a Pickersgill High uniform, and let out a cry as she tried to stop the bike in her sports shoes. She hopped a little bit and the front wheel fell to one side and hit the gutter.

Peter kept walking towards her and could see a lick of grease from the chain about halfway up her calf. The girl's legs were lovely, he thought. He had looked up at her face and saw her staring back; she seemed a little unsure about him as his look became a stare.

She was very pretty. Lovely. A splash of freckles across her cheeks and deep brown eyes. He knew he should stop looking and try to say something but he couldn't make any discernible sound except for a catching noise in his throat, like one of the emus in the tiny enclosures at Alma Park Zoo.

The girl held his gaze, but Peter finally managed to look away by checking his wristwatch; he did so in such a jerky manner it took her by surprise. He flicked his arm out, up and in towards his face like an action toy. The sort with a panel in the back that you squeeze so its plastic arms and little balled fists punch out at some imaginary adversary.

And that was undoubtedly what this girl thought he was going to do, this staring boy in his city-school blazer. It didn't get any better when he finally managed to say something in a voice that sounded as if he was being choked: 'It's seven thirty-five and thirty-eight seconds.'

At the sound of his voice something died inside him and Peter was brought back to the present, standing at the counter of the bakery. Utah had moved on to his breathing problems, brought on by his emphysema. 'And never even smoked in me life. It's something in me lungs. Doctor said it was me being a house painter.'

Peter nodded and heard the woman in Lycra order.

'A coconut water, thanks – one of the organic ones without the flavour, Nell.'

The girl with the pierced nose smiled back and asked how far she'd ridden.

'Oh, just over to the next peninsula and back.'

'*Just?* Oh, give me a break!' said Nell. 'You're a freak!'

And the woman in the bike clothes made a half-laugh half-cry sound. 'Oh, thanks.'

It was that same noise she had made all those years ago, when she was in her school uniform with the oil mark on her brown legs, just above the white ankle socks. And Peter had taken a breath and said in his near-to-normal voice, 'Are you okay? Do you need a hand?'

She had made that noise and then said, 'The chain's come off.'

Peter had nodded and said he would put it back on for her.

She had smiled while he held the bike as she kicked her legs over the saddle and passed very close to him, close enough for him to inhale the smell of her shampoo.

As he remembered this now, he tried to inhale that clean scent again but instead, all he got was a smell of baking and Utah and yes, of all things, hot savoury meat. Like warm luncheon meat.

Utah coughed, swallowed and ploughed on, not quite believing his good fortune that his new Cornish-pastie mate was stopping for a chat. 'A house painter, you see, 'cause when I was doing me trade there was lead in paint. Lead got in me system.'

Peter Kennedy remembered more about the morning of the bike and the chain.

He had put his bag down and squatted by the bike. But as he remembered it now, he wasn't Peter Kennedy in his school blazer, he was Peter Kennedy, the architect, and instead of his bag, he put down his chocolate milk and his Wagyu beef and his feta pie and his pastie.

He had been there with her for a while, long enough to see his bus come over the top of the hill, but he didn't mind.

She had begun to talk.

She had come down here early, she said, before school, to buy some foolscap and new pens to finish an assignment for History.

'Just before the chain came off I realised I'd forgotten my money,' she said and she made that half-laugh, half-crying sound.

Peter managed to put the chain back on as his bus rolled past. 'I usually catch that,' he said.

'I'm sorry.'

He liked her freckles and he had smiled.

Then he heard Utah again.

'And me legs, then, 'cause of the gout and lead in the system and that's when it's the veins that kick in. Varicose veins, pretty bloody big. No way I can get up to the Vietnamese by the water tower on a morning like this.'

Peter had been seventeen, almost a man. He'd given her a foolscap exercise book and a couple of pens from his bag. 'Here, take these.'

She had tilted her head to one side and smiled. Her freckles rose to her eyes. 'Thank you. I'm Lisa.'

'Peter,' he had said and to his relief his voice had sounded almost normal. Perhaps that was why he had added with an attempt at nonchalance a great line in casual romantic conversation: 'I have lots of Kilometrico pens, my nanna gave them to me.'

Kilometrico pens. He said it as if he were some Arab sheikh giving her one of his many prize stallions from the palace stable. But no, what he was offering were a couple of plastic pens with a smiling worm leering out from their middles.

When he heard himself say those words, whatever hadn't already died inside him earlier when he had blurted out the time, gave up the ghost, keeled over and expired.

He knew he must have seemed like a total idiot, standing there in his blazer and long trousers, but to his amazement Lisa had smiled back at him and taken his exercise book and Kilometricos, before waving goodbye and riding away. Peter had busied himself with fiddling with his bag, but made sure he could still see her and he noticed that she looked back. Quite a few times.

He'd thought about her freckles and the mark on her legs all that day, which was fortunate because he was kept back after school for arriving late.

He had sat in a classroom with two boarders from western Queensland, who had been caught fighting in the showers and a strange boy from Mount Gravatt, who talked to himself during mass.

The four of them were supposed to do work, but the old teacher who supervised them sat reading the *Telegraph* while the boarders tried to stick each other with the ends of their compasses and the boy from Mount Gravatt sat and spoke quietly to himself. Peter spent the hour staring at a maths book and seeing only that mark above her white socks and her eyes. He checked the flashing face of his watch once to see how much longer he had to wait, but he needn't have bothered; all he could see was seven thirty-five and thirty-eight seconds. And Lisa.

When he came home later than usual that afternoon, he found his mother smiling at him from the verandah and his father standing in the garden hosing the lawn, while Pearl and Gary watched him through the windows.

Ken held the hose in one hand and a stubbie of home brew in the other.

Peter walked across the front yard and his father studiously ignored him until Peter had almost passed him, then he uttered an almost imperceptible and conspiratorial 'Eh.' Peter turned back to see his father's sly nod and raised stubbie. He stared at his father but Ken had already gone back to hosing his couch grass, with a smile on his lips.

'Well hello, Mister Late for School,' his mother called out.

'I had a reason.'

'Yes, I know. Your friend dropped something off for you.'

Peter wondered what she might be talking about, and then Pearl shouted from the windows, 'Yeah, your friennnd.'

'Friend, yeah,' added Gary.

Mary shushed them and then disappeared inside before reappearing with the exercise book Peter had given Lisa that morning.

Some pages had been carefully removed but then, on a page near the back, opposite a rough sketch he had made of a house, was something written in writing that wasn't his:

Thank you very much for helping me this morning, Peter Kennedy. My name is Lisa Sykes. And beside that she had written her address and her telephone number with the note, *I've got your Kilometrico pens; perhaps you can come and pick them up.*

Lisa had very neat writing, like most girls, but at a boys' school he hadn't seen that much of it. Peter read it over and over until some water was flicked at his feet.

'Come on, son, I want to hose there,' said Ken.

Peter moved away and then stopped when he saw on the page of his sketch she'd written something else.

It's a lovely looking house, but the roof overhang is a little too big, even if it is three levels, don't you think? And three levels wouldn't be approved anywhere in Pickersgill.

He read that again, too, and could see that the roof over-hang on the drawing was obviously too big. But it was only a sketch, a doodle, and he hadn't been thinking anyone in Pickersgill would want a house like the one he'd drawn; she should know that.

But then he remembered her smell and the mark and the freckles. And that sound she had made. Closing the book, he walked up the stairs.

That's when Pearl had yelled out, 'Kilooometricos!'

•

It seemed that Utah didn't have much more to say about any other ailments as Peter stood there, thinking back to that afternoon, remembering and then mimicking Pearl's drawl: 'Kilooometricos.'

Utah was clearly trying to understand what the big man was saying. 'Mate, it's not kilometres to the water tower just up the road there, but yeah, it might as well be, the way things are this morning.'

'Sorry?' said Peter.

'Kilometres, mate, you said kilometres.'

'Lis, you right?' said the woman with the nose stud to the woman in the riding outfit.

'Kilometricos,' said Peter Kennedy, still thinking of Pearl.

And he heard the half-laugh, half-cry and turned to look into the brown eyes of Lisa Sykes, standing in her Lycra beside him at the counter.

They stared at each other for a while.

'Kilometricos,' she repeated softly.

'Yeah, well, I might scoot,' muttered Utah, and shuffled off to his bike.

Peter continued to stare, thinking, Her freckles, she doesn't have any freckles.

Chapter Nine

There was silence for a moment.

'What are you doing here?' Lisa finally asked.

'Buying breakfast.'

She looked at the tray of food. Peter looked at the organic coconut water.

'Just rehydrating,' she said.

It's a funny thing, time, he thought. It seems to stop in a moment, just like that, a few seconds but long enough for a mind to run through a lot of memories. And he knew where they would end.

He had, of course, gone to collect the Kilometrico pens after an awkward phone call, dressed in his good blue jeans and a cheesecloth shirt with a denim collar.

The Sykeses had a two-storey brick house with a very neat garden. There was a tree in the front that was exactly like a big version of the little plastic trees that people stick on model railways. It stood in a concrete circle surrounded by white pebbles.

There was a rubber plant to one side and a thin row of gerberas that always seemed to be in flower. A driveway led to a garage attached to the house, and a curved mauve-coloured concrete pathway stretched from the gate and the ornamental Royal Post Office letterbox to the front door, which had two panels of coffee-coloured glass on either side.

He studied the roof; there was very little overhang, he noticed, and hardly any eaves. They had skimped on building, but almost everyone in Pickersgill could have been accused of that.

Walking inside he could see that most of the ground floor was taken up by the double garage. There was also an office and a bedroom and a narrow hall, with stairs leading up to the living area.

This was the home of Karl and Maureen Sykes and their three children, Lance, Lisa and Leanne.

The family, like the garden and the house, was very neat.

Mr Sykes was a sergeant of police at Kalangar Station out past Pickersgill and was in his forties. He had hard, pale eyes, an angry brow and a very stern copper's manner. He spoke English as if it were his second language, which was odd because it was the only language he spoke.

Mrs Sykes was a tall woman who had been willowy but had grown increasingly wobbly with age. She had been a very good tennis player when she was young, apparently, and for some reason that was never explained to him, Peter Kennedy's mother had said it was because she was Dutch.

Mrs Sykes hardly ever said a word but was quite friendly in an odd, half-smiling way, while her husband always had something to say, usually in an angry manner, except for the times when he would find something that would amuse him. Then he would smile, nod and laugh, say something to himself as if he was the only one who'd get the joke, and then go back to being cranky.

Perhaps the father of two very attractive girls has to be suspicious? Or perhaps the father of a slightly odd son was reason enough to behave in an unsociable manner.

Lance was short for Lancelot, which the young man himself was fond of saying. Peter Kennedy knew he was a bit odd from the first time he saw Lance in the House of Sykes. Standing there in his Bruce Lee Kung Fu master pyjamas.

He was wearing them as he opened the front door. Then he let out a yell and struck a Kung Fu pose.

Peter Kennedy stepped back in shock and then heard an angry voice yell, 'Lance!'

That's when he met Sergeant Sykes, who opened a door from the garage and stood there holding a little green tree and a tube of Tarzan's Grip glue. Behind him was a model railway; a freight train clicking its way through snow-capped mountains dotted with chalets.

'Ah, yes, you,' said the man with the tree. 'Lance, show him upstairs.'

Lance must have been two years older than Peter, and he pointed to the white-belted Kung Fu outfit that he wore. 'This is not action wear. It's sleepwear. Dynamic sleepwear.'

Lance was the boy who always played the electronic organ in the shopping mall down at Pickersgill Central. He was also, Peter realised, the guy who liked to run, everywhere. Peter would see him sprinting along the beach and around Bell's Paddock while Peter was at rugby training. Running full pelt and as happy as Larry.

'Mad as a cut snake,' was what his rugby coach, Murry Sinclair, said whenever Lance would scream around the oval, but he always added wistfully, 'He'd make a great winger – fast as the wind and a head full of shit.'

'Okay,' said Peter Kennedy, looking at the pyjamas and he and Lisa's brother looked at each other. Peter remembered his rugby coach's words.

Lance made another Kung Fu move and then Peter heard a 'Hello' and there at the top of the stairs was Lisa.

'I'm going back to my organ,' said Lance, and he disappeared into his room as Peter Kennedy slowly climbed the stairs.

To the strains of Lance's Hammond organ playing 'Popcorn' he walked up to the top level of the Sykeses' house.

He would walk up those stairs off and on for nearly two years and not once would he ever feel truly at ease.

There were a number of reasons, not least of which was that Sergeant Sykes always looked at Peter as if he was up to something, which he quite possibly was, especially with Lisa. Well, they were up to things together, but it was Peter Kennedy who got the baleful stares from the sergeant. He never really had conversations with anybody in the house, not with Leanne or a smiling Mrs Sykes, certainly not with Lance and not even really with Lisa.

For Peter, it was a case of putting up with 'the Olds'.

During that time he never got over the fact that Lance Sykes was studying to be an air traffic controller. He passed with flying colours and headed off for a career in aviation. And he was nearly always playing something on the organ. It was strange to Peter Kennedy that the family took so much pride in Lance and the organ. By the late seventies fake-walnut veneered electric organs seemed to be a thing of the past. But the Sykeses had kept the faith.

One of the few times that Mrs Maureen Sykes had said anything at length to Peter was early one Saturday evening when he and Lisa were heading off to her high-school formal. Sergeant Sykes was at work and Mrs Sykes had been smiling at Peter while he waited for Lisa to make her entrance from her bedroom. Lance was downstairs playing 'I Never Promised You a Rose Garden'.

It took a while before he noticed his girlfriend's mother because he was staring, and not for the first time, at a framed cover of the *Australasian Post*.

The magazine was a news pictorial that came out every week. It was a collection of comics and adventure stories, and some scandal, usually involving movie stars or pop singers of a certain generation. It was a dad's mag. Or the Barber's Encyclopaedia, because every barber had one. There were fishing tips, stories about cars, and a slew of half-blue jokes of the week. There was also a big crossword at the back called 'Mr Wisdom's Whopper'.

Ken Kennedy would buy the magazine each week, and on a Sunday afternoon he would sit with Mary and they would work their way through the puzzle together.

But it was the covers that always drew Peter's attention. A young woman, usually in a bathing suit and occasionally a wet shirt, would smile out at the reader.

Sometimes the model would be looking up from a pool ladder, as if she had come from a dip, or she'd be stuck in a slightly awkward pose at the beach. The girl would always be happy and either adjusting her bathing suit or holding onto something.

The *Australasian Post* cover in the Sykeses' house featured a girl in a white one-piece bathing suit kneeling on the beach with her heels tucked under her and waves lapping the shore in the background.

She let one hand rest by her side and in the other she held a coconut with a red-and-white striped straw coming out of it. The straw wasn't near her mouth, just held awkwardly in front of her as she smiled.

She was very pretty but her smile didn't reach her eyes, probably because she was getting cramps in her legs from holding the pose for so long. Or perhaps she was worried about the cold water rolling in and lapping at her bottom. Or maybe she was thinking what her father would say.

And why wouldn't she, for her father had exploded when he had seen it.

Karl Sykes had known that Lisa had gone and had the odd photo taken. But when she told him she was going to be in a magazine, he had thought it was the *Sunday Mail*'s colour supplement or the school pages of the *Pickersgill Courier*.

Not the front cover of the *Post*.

Not the Barber's Encyclopaedia.

She hadn't told anybody except her mother and her mother hadn't told anybody until the day the magazine appeared in the shops.

Mrs Sykes had gone down especially early and bought two copies from the Pier Newsagent and had shown it to her husband. Shown him the cover photo of their daughter. And her coconut. And a few words not far from her mouth saying, *Queensland beauty Lisa loves the beach and fresh coconuts. See inside how an Australian coastwatcher found a message on a coconut that saved JFK.*

There was also a story about Liberace's gardener and one about the secrets of palmistry.

Lisa Sykes on the cover of the *Post*. His daughter.

Lisa Sykes on the cover of the *Post*. His girlfriend.

It wasn't like it was anything to get too upset about – the bra advertisements for McDonnell & East in the *Courier-Mail* were more explicit.

Even though her father was angry he still framed the cover and placed it above the good sideboard in the living room.

Peter Kennedy would glance at the cover from time to time and then invariably turn to see Sergeant Sykes staring balefully at him.

One time, though, Peter didn't hear him coming. Lisa's father should have been at work, and the fact that he had entered the house and walked up the stairs so quietly was slightly unnerving.

'The stealthy tread of the copper,' Sergeant Sykes had later hissed to Peter as the two of them stood alone wiping the dishes in the kitchen. 'Just remember the stealthy tread of the copper, Peter. Just remember.'

Peter Kennedy was gazing up at Lisa and her coconut when he suddenly felt a looming presence, an uncomfortably close breath and the smell of kabana sausage.

'Get your eyes off my daughter, Kennedy. I know what you are thinking. I know what you do with your bad jams.'

Bad jams. A chill ran up his spine. Peter Kennedy had heard this only once before. At a Family Lecture at the Pickersgill CWA Hall. It was a talk entitled 'Now That You Are Changing' by a woman called Rhona van Pipe. She was a self-appointed Decency Advocate and Life Educator who held yearly talks for the school children of the Peninsula. Her husband, Barry van Pipe, was a one-term mayor who encouraged the local families to let their children hear the wisdom of his wife.

It was an afternoon off school anyway, so why argue.

At the age of thirteen, his first year of high school, Peter Kennedy sat and listened to a woman who knew next to nothing about life speak about LIFE.

She wore the armour of a life lived completely on Pickersgill Peninsula: blind ignorance.

For her talk Rhona van Pipe had a few slides. One of the Queen and one of Price Phillip. And one of a can of State plum jam.

'When a boy . . .' a slide of the Duke of Edinburgh aka Prince Phillip appeared on the bed-sheet screen, 'meets a girl . . .' A slide of the Queen appeared. 'At a particular time, a time of change, the boy may find that certain parts of his body . . .'

And for some unaccountable reason a rough line drawing of a male figure complete with a tin of State plum jam, placed where his genitals should be, flashed up on the bed-sheet screen.

'These feelings may cause a boy to have a change in his jams.'

The slide changed to the same rough drawing, only with a larger and quite angry looking tin of State plum jam-genitalia.

'You must control your jams. You must control your bad jams because if you don't then your sweet jams will become *baaad* jams.'

And then a succession of slides with a smiling Duke of Edinburgh and an open tin of State plum jam with a plastic bug, perhaps a cockroach, resting on the top of the jam flashed up intermittently.

Bad jams.

'You must resist bad jams.'

Peter Kennedy had no real idea what the talk was intended to communicate about life, but he knew that not long after watching the slides, his bad jams were all that concerned him. And he dealt with them in the traditional manner.

Bad jams.

It was a solo effort up until the time he met Lisa and her bike chain, and then they both did rather enjoyable things with their corresponding bad jams.

Bad jams. Who would have thought that Sergeant Sykes would have been an avid devotee of Mrs Rhona van Pipe?

Bad jams. He could have laughed, but in Sergeant Sykes' mouth 'Bad jams' sounded strangely sinister. And besides, that was exactly what he was thinking of doing.

He froze and said as innocently as he could, 'Mr, Sergeant Sykes, I was looking at Lance . . . And Bernard King.'

There was a pause.

Downstairs Lance was playing 'Life is Great in the Sunshine State'.

'What?'

'The *Pot of Gold* photo.'

There was a longer pause.

'Bernard bloody King,' Mr Sykes seethed.

The wall was shared by a graduation photo of Sergeant Sykes from the Police Academy, Leanne in a ballet dress, the *Australasian Post* cover and, most spectacularly, a photo of Lance at an organ, dressed in a silver suit, white shirt and a banana-yellow bowtie. Around his shoulders was the arm of cook and TV personality, Bernard King.

This was because Lance had gone on the television talent quest *Pot of Gold* on Channel 0. Bernard King had been a judge.

This was the photo that appeared in the *Pickersgill Courier* under their unique headline 'Local Young Organer Wins'.

'Old Bernard, eh. Bernard bloody King and Lancelot Sykes. Well, how'd you be?' Ken Kennedy had said the Wednesday evening the *Courier* came out.

'He did well enough to win,' said Mary Kennedy when she read it.

The story was on the front page. 'It says he played a medley of "Flight of the Bumble Bee", the theme from *Jaws* and "Congratulations".'

'A bloke at the pub said the juggler would have won, but he dropped a club,' said her husband. 'And what about Bernard bloody King! What about his outfit?'

'Now leave Bernard King alone.'

'Beg yours?'

'I like his cooking show.'

'Oh Holy Mary.'

'Ken.'

•

Can you have a memory inside a memory? Peter Kennedy didn't know because usually he didn't think about memories, and it was still only a few seconds since he had seen Lisa Sykes in her Lycra in the bakery.

But here he was remembering a conversation between his parents years before he had even helped Lisa mend her bike chain. Somehow it led down a lane to hot kabana breath on the back of his neck emitted by a large, bad-tempered policeman.

He should deal with that memory first.

He had turned to face Sergeant Sykes.

'All right then, Kennedy, but I'm watching you,' he said and pointed at Peter with a scale-model replica of the Indian–Pacific engine in his hand, then he stomped back down the stairs.

There was a point, Peter supposed, to these memories within memories, because it was Lance's appearance on *Pot of Gold* that had caused Mrs Maureen Sykes to smile and point at the photo that evening.

Peter had been gazing at Lisa's cover again but Maureen Sykes had assumed that the Kennedy boy was looking at Bernard King. After all, his mother had said at tennis club that she enjoyed Bernard King's cooking show, she thought it was fun, so perhaps the admiration of Mr King might run in the family.

'Bernard King said Lance showed great style. That's what he said, that's why he won.'

'He did well; that juggler was pretty good,' Peter said, as if he had seen the show himself.

'Oh, was I worried about him!' said Mrs Sykes and then she leant in close to him. She smelt of oil and copha, because she had been making chocolate crackles with Leanne for her daughter's Home Economics class.

And she whispered, 'You know Lance wasn't the only one on the telly.'

'Really,' said Peter Kennedy.

'I was on the telly, too.'

'Really?'

'Oh, yes, would you like to see the photo?'

Peter nodded and from the drawer of the sideboard she pulled out a news clipping. It was from another edition of the *Pickersgill Courier* and showed a larger photo. 'Local Woman Gets the Treatment' was the headline.

There, looking very young and willowy, was Mrs Sykes – she was only a mother of two at the time – smiling in a startled way while a man in a suit had his arm around her shoulders.

The man was Raymond. Pronounced Ray-*mond*, as in 'pond'. He was a short man with grey hair swept up and back like a freshly puffed-up couch cushion, and a little thin moustache.

'I was on the telly, and in the paper.'

Peter looked at the photo and back up at Mrs Sykes. 'Yes, my mother saw you on the TV.'

'Really! Oh that was years ago! Ray-*mond* of Queen Street.'

Peter had seen her too. He and Pearl and Mary Kennedy and Aunty Eunice had watched the show one wet day when they were both home from Grade One with colds.

Ray-*mond* had a hairdressing salon on Queen Street that was called with great originality, Ray-*mond* of Queen Street. He used to host a ten-minute segment on TV just before midday where three customers, whom he had chosen to demonstrate his hair-styling prowess, would sit on stools and would be rotated by Ray-*mond* so all at home could see what coiffs he had created.

The fact that the ladies on the stools nearly always towered above him, especially if he had gone to town on their hairstyles, was never lost on Mary Kennedy.

'Hello Ray-*mond*! Who have we got today?' she would ask.

'Allo to yeurrr luffley ladiz. We ave eeaw Butty, Jaooon anda Moreeeeeen.'

Three stunned-looking women the same age as his mother grimaced out from the TV, but it was Maureen who caught Mary's attention. 'Oh, it's that Dutch woman – Sykes,' she said.

It made some sort of sense to Peter; this was the Dutch lady that his mother always complained about when she came home on Wednesday mornings from the tennis club.

'It's all right for some to go into Brisbane for a trip to Ray-*mond*'s. Every month she goes in, you know,' said Aunty Eunice.

'I suppose it's her money. I just wish she'd let someone else win the tennis comp occasionally,' said Mary.

'How does she afford it on a policeman's salary?'

'Oh, Eunice, I think her mother left her some money. Look at her, look at her hair.'

The segment followed the usual formula – Raymond would chat a little too long to his first two lufflies and then try to whip his third around quickly.

'Allo, Moreeeeen, ow are yuuu?'

Mrs Sykes' teased hair shot out like a lyrebird's tail on full display. Ray-*mond* almost disappeared behind it. She tried to say something, but no sound came out.

'Well, eaaaw, look at eet.' And Ray-*mond* twirled her around on her stool like a top.

Mary Kennedy and Pearl laughed.

Peter had thought Mrs Sykes looked frightened.

'She's like a laughing clown at the show. Go on, Pearlie, pop a ping-pong ball into her mouth,' said Mary, laughing.

Peter had never liked the clowns at the sideshow. Never. When he was only five Pearl had insisted on playing them. Their wide-open mouths, bright red noses and the funny eyes with little crosses where pupils should be had scared him. He had tried to throw the ping-pong ball down the clown's throat, but all he could do was stand there staring at their open mouths.

Pearl had stood next to him, telling him to hurry. The man in charge of the stall had joined in. 'Come on, Champ, do the right thing. Pop it in, they got no teeth so they won't bite.'

Peter had tried, but he was frightened. He put his hand into a clown's mouth but he hadn't been able to let go of the ball, and the clown had turned his head this way and that. Peter had cried, and the man had laughed. And so had Pearl.

Peter watched the frightened lady on the screen and he had closed his eyes shut to make her go away.

And there she was, standing in front of him now, holding her photos, smiling with an open mouth.

'My style didn't last very long. It rained on the way back from the TV station at Mount Coot-tha, and I had to sit on the train with my hair a mess. Karl wouldn't let me go back to Raymond's, he said it was a waste of good money. Set it myself now.'

Peter Kennedy looked back to Bernard King and Lance as Mrs Sykes put her news clipping away in the drawer.

'You should put your photo on the wall, of you and Raymond,' he said.

'Oh no, no. Nobody wants to see it.' She held her hand over the drawer. 'Nobody.'

Downstairs, Lance was still playing on the organ. 'Mull of Kintyre'.

Peter could hear Lisa calling out for her mother to help with her dress, and as she started to walk away, he said to her, 'Mrs Sykes, it's a lovely photo. Thanks for showing it to me.'

She opened her mouth but nothing came out. Lisa called again and Peter began to fidget with his feet. Mrs Sykes stood still and then out came a soft little, '*Oh.*'

Lisa called again and her mother went to help.

It was the longest conversation Peter had ever had with her, and really the next to last thing she had ever said to him directly.

That final handful of words came a while later, on a Sunday evening at the Sykeses'. It wasn't long before Lisa was due to leave Pickersgill, having decided to complete her studies at Sydney University.

Peter had found this out a week earlier when he and Lisa had gone for a walk along the beach. Lisa said she had something important to tell him.

It was an uncomfortable few minutes because he wasn't sure what that something might be — a young man's mind can race to some very predictable conclusions. And Pickersgill Peninsula was a small town so having to tell someone directly that something had happened was commonplace and usually the predictable conclusion turned out to be right.

An image of himself with a young mother pushing a pram down the grocery store aisles flashed before Peter's eyes.

Lisa looked at him and annoyance furrowed her brow. Then she told him something.

Peter let out an audible sigh. Of relief.

Lisa had looked away and made her sound. She'd cried and he felt a bit sad. They had held each other. And it was decided they would see what would happen.

Both of them knew it wouldn't be much.

They didn't tell their parents; they weren't the sort of young people to do that. They just kept mooching along doing what they were doing until the date they had set in their minds when they would go off and do something else. It was a particularly Pickersgill way of going about your life. And that's why Peter Kennedy was at the House of Sykes that Sunday.

Leanne was away on a Girl Guide camp and Lance was downstairs fingering up a storm on the Hammond. 'Macho Man' bled into 'New York, New York'.

Just a normal night at the Sykes home.

Mrs Sykes was in the kitchen.

Sergeant Sykes had done weekend duty and was a little more grumpy than usual. He sat in his chair, Lisa sat in the other lounge chair and Peter Kennedy sat on the three-person couch alone in the middle of the room, as far away from the other two as possible.

There was no conversation, no words exchanged, just the tunes from Lance and the noise from the kitchen. This, surprisingly, was quite loud because there was only a Spanish arch and no door separating it from the Good Room, as Sergeant Sykes called it.

All the while Peter, Lisa and Sergeant Sykes watched the television. A newsreader with a comb-over and a plaid jacket announced that he was Nev Roberts with a news update. 'More claims today of widespread police corruption were dismissed by the Police Minister, Mr Russ Hinze.'

'I don't want this rubbish. Can't we watch the vets in England?'

'That finished last week, Dad.'

'At least turn this idiot off.'

Mr Sykes got to his feet, stomped to the television and switched the channel to the ABC. 'This'll do.'

Birds on an island somewhere were doing what birds do while the breathy tones of David Attenborough stated the obvious.

'A bird protects its nest,' David Attenborough said as the bird protected its nest.

Two birds nuzzled close together and David breathed, 'And now it's time for mating.'

One bird jumped on another. David said nothing. Mr Sykes coughed and looked at his daughter and then across to Peter Kennedy. Peter watched the birds. The scene went on for some time, longer than he could believe was possible. Even David Attenborough was silent. He could hear Mrs Sykes stirring something in the kitchen and Mr Sykes breathing in his chair.

'I think we get the idea. They shouldn't have to show this sort of stuff,' said Sergeant Sykes.

The birds finally stopped mating and started flying. Mr Sykes coughed and in the kitchen something was dropped into the sink. The frying pan sizzled away.

The birds sat on some eggs, squawking at other birds that came near.

There was a little moan from the kitchen that went unremarked and then another.

Finally, 'Are you right?' said Sergeant Sykes.

No answer came for a few moments and then as the eggs began to crack there was a soft, 'Yes.'

The birds now magically had chicks and went about feeding them, diving into the water catching fish, half-digesting them and then regurgitating them down the yawning throats of their fat fluffy chicks.

Trying to regurgitate the fish was more graphic than the mating, and went on longer. Peter watched the parent birds, sticking their beaks down the throats of the chicks, their whole heads almost disappearing, all the while heaving with their stomachs. He coughed. Then he gagged and clapped his hands as if he was trying to break some spell.

'What's wrong with you?' said Sergeant Sykes.

Peter coughed again. 'It's the birds. Sticking their heads down the throats of the chicks.' He swallowed and then coughed. 'It's a bit, icky.'

'Icky?' said the sergeant. 'A bit icky?'

Peter wished he hadn't opened his mouth.

The birds were still heaving away.

'A bit icky?' repeated Sergeant Sykes, as if he was considering the phrase very carefully. He turned back to the screen and the birds, then suddenly hawked and half-coughed as though he was going to spit. He shook his head. 'Yes, it is too much. Not very comfortable, really.'

He glowered at the screen and coughed again. The birds still had their heads down the throats of their offspring.

'You really wouldn't call this entertainment, shoving a beak down another bird's throat.' He looked straight at Peter. 'Icky?' he sneered. 'It's a lot more than icky. It's nature. Damn disgusting.'

'Well, why don't you try having someone's bad jams down your mouth and see how you like it.'

It was the loudest and clearest thing Peter had heard Mrs Maureen Sykes ever say. It was as if she were an actor making sure every member of the audience, even those way up the back of the theatre, could hear every word.

Downstairs, Lance paused before starting a rousing version of 'Look What They've Done to My Song, Ma'.

Watching the birds again, Peter panted a couple of times, trying not to laugh. Out of the corner of his eye he could see the sergeant seething in his chair, his fists balled in white-knuckled rage.

Peter turned to Lisa and was greeted with her glazed *Australasian Post*-cover smile.

Mrs Sykes appeared from around the corner and smiled, too, her eyes fixed on the light hanging in the centre of the room. 'Dinner's on.'

The four of them sat around the table eating some rissoles, mashed potato and gravy. Lance was still pumping away downstairs at the Hammond trying to perfect the chorus of the tune that he played over and over. Nobody spoke. Except for David Attenborough. 'Dinner is served again. The chicks obviously have a fondness for home-cooked meals.'

Sergeant Sykes stared at Peter with such studied belligerence that Peter could barely eat.

'Eat up,' said Mrs Sykes, adding rather wistfully, 'Look what they've done to my brain.' And she looked at Peter Kennedy with hopeless eyes.

Lisa still wore her *Australasian Post* smile and, as he sat there, Peter felt glad she was going to Sydney.

They ate without speaking, and listened to the sound of birds screeching on the TV and Lance's organ.

It was on the fifth rendition of the song that Sergeant Sykes roared, '*Laaaaaaance!*'

The organ trailed off as if Lance was trying to discern whether someone had bellowed his name.

And, just as Mr Sykes was moving a shovelful of rissole and mashed potato towards his mouth, Lance cranked up the brain tune again, sounding like Count Yorga in his lair.

Peter laughed so hard that gravy came out of his nose.

That was the last time he visited the House of Sykes.

He saw Lisa off at the airport, but hadn't seen her again until now, in this bakery.

He never saw Mr Sykes or Mrs Sykes again, although he was aware of what life had dealt them by way of his mother's weekly phone calls.

Things certainly had taken a few twisting turns.

'Have you heard?' said his mother when she rang him at his share house in Milton a year after that fateful dinner.

'What would I have heard, Mum?'

'Mrs Sykes, Lisa's mum, the Dutch woman.' His mother almost panted.

'What about her?'

Down the phone he heard his father yell out, 'She's gone all Dutch on us!'

'Ken!' his mother yelled out.

'She's turned,' his father yelled.

The dogs barked.

'Ken, shush,' and his mother turned back to the phone and her voice was pleasantly conspiratorial. 'She's left Mr Sykes and become a lesbian.'

Peter had stood holding the phone. Somehow he wasn't surprised.

'A lesbian, she told us at tennis this morning.'

Ken Kennedy laughed somewhere in the house. 'Mary, you are a gossip!'

'A lesbian, who would have guessed?'

As for Mr Sykes, well time had caught up with him. He wasn't mentioned prominently in the Fitzgerald Inquiry but it was made very clear that the Queensland Police Force could do without his services.

When Peter heard the news it made some sort of sense to him. Mr Sykes did have very big train sets and he must have found the money somewhere to pay for them. He had moved away from Pickersgill after he left the force and according to news via the tennis club, he was living with a Filipina lady in Mackay.

'He was one of those blokes who knew how to hide the bruises he caused,' Ken Kennedy had said at the time. 'That poor bloody family of his.'

•

Peter Kennedy stood with his pastie and his chocolate milk.

'You still like your coconuts,' he said.

Lisa looked up at him and her brow tightened, and for a brief moment the shadow of her father crossed her face.

'I'm back to have a look-see at a few things,' he added.

She nodded. 'I'm at the council here now, in planning.'

'Oh.'

She nodded again. 'You're looking well.'

'Well fed,' he said.

She laughed a little. Her face was smooth, and she made her little sound. 'I might see you around.'

He nodded and asked, not because he was trying to be smart or funny but because after those few seconds in the bakery he actually wanted to know, 'How's your mother?'

Outside the bakery two seagulls had landed and were screeching at each other over a scrap of food dropped by a customer.

Lisa smiled tightly, her *Australasian Post* smile, picked up her organic coconut water and said, 'She's good.' Then she left the bakery.

And the seagulls screamed again.

Chapter Ten

The land registry office was found in the annexe of the Council Chambers, a building that was described as recently as the past Easter as, 'still frighteningly modern', by the incumbent mayor Edwyn Hume. Considering it was built in 1961, this gave a fair indication of Pickersgill's political representatives and their appreciation of aesthetics. Also as most people in and about the area generally agreed with their four-term mayor, it was, to Peter Kennedy, a fair indication of the sort of place Pickersgill was; a place where something different was regarded as suspicious.

The council buildings were down by the main jetty, in the heart of the CBD and featured a circular council chamber. Above the roof of the chamber a great sheet of steel had been draped and then fastened down at the corners. It was an effort that bore some resemblance to the National Science Museum in Canberra. For the locals it had become a bit of joke, as if they were embarrassed by the idea of trying something too different, Peter thought, a little too try-hard. *Remember, don't get above yourself, this is Pickersgill.*

Some said it looked like a parachute descending or a navvy's knotted hanky draped over a head or, as Mary Kennedy had always said, a badly iced cake.

To the right of the chamber, stood a clock tower which had the same stucco finish as the walls of the main building.

Peter remembered his father chatting to Howie Whittaker about the Council Chambers at one of Ken Kennedy's Christmas parties for his employees and contractors.

'What's the point of building in brick when you cover it up with all that stucco? People build in brick to let other people know that they've got enough coin to do so. Covering it up is a bit too try-hard,' Ken had said.

'I wouldn't mind what it was covered with if you knew the thing was telling the right time.'

This was true; the four-faced clock was itself an eccentric piece of work. Nobody had been able to fix whatever it was that made the thing do what it did, which was tell the time *almost* correctly.

It sort of crept up on you that the time on the clock didn't quite correspond to the time broadcast on the radio or that showed on your wristwatch, and all of a sudden it lurched forward or drifted back.

There was no pattern to these inconsistencies, and depending upon which clock face you looked at you more than likely saw four different times of day. As people on the Peninsula couldn't help but pay attention to the times it gave – it was, after all the town clock – there was always a margin of error for meetings, school pick-ups and deliveries to allow for the town's four different time zones.

To Peter the Council Chambers and clock had always been a set of buildings that excited him – there was something about them he found amazing – but the fact that they were largely derided also made some sense to him.

At a twelfth birthday barbecue party on the beach for him and Pearl, Ken had made a speech about how grateful he was for his two lovely children and also to be having such a lovely day in such a lovely town. Then he asked his birthday twins what their favourite thing was in Pickersgill.

'The Chambers,' Peter had said.

'What?'

'The Council Chambers.'

'Stop your arsing around, will you?' His father had laughed a little and other people had joined in.

Peter had just stared back at him.

Then Pearl had blurted out, 'My family! All of you!'

'Well said, Pearlie,' said Ken.

Pearl was given a little round of applause, and then Ken had added, 'But that doesn't mean you're going to get good presents, from me or them.'

'Don't need 'em!' said Pearl, laughing.

Peter had wanted to say he hadn't been arsing around, that he wanted to be able to make something like that building himself, to make something that nobody else in Pickersgill could make. Something that wasn't like the houses that his father built or the chamferboard homes or the little shops.

The Council Chambers had style, it was supposed to be special, it celebrated the idea of civic representation. Even if the councils that sat in the beautiful timber-walled chamber were all made up of men with bad haircuts coated in Brylcreem, who shed mountains of dandruff like desiccated coconut falling off old lamingtons down onto their shoulders or onto the large polished round table in the centre of the room. That they were men who didn't do anything really grand or terribly important didn't matter.

Peter remembered going there on a school trip and walking into the chamber and thinking, this is where someone like King Arthur might sit.

Instead, he had been greeted by an alderman who had come in for the afternoon to say hello to the kiddies. A man by the name of Dick Provan, who had a shoe store down the road.

It didn't matter to Peter Kennedy that standing there before him was a red-haired man wearing smart dress shorts, a cheesecloth shirt and biros tucked into socks; he *could* have been Sir Gawain.

It was all down to the way the building looked, how it felt. Peter believed that anything was possible in the Council Chambers.

And he knew then that he wanted to design something like that and see it built. The Chambers had seemed as if it had arrived from Mars when it was finished. Even today, it was like no other building on the Peninsula, not even some of the more outlandish of the new houses that were being built down by the harbour.

These were concrete-and-glass efforts that really weren't much of anything – neither inspiring or offensive, just big homes with big views of the bay. There was one home, though, which fascinated him, not just because of what it looked like but also for what it came to represent to Peter.

It was the last piece of work a Sydney architect called Bryce Halibut had completed before entering a rehabilitation centre in Byron Bay and then becoming a short-story writer.

Made of caramel cement and lots of blue and orange glass, it looked like it had come from a seventies' shopping centre or coffee set. Nobody had ever really lived in it, simply because it was almost impossible to have any privacy.

On a clear evening you could see the toilet in the third bathroom on the fourth level illuminated in a perfect *Gone With the Wind* technicolour sunset and you also had a fair view of whomever was attempting to use it.

Nobody would have imagined a design like that would ever be approved but it had been, and nobody really cared. After all, why would the council deny one of the wealthiest local residents? Bull O'Toole called himself a Real Estate Wealth Creator Fund Manager. Whatever that may have actually been, he was an immensely successful one.

He ran a company that many people in Pickersgill and the surrounding areas had used to increase their fortunes during the great growth years of the nineties and the noughties, and it seemed that Bull O'Toole could do no wrong. He was proud of the fact that he had no letters after his name or years of study behind him, but had nevertheless been successful because he lived in the real world and had common sense. So successful and so local.

Bull O'Toole had decided to make a statement in commissioning this house.

When it was finished he decided to throw a party to celebrate, to which the mayor and council staff were invited. This raised a few eyebrows because Bull and Edwyn Hume, or Eddie as he was known in the seventies, had played against each other in a Rugby League grand final.

During the game, Bull had king-hit Eddie from behind and knocked him into next week, but instead of being sent off, he'd gone on to win Man of the Match for the Valley Die-hards.

Bull had the good grace to apologise to Eddie and thank him for being such a great competitor and Eddie had shaken his hand and embraced him, probably because he would have collapsed if he hadn't. When he was asked by a reporter from 4IP Colour Radio, 'Eddie, how do you feel about yet another Marlins loss, even one as gallant as this, in yet another grand final?' Eddie gained a certain notoriety when he replied, 'I never heard anything and never touched nobody, her or her sister.'

Eddie Hume wasn't the same after that game but had managed somehow to make a career from being concussed. He even ran a campaign with a picture of himself being poleaxed by Bull O'Toole with the slogan 'Edwyn Hume – not afraid of the hard knocks!'

At the opening of Bull's glasshouse mountain the architect, Bryce Halibut, had made a brief and energetic speech. 'People live in houses like this in Colombia and Bolivia all the time, houses inspired by the great Aztec cultures of the past. The sun gods and sacrifices, the beauty of pagan worship and the mysterious foresight and understanding of the Mayan culture all have, in some way, a home here in this building,' he said, in between sneezing and wiping away at imaginary traces of whatever product from Bolivia he may have been acquainting himself with a little earlier. 'Also, I have been influenced by Spain, the birthplace of the Conquistadors, in the ensuites and bathrooms; they signify the colonisation of South America by the Old World. And now I like to think that here in your beautiful peninsula you will enjoy the lifestyle of the South American culture, the culture of the new millennium.'

With that, he had sneezed again, shaken the hand of Edwyn Hume and raced off to a Spanish-influenced bathroom to inhale a little more South American 'culture'.

Then the mayor had dropped his comment about the Chambers in comparison to this 'very interesting building' that would be the home of Bull O'Toole. Bull appeared even more agitated than his architect.

In hindsight the event was more of a fateful goodbye than an opening party, for Bull was never able to live in his interesting home. This was not only because of the obvious lack of privacy, but also because his financial resources were even more see-through than the walls of his great glass mansion. The banks, more scrupulous than ever thanks to the global financial crisis, didn't appreciate the amount of credit he had been on-selling to his clients, backers and markets.

Edwyn Hume's great statement to the board of inquiry into the collapse of O'Toole's investments and the level of the council's involvement and particularly his own as mayor, was that 'The wheels of justice turn slowly, but I think the events that happened in the Grand Final of 1976 have been squared with the jailing of Bull O'Toole.'

Mary sent Peter the clippings from the *Pickersgill Courier* and he had read them in the study of his comfortable home.

Edwyn Hume's statement seemed to sum up so many things to Peter about the place when he had grown up. Greed and a sense of entitlement.

The belief in good blokes and the ethos of the sporting champion. The belief that because someone was a good bloke he must know exactly what he was doing. That life wasn't so specialised that you could build wealth and big buildings and have the things you want without actually having to think about it. Yes, you got them because you deserved them.

Peter Kennedy looked at that house in the clipping and wondered about those people who had lost so much of their savings because they had believed in Bull O'Toole and the idea of continuing growth. They might not have believed that Bull was a financial genius, but deep in their hearts they felt that they, too, deserved that growth in their wealth. They deserved it.

Pearl had lost money. And his parents. Maybe even Gary. Lots of people.

That great stupid house stood empty, reminding them all of what they had lost. So symbolic was it to Peter that whenever he heard people talking about how tough things were – be they a pinched-looking economist on *Lateline*, or grim-faced politicians, or people in an airport lounge whispering about how scared they were of what was happening in Europe – he thought of that house. Watching people on the news who had been retrenched or were rioting against austerity measures always made him think of that big glasshouse, how everybody had let it be built, how they had all been complicit to that view of the toilet at sunset.

He sat outside the Council Chambers, on the park bench next to the clock tower, and ate his breakfast – his tray of pasties and chocolate milk – and slowly realised that if Lisa Sykes was working in planning here at Pickersgill Council then she must have been a part of the approval process of Bull O'Toole's house.

And then he checked the time on the clock tower; ten to one.

He stood and walked into the Chambers and, glancing at his watch, he saw that it was barely nine o'clock. To his surprise he found himself laughing.

•

Peter sat in the land registry office for hours beneath a portrait of a smiling Queen, sifting through title deeds, old town planning declarations and provisions and decrees from the Queensland Parliament.

As far as the showgrounds were concerned he could see that they had been gazetted Crown land since the end of the Second World War. They were at the entrance of the town of Pickersgill, following on from the botanic gardens.

Peter could see from the plans that this area had never really changed over the years. Resting on a gentle rise, it was elevated above the rest of the town, and the site had always been little more than a piece of scrubby grassland.

While other areas of the Peninsula had become a collection of little farms, the showgrounds had retained a sense of space and were used to graze cattle in the early years after European settlement. This was in part because there was a ready water supply; the land had a spring that continued to seep up from the right-hand corner of the allotted showgrounds area.

The seeping water ensured that a thriving population of mozzies were kept busy feeding on anything warm-blooded. Also, because the ground was almost constantly soggy it was always assumed that the land wasn't appropriate for residential development.

He studied an interval map of the entire Pickersgill region and saw through the twenty-year interval growth plots that the area closest to the shore had been the first settled and the later development had crept further inland. And with each succeeding plot map he saw how the empty spaces had been gradually coloured in over time, like some school project, and names had been given to the area. They were a mixture of transplanted English names for the beaches and suburbs – Rye, Ramsgate, Seaford, Cowes, Hove and Bexhills – and the most mundane and obvious of geographical descriptions. So a rocky outcrop at a point became Rocky Point, a hill with a bare space of stone became Bald Hill, which was where the water tower now stood, apparently not far from the Vietnamese bakery that Utah could only reach on the good days when his gout wasn't playing up.

There had also been the slight nod to the original inhabitants of the Peninsula, with a smattering of Indigenous place names filling in the gaps: Googong Point, Burrundong and Wanda Beach.

Peter discovered that all the construction on the showgrounds had been carried out under the guidance of a community trust board.

The buildings were clumped together in a village covering roughly three hectares while the rest of the area was made up of a trotting track with a sporting oval inside it, and to the north, a wood-chop square and a bar. That left nearly thirty hectares, of which about a third was filled with stalls, sideshow alley rides and various exhibitors' stands when the show was on. There was a lot of space there. Waiting.

As Peter worked his way through the documents he wondered why no one had appropriated the land for development before.

What marked them out as having potential for high-density development was their elevation. The gentle hill had uninterrupted water views, so even with the high-rises that were built along the beaches you could still enjoy the bay from one direction and the mangroves that seemed to stretch to the horizon from another.

Peter flicked from the land and title registry records to the planning folios that showed in more detail what kind of building had taken place on the site. None had any real historical provenance, unless you counted the early aluminium cladding used on the Poultry Pavilion in 1958 and the variation on that theme for the Horticultural Hall with its PVC white picket fences in 1969. They were hardly pavilions and barely halls, and it was almost too generous even to call them sheds, but as he flicked down the records of construction he saw that that was how whoever had built them wanted them to be recorded.

Peter sighed heavily. They really had no idea; halls, pavilions – they were simply Besser-block sheds.

He suddenly felt irritated: anyone could be doing this, and his being here wasn't worth the hassle of what would inevitably be waiting for him at home. Kate's 'talk' would only become more of an issue. He reached for his phone. There were a number of messages and missed calls. From his home. He'd forgotten to ring that morning. He considered listening to the voicemail but then grunted; he'd ring Kate after he'd spoken to Greer Harvson. As he pressed her number he grabbed the latest development map of the north-east region of Brisbane.

'Peter.'

'Greer.'

'What's wrong?'

'What do you mean?'

'You're not eating anything and you're on the phone, so, again, what's wrong?'

'Give me time. Listen, what exactly did you want me to find out up here?'

'We want to know if there's a reason why we couldn't consider a development in the areas we talked about.'

'It's gazetted Crown land but you lot are big enough to try to overturn that, given enough time. You've got a water table problem but, again, if you really want it you'll just have to pay the reclamation costs.'

'What are we looking at?'

'Fairly substantial – it's a big site.'

'Prohibitive?'

'If you want the land then you'll spend it.'

'What else?'

'Look, Greer, it's a lay down really. This whole area north-east of Brisbane has changed so much that development is the way you do things. It turns the economy over here. It's not like Noosa; you won't have people jumping up and down.'

'Yep.'

'You can take a place like Caboolture on a development map and it's wall-to-wall; zone 4. Everywhere it's curbed and channelled. My grandmother had a farm there twenty-five years ago. Now it's a Kmart.'

'Does she shop there?'

'No, she probably haunts it, though.'

'I'm sorry, Peter.'

'Don't be – she was a pretty scary lady.'

'And the site we looked at?'

'Well, it's the showgrounds. It's peopled by the folk who still think Toranas don't go anywhere to die, that they're still tooling around on the streets.'

Greer laughed a little.

'Well, Greer, it's run by people like my parents, and they're pretty old.'

'And?'

'You know, natural attrition in a demographic . . .' He heard himself and winced.

'God, Peter, they're your parents.'

'Yeah, well, you know what I mean.'

There was a slight pause.

'Where are you ringing me from?'

'From the land registry office at the Council Chambers.'

'Peter! I told you not to let anyone know what you were doing.'

'Greer, nobody knows I'm here or why I'm here – and that's including me –'

'Peter –'

'If you want this land it's yours to take –'

'Peter, get off the phone and check; see if there's anything that can get in the way.'

Peter realised too late he should have rung home before Greer.

'All right, I'll speak to you when I've got something in my mouth.'

Greer hung up.

And then he looked up to see Lisa Sykes in her tailored work clothes and beside her the four-term mayor of Pickersgill, Edwyn Hume, smiling down at him.

Chapter Eleven

Peter still had the phone in his hand so he kept on talking. In a manner of speaking. He *uh*-ed and *yeah*-ed and *ah ha*-ed into the lifeless phone. And Edwyn Hume kept smiling at him. And Lisa Sykes, looking startlingly young, stared at him. Her face was tight.

Peter said, 'Sure, sure, yeah,' to nobody.

This was embarrassing. He was lying – or about to – and in the meantime he tried to work out how much they had heard. He had interval development maps and a list of the showgrounds developments in front of him.

How much had they heard? Well, it didn't really matter because it was pretty obvious what he was looking at.

This, he realised, is what happens when you go back to where you're from and forget to ring your family and, even more amazingly, when you tell your sister she would be a good shot putter when you are almost ten and watching the 1974 Commonwealth Games and making her cry.

Jesus, he thought. Where did that come from? I'll smell luncheon meat soon.

He knew he couldn't keep grunting for much longer into the phone but had to brace himself; unfortunately he was an Olympian when it came to unconvincing lying.

He held up a hand to the two people who stood over him and smiled and then, summoning up all his powers of imagination, said into the dead phone, 'Okay, darling, I love you too. See you soon,' as if he were ordering something from a drive-through. And he felt slightly ashamed that even though he hadn't actually bothered to call them, he was pretending to talk to his family now.

He could see Edwyn Hume standing and smiling, his head wobbling from side to side like one of those wobble-headed Elvises that people used to stick on their dashboards.

He picked up the phone again and realised he hadn't told Kate that he loved her for a long time. He bowed his head for a moment and as he did so, his eyes rested on the planning folios for the showgrounds and he realised that the five buildings completed there after the 1969 PVC-fence experiment were constructed by Kennedy Master Builders.

He looked again. Ken Kennedy.

No, Peter wasn't a great liar – not for want of trying. It was simply a case that the gift wasn't there. And it wasn't as if he lied all the time, or as if he even lied about important things, although what the important things were he couldn't quite work out.

What *did* he lie about? Well, about forgetting parent–student nights, eating stuff on the sly, the paying of bills and anything to do with the dog; he lied about Bingo quite often. In fact, he stitched Bingo up more than he should.

What *didn't* he lie about? He couldn't think of anything but he knew it must be okay to lie sometimes; everybody does.

He knew what he did when he didn't lie, when he didn't want to do something or see someone. He would just take a deep breath, stare and say nothing. That usually worked, but not here, not this time.

And anyway, this wasn't going to be a big lie. This was only work. And so it was more a case of lying in the way an occasional golfer plays golf. You know, you pick a club, hold it in your hands, swing it and think that you could easily master anything that could be performed by seriously trying. Everybody thinks they can be Tiger Woods when they toy with hitting a golf ball.

And really, anybody *can* hit a golf ball. Just like anybody can tell a lie. So he might as well pick up the club and swing a lie like Tiger. And who knows, he might hit one right where it should go. Anyone can get lucky.

Christ, he thought, I can't believe I'm thinking like this. But a part of him wondered, perhaps all men think a little like this. And then he thought, maybe swinging a lie like Tiger Woods wasn't the best way to go about this; old Tiger ended up a lot worse off, after all. And having to do too much explaining to too many people.

Even so, Peter took a breath and decided he should have a crack; the situation couldn't get any more embarrassing.

'Lisa, Mr Mayor.'

Edwyn Hume wobbled his head this way and that and smiled even more. 'How are you, Peter? Look at you, what a place to find an architect like you.'

Peter Kennedy smiled.

The mayor smiled even wider while Lisa Sykes still held her face tight.

'And don't call me "Mr Mayor". You know that's one of the benefits of having a multi-faceted first name in politics. Take Edwyn for example.'

'Really?'

'Yes, really. Multi-faceted: Edwyn for the memorials for the parks, Eddie for the old ladies, the young ladies, the not-so-young ladies and the kiddies, and Ed for the blokes.'

'So what do I call you?'

'Well, you're not a memorial in a park and you're not an old lady or a little kiddie so you can call me Ed.'

Peter Kennedy wondered if the mayor was in a state of permanent concussion the way he spoke; nice and slow and enunciating every syllable a word had to offer and then a few extra thrown in for good measure.

'Ed-duh,' the mayor repeated.

'Okay, Ed-duh it is. How are you?'

'How are *you*?

'Good.'

'Good-duh. Lisa, here, bumped into you this morning? And then we heard you were-uh in the land registry. And the titles registry.'

'Yes, I was.'

'And-duh, here you are with the map of the showgrounds.'

'Yes, here I am.'

'And-duh, Lisa works in planning here with us.'

'Yes, she told me. I was actually thinking of that after I met you this morning, Lisa.'

'Oh yes?'

She sounded like she should be furrowing her brows by the tone of her voice and there was definitely a slight movement there between her eyes, a twitch, like when a DVD suddenly jumps and rides over a scratch.

'Yes.'

Nobody said anything for a moment and Peter saw the mayor glance at the papers before him. Normally he wouldn't have said anything, but he was treading water. 'I thought – and I hope you don't mind me saying this – but I thought . . . Well, I thought . . .'

Christ, what *do* I think?

'Well, I was thinking . . . about that multi-level house on the beach that Bull O'Toole built, and I was –'

Lisa finished the sentence for him. 'Wondering if I was working in planning when it was approved?'

'Yes, I was,' said Peter Kennedy.

'Okay.'

'Yes, well . . .' said Edwyn Hume. 'Sometimes, you know . . .'
Nobody said anything for a moment.

'Whatever old Bull did he's-uh, paying a price for it.'

'So they say,' said Peter and he had no idea whether Edwyn Hume was talking about the Grand Final punch or the collapse of the finance company.

'It was an exciting design that didn't come to fruition in reality. I was sure it would be something special,' Lisa said.

'It is interestingly modern and certainly a talking point.' Edwyn Hume coughed and then smiled. 'The thing is Peter . . . What's a nice architect like you, with a pretty friendly relationship to a major development company that has close connections to some of the finest developments in Pickersgill, doing looking at the showgrounds?'

'Well, Ed-duh, it's not what you might think it may be about.'

'I don't know what it may be about-uh, because I am here and you are here and we are-uh, well, here we are, aren't we? Just asking you what brings you back home, Peter?'

Put the ball on the tee, feet shoulder-width apart, keep your eye on the ball, slowly swing back and release the arms then the hips and keep the arms and wrists strong and keep your eyes on the ball.

'Back for the show and for the Big Valley Bingo charity night –' He paused. Now swing through, nice and controlled. Don't try to hit the cover off the lie. 'And back here today for my dad.'

Edwyn Hume stopped.

'Ken? Kenny Kennedy. Your dad Kenneth?'

'He could have gone into politics with a name like that, couldn't he, Ed-uh?' Peter said, smiling.

'Well, yes, very multi-faceted.'

'Indeed.' Now swing. 'I wanted to get a record of the things he built. Collate them, find out about them. He's getting on and he never really spoke about what he did that much. You see, I didn't even know he built these sheds here, five of them, at the showgrounds. Kennedy Master Builders.'

That one went straight down the middle. Effortless. A hole in one. Go Tiger! It felt like he didn't even hit it, like he wasn't even lying.

'Yeah, I, uh, wanted to find out more about what he did. I have a tendency to get lost in work and not pay attention to what's going on around me. Just trying to catch up, I guess.'

Go Tiger.

The mayor smiled. 'Good for you. You'll be busy, you know. He built quite a lot of places on the Peninsula and-uh, they are pavilions, Peter, not sheds. He built eight of them up there, at a cost to himself too, you know – never charged for labour, only the materials. But well done.'

Peter Kennedy shrugged his shoulders and turned away.

'Must admit, Peter, I thought you might be up to something. Nothing wrong, mind you, but you know council amalgamation might be in the wind and-uh, well . . . Eh, Lisa?'

'That's right. If boundaries change then the gazetting of land can change too; the state government can redraw almost any article of land if there's enough interest from particular developers or other parties.'

How much did they hear? Peter wondered.

'But good on you,' repeated the mayor. 'You'll have your work cut out. The old records aren't cross-referenced or indexed, are they, Lisa?'

'No. You'll have to sift through the old hard copies, I'm afraid. They're indexed.'

'So-uh, that's the rest of-uh your day gone, Peter,' said the man with the multi-faceted name.

And for the first time since he saw her balancing on her bike, Lisa Sykes smiled.

Peter held up his hands and grabbed another club. 'Oh, well, that's what I'm here for.'

The two people standing before him didn't notice, but he knew he had sliced the ball very, very badly.

•

The staff at the land registry office had been kind enough to let Peter go into the archive area in the basement and work through the mountains of old plans. It wasn't hard but he knew he would have his work cut out.

He had sat there in silence for the first fifteen minutes and then decided to listen to his voicemail.

Messages from home. All from Kate. She had obviously

been thinking hard when she left them; they became briefer and terser.

The first was rather pleasant; Ellie was in the car with her and chirped in with a 'Hello, Dad!' Kate reminded him to give them a call and not to forget to let them and the school know whether he would be at the father–daughter night.

Then about four, 'Peter, it's me, call back when you can', and finally a grim, 'Peter, call.'

He hesitated then rang the home number before Kate's mobile. There was no answer so he left a message. 'Hello there, it's me, Peter-slash-Dad. Everyone up here at Planet Pickersgill is on normal form. Caught up with work. Will call you again tonight. Hopefully home tomorrow evening. Cheers.'

Then he had sat for a bit longer and said slowly to himself, 'I should have swung the club.'

It took him until just before five, the council offices' closing time, to finally complete the list of buildings that Ken Kennedy had built in Pickersgill: one hundred and twenty-four.

There were plans for each of them, and Peter had traipsed to the photocopier a hundred and twenty-four times to peel off a copy.

The homes were modest and compact and spoke of another time, when people made do with whatever resources were available.

The first house Ken had built was in 1959, the year of his marriage to Mary. Over the next thirty-five years he had averaged three homes a year plus the odd shop and then a spate of building up at the showgrounds. It was a good output by a small business and Peter had to give his father a fair piece of admiration.

Every home he built always boasted a verandah.

'You can't have a home here without a verandah. Where else are you going to pee off?' Peter's father had proclaimed this at the dinner table one night when he had asked his father why all the houses he built had a verandah.

He had heard two teachers at primary school talking about a house one had recently had built by Kennedy Master Builders.

'Oh, you'll enjoy the verandah, he always puts one on,' one teacher had said to the other.

'Yes and the inside toilet! We have two, you know.'

'Two toilets!'

That's why Peter had asked about the verandahs. And he also wanted to know why the big house in pride of place on the crown of the hill – their home – only had one toilet.

Ken had told him not to worry, because that's what a verandah was for; the second toilet. 'That's the perch you pee from, young Pete.' And he had laughed and Mary had chided him.

'Ken, not at the table. Your father thinks it's important for a family, or anybody who lives in a home, to have a place where you can touch the sky. That's what he told me.'

'Well I do. Just you remember, everyone should be allowed to touch the sky and a verandah gives them a leg-up.'

His mother had smiled and then leant over to her husband and kissed him gently.

Peter sat now looking at the plans for the thirtieth home his father had built. It had two toilets and a verandah. He wondered if it was the teacher's house and whether she had ever tried to touch the sky.

He doubted it, but at least his father had seemed to believe she would.

It dawned on him later when he was copying the plan of Dr Langdon's home at Hove, that he was holding his father's life in his hands. And not only his father's.

He remembered this house – a four-bedroom brick building, the first big home his father had built – and it was very special; it had a pool.

Not a circular above-ground Clark pool like the one they had jumped around in in the backyard of the big house, but a proper below-ground job with a row of tiles around the lip – a light blue followed by a deep royal blue – that shone so that they appeared as if they were made of glass. Even more remarkably, the pool had shallow and deep ends complete with two sets of ladders.

Peter Kennedy knew this not because his father had told him but because one afternoon, as he and Pearl had left school with Gary walking in between them, they had heard their mother singing out to them from the car, 'Come on, your father and I have something to show you.'

He knew then that it was something special because they were only ever picked up from school in the car when something really important happened, like when they all had to go and have injections together, or a trip to the hospital to see Nanna when she had her gallstones out.

But his mother wouldn't tell them what it was. And she drove to Hove of all places and then up the drive of a big brick house.

They had walked from the car around the side of the house and she had called out, 'Ken!'

'In here!' came his father's voice.

The three kids had looked around but couldn't see anyone. 'Come on, in here! It's beautiful!'

First Peter saw a hand waving and then nothing and all of a sudden Pearl screamed as her father's head popped up from below the ground and bobbed down and then popped back up again, with his big smile breaking his face open.

They ran to the top of the pool and there below them on the bottom was Ken Kennedy, with fish and chips and two big bottles of Tristram's soft drink set out before him.

'Come on! Come down here with the fish!'

They had climbed down the ladder, at *the deep end*, and sat on the bottom of the empty pool and had a picnic.

Then they had walked up and down pretending to swim. His mother in her hairnet, the shirt she wore when she worked around the house and her grey stretch slacks; his father in his work boots, Stubbies and T-shirt. They walked up and down the pool with their arms doing breaststroke and butterfly and freestyle.

Pearl and Peter had backstroked together into Gary and their little brother had laughed himself silly.

'Care for a dance on the bottom, love?'

'Oh, very Esther Williams, Ken.'

•

Peter Kennedy sat in the archive basement now, looking at the building plans for this house and suddenly laughed, just as he had when he and Pearl had bumped into Gary, remembering the wonderful silliness of it all.

He had completely forgotten that afternoon. How could he have? It was . . . It was – he could hardly believe it – so much fun.

He spread the plans flat on the table. And he looked at the paper and visualised the tiles glistening. Then he noticed a series of numbers at the bottom, almost like a serial number. But not in the place where the building specifications or document numbers were usually placed.

He hadn't noticed it before. The way it was written in was unusual. In pen in his father's hand. He could tell because of the way his father always wrote his fours and sevens; a triangular four and the German seven with the two strokes through the body of the number. At the end of the number was written what seemed to be a name: *Gurton, J.*

When he had finished copying the final plan of his father's last home, he sat down and tallied up the plans with those numbers and a series of different names. In all they totalled thirty-eight. Peter could make no sense of them.

That's when he heard Lisa Sykes call to him. 'We'll have to turn you out, I'm afraid.'

'Oh, I'm done. Thanks.' He walked over and began to collect the papers.

'How are your family?'

'Haven't spoken to them, I'll do that when I get back to my parents' place.'

'Didn't you speak to them earlier?'

He remembered Tiger's swing.

'Yes. Yes, earlier. I thought you meant since then.' He gestured with his handful of plans. 'I've been busy.'

'Are they coming up for the show?

'Uh, no. Don't know. We'll have to see.' He smiled, he was sure he'd hooked a ball. 'It's been really good to see you again, Lisa.'

She looked at him for a moment and then tried to frown. 'I'm really glad you did this. For your dad – I didn't know. I thought perhaps you were . . . doing what I thought you might have been doing.'

Yes, he decided, he had hooked the ball. He went back to his preferred response to unwelcome questions – the blank stare and the deep breath.

'I mean, I'm sorry. I wanted to say that before – But, you know, with Eddie Hume . . .' She shrugged a little.

So, thought Peter, she'd be one of the 'ladies' in the world of Mr Multi-faceted.

'I know you don't design any more. I read that somewhere. You're a conceptualist developer. So, you know . . .'

They stared at each other. He stared longer than her.

'I'm glad you did this for your dad. He's a lovely man and I hope you design again. It was nice to see you . . . And thanks for asking about my mum.'

Maybe he hadn't sliced. Or hooked.

'She always liked you.'

For a moment he was sure she was going to say something else, but instead she tried to frown again and under the fluorescent lights he realised why she looked so young.

'Might see you around.'

'Might. You never know.'

And as he left he thought of three things. One: the bike chain incident seemed so very long ago. Two: he didn't want to play golf with Tiger any more, and three: he wanted to know, despite himself, what those bloody numbers and names meant.

Chapter Twelve

As soon as he had started Red Getz the phone vibrated. He really should set the thing to make some sort of noise so he knew when somebody wanted to contact him. But then maybe he didn't really want to talk to anyone; it was always easier to deal with someone when you already knew what it was they were after and that was the whole idea of leaving a message.

But he answered now because he thought it would be Kate. He pressed the green 'accept call' button, took a breath, then held the phone to his ear. It was his mother's voice. 'Peter, Peter? Peter, hello?'

He let out a sigh. 'Yep.'

'Peter.'

'Yep.'

'Peter, where are you now, dear?'

'Sitting in my car.'

'Your Noddy car? Are you on your way back here?'

'Yep.'

'Oh, lovely.' There was the noise of somebody talking in the background and then his mother's voice faded. 'No, no, no; it will be all right, you wait.' Then, 'Hello, Peter?'

'Yep.'

'Could you stop off at the shops and pick up some salad, please?'

He sighed again. 'What sort, Mum?'

'Oh, just some pre-made stuff in a packet and some milk, please, a large bottle. Thank you.'

'No worries, Mum.'

And he rang off and considered changing the phone's settings and decided not to; he would ring home from his parents' place later.

•

At the entrance to the shopping centre Peter saw people sitting along a row of low wooden benches. And that's all they did; sit. He couldn't divine whether any of them knew each other or whether they were just a clutch of roosting strangers.

The men all wore baseball caps. Some sat with their mouths agape, otherwise barely moving apart from an occasional scratch of an elbow or thigh, perhaps a roll of the tongue around the mouth, or a sniff.

One broke ranks, did both and folded his arms.

The two women just slumped.

There was a sign near the seats: 'Our Guests' Lounge.'

Venturing inside, there were some more of Pickersgill's citizenry. The people at Brisbane airport had been dressed formally in comparison.

Sun-burnt men in fluorescent safety jackets and trade-work clothes mooched around with tired eyes, too-young mothers, who seemed barely older than Peter's daughter, pushed their children in strollers. He felt a pang at the memory of Lisa Sykes saying she had something to tell him, all those years ago. This could have been me, Peter Kennedy thought.

He walked into the supermarket, down the aisle, and grabbed for the brand of milk that was always in his fridge at home, and a little girl followed him.

Her young mother grabbed her. 'No, Charade, not that one – that's the expensive one.'

Peter smiled down at the little girl, who stared back and then walked away.

He had never, he realised, considered which was the expensive milk and which was cheap. There was only milk.

Around the next aisle he saw girls as young as or maybe even younger than Ellie, giggling over what chips to buy, dressed in denim shorts that were almost non-existent.

In the fruit-and-veg section, he tried to decide which pre-packed salad his mother would want.

'No need to wash!' was emblazoned across the top of one packet. This time he decided to compare prices. Pre-packaged salad was dearer than the unwashed green leaves.

He chose not to wash.

Then he saw a long open fridge. He walked over and searched for it: luncheon meat. A small log lay before him.

He picked it up, feeling its spongy coldness. It felt decidedly unpleasant. He put his basket down and rotated the log in both hands, as if he were a manufactured-meat connoisseur. A little like the way a wine expert will sniff, swill and spit the wine.

He became quite fascinated with how awful the luncheon meat felt, holding it in one hand and slapping it three or four times into the palm of his other, making a wet squelching noise.

'Oh,' he said. 'Oh.'

He held the log at arm's length and slowly turned it around until he came to the ingredients list and he read: '*Meat, including pork, seventy-seven per cent, water, salt, soy protein, starch* . . . What's that? *Maize and tapioca, spices, emulsifiers* . . . A whole heap of numbers . . . Jesus, how many numbers *are* there?'

He hadn't realised that he was reading the ingredients out loud.

'*Dextrose, flavours* . . . that'd be sugar, more fucking numbers, *hydrolysed vegetable protein, yeast extract*, more colour, more numbers and *fermented rice*. Holy Christ!' he said, holding the log upright in his hand as if it were a vital piece of evidence and he stood before a jury. 'And I stick this bloody thing in my mouth!'

He suddenly noticed the little girl from the dairy section staring up at him, open-mouthed.

'Hello, there,' he said, still holding the manufactured meat out like Yorick's skull.

There was a shriek.

'Charade, Charade! Get away from him!'

The girl ran off and trailed after her mother.

'He was speaking to the sausage.'

'Just get here.'

Peter stood looking after the girl and then was jerked back into action by a voice that seemed to come from one of the cardboard cut-out staff members. 'You right there, sir? You right?'

He got a fright; he could see now that it wasn't a cardboard staff member but a real one. They wouldn't use this guy as a cardboard cut-out. He was dressed in a uniform three sizes too big and had a thin moustache and a tattoo of a snake writhing up his neck towards his chin. He was very pale and very thin.

'Problem with your luncheon meat there, sir?'

'No . . .' Peter said slowly. 'No.'

'Are you going to purchase that?'

'No.'

And he very gravely handed over the luncheon meat sausage to the skinny man with the snake climbing up his neck.

It felt vaguely ceremonial, the sausage handover. And even more so when the thin man very carefully put the luncheon meat back in the fridge, as if he were placing the last Jack of Diamonds onto an ornate house of cards.

Peter looked down at the stacked logs in the fridge, at the house of manufactured meat. They were lined up like armaments that were waiting to be stuffed into a device and shot off into the distance to destroy some godforsaken village in a forgotten war.

He turned and walked to the check-out in a daze; his hands actually felt a little contaminated.

Standing before him were the young girls in the denim shorts. They had small bags slung over their shoulders and were wearing make-up. Three of them were looking through a copy of *Cosmo* as they waited.

This time they weren't giggling about what chips to choose but the magazine article. Over their shoulders he could see what they were reading.

Sex questions answered! Question one was *Should I give him oral before we start having sex or will he peak too quickly?*

Peter looked away.

The girls went through the check-out and as Peter paid he heard one girl say to her friends, 'You got change? Put it in the dog. Always put some of the change in the dog!'

'Nice puppy dog,' said another, of the plastic Seeing Eye Dog charity box.

And they did. They were probably younger than Ellie and all in a rush to grow up. Maybe they thought the sex questions were only tosh, a bit of fun? He hoped so; they were so young. He watched them walk away through the shopping centre's guest lounge and out into the evening.

Peter walked back to Red Getz, still wondering about those numbers on the bottom of the building plans. Those bloody numbers.

As he pulled up outside his parents' home he felt the hum of the phone. It was Kate.

'Hello?'

There was no reply.

'Hello . . . Hello? Hello!'

'How does *that* feel?'

'What?'

'How does nothing at the end of the phone feel, Peter?'

'Oh, Kate . . .'

'Don't "Oh, Kate" me. Why don't you ever have your phone on?'

'It was on the silent thing and I've been . . . Look, I left a message.'

'Well done, you!'

She was thinking hard all right. So he said nothing.

'I don't want to get mad, Peter, I'm sick of that. I just want to know if you are coming home tomorrow for the father–daughter night. If you're not you'll have to sort something with the school.'

'Yep.'

There was a silence from the end of the phone.

'Yep,' he said, louder. 'Kate?'

'Peter,' her voice sounded sad. 'Peter . . .'

He wanted to say what he had said to the dead phone earlier in the day. He wanted to, but he didn't.

'Is Ellie there?'

He heard Kate sigh. 'No, it's her swimming carnival tonight and you don't even know what races she's swimming in, do you?'

He could have said nothing, but instead he said, 'No.'

And his wife hung up.

He sat in the car with the phone to his ear and said softly, 'I love you.' And then he put the phone away in his bag, collected the shopping, squeezed out of the car and, as he locked the door, said, 'Freestyle, in the individual and relay.'

He got to the first step when he was assaulted by the familiar tones of Orlendo Lane. 'Here is the *big fellllllllooooow*!'

There was Orlendo, standing at the top of the stairs under a sprouting hat. Or was it a wig?

'Orlendo.'

'Peter.'

'What are you wearing there, mate?'

'It's my Limahl look.' And then Orlendo's voice went all soft and warm. 'Peter, do you remember Limahl? *Never Ending Story*?'

The phrase *fuck me sideways* strobed across Peter Kennedy's mind's eye as if it were written in scalding lightning, and at that moment he came as close as he could remember to actually saying what he thought without waiting to censor himself.

Not quite, though. He breathed and looked at the tall thin silhouette that appeared as if it had the neck, torso and limbs of a man with the head and plumage of a Chinese silkie chicken.

He sighed and said, '*Never Ending Story.*'

'Yes,' purred Orlendo.

'The dog, the flying dog. And Columbo was in that film,' said Peter Kennedy warily.

'Yes, first "Columbo" – aka Peter Falk. Common mistake to make; he was the granddad in *The Princess Bride* not *Never Ending.* Now they were very similar, but *The Princess Bride* was quite mainstream, if you like; *Never Ending Story* was definitely more Euro.'

Peter Kennedy nodded. Orlendo was right. Peter Falk was the granddad in *The Princess Bride.*

'Yes,' Orlendo continued, 'slightly darker, a little strange – hence reminding everyone of Limahl; strange. But you're definitely on track with the flying dog. The dog, of course, was actually a flying Chinese *dragon*, but what prompted me, big felloooooooow, to go with the Limahl look, was when I saw a golden retriever this very morning and the resemblance between the two is uncanny. Hence I've gone Limahl. What do you think?'

'Limahl was like the golden retriever?'

'No, my mistake. The flying dragon looked very much like a golden retriever if you do the eye-squint. The association with Limahl came with the film's very memorable song.'

'Yep.'

The was a pause. And Peter filled it. 'Orlendo, I think I can say we are the only two people in the universe who are talking about Limahl. I don't think he's talking about himself. It's a daring choice.'

The Chinese silkie nodded. 'Thanks.' Then it turned its head towards the door. 'The big fellow's here.'

An awful thought struck Peter: How many of them are there?

He found out when he walked in.

There was Pearl and a young teenage girl he didn't know. His mother and the Chinese silkie chicken, his father, and then there was the man whose hand his father was holding. Wayne Dixon.

Peter looked at them all. And they looked back at him.

Why is my father holding Wayne Dixon's hand?

'G'day, mate,' said Wayne enthusiastically. He was dressed in going-out clothes: white runners that he never used for running, a pair of Levi's, pulled up high, an Abercrombie & Fitch tartan shirt and a jumper thrown over his back, the sleeves knotted around his neck. He was very clean. And fit. And ready to go out.

Why is my father holding his hand?

Ken broke the silence. 'Hello there, son.' He stood, leaving Wayne Dixon's hand gently behind. 'We're all waiting for Gary to come on the weather.'

Wayne stood up. 'Just popped over to say hello to your Olds.'

'Oh, charming,' said Mary Kennedy.

'I think I might scoot down to the shed,' Ken continued, 'and box those beers for you to take over to the Produce Pavilion, Orlendo.'

'My word,' said Orlendo.

'Hi,' Peter Kennedy said, to the room.

'What have you got there, Peter?' asked his mother.

'Shopping. The shopping you wanted.'

They all looked at him. And the plastic shopping bag.

'Yes, what is that you bought again?'

'Milk and salad mix. You don't have to wash it.'

They stared at him. He stared back.

'The salad. You don't have to wash the salad,' Peter repeated.

'Oh, that's handy. Well, pop it in the fridge.'

He breathed in and was about to go into the kitchen when Pearl said, 'Peter, this is Elenore, she's staying with us for a time.'

'Hello there,' he said and stood there for a moment. 'Nice to meet you. I have a daughter your age; she's swimming tonight. School carnival. The freestyle. Individual and relay.'

He stood for longer than he meant to, before his father patted him on the elbow as he headed down the steps towards his shed.

'I like to swim,' said the girl.

Peter smiled at her. 'Well, it's a good thing to do.'

He walked out to the fridge as Wayne Dixon said, 'Gary's coming up after the ads.'

This is all very strange, Peter decided. There's a lot of staring and popping in and out going on here tonight. It didn't improve when he opened the fridge; he saw a lot of milk and even more lettuce.

'Mum, why'd you ask me to get the shopping?' he asked quietly.

'How do you mean?'

'You asked for milk and a salad and you've got lots of both.'

'Never mind, pop it in the fridge. You can never have too much of a good thing.'

'Now I don't, I don't know about that,' said the Chinese silkie that was Orlendo who used to be Len.

'Here he is,' said Pearl. 'Here's Gary.'

'Will he mention it?' said Wayne Dixon.

'Did last year,' said Pearl.

'He'll do it,' said Mary Kennedy.

Peter stood at the fridge listening to them. Their voices. He remembered how sad Kate had sounded. He couldn't remember hearing her like that before, as if she had not given up but had resigned herself to bad news, or something nobody could do anything about.

Then he did what he always did when he got close to working something out that had to do with the whole scheme of being human: he placed it in the 'to do' tray somewhere in his brain and tried to find some other compartment in his mind to fiddle with. What, though?

Then he heard Gary chatting away with the newsreader about the weather and how the weekend was looking fine and tomorrow, too. This was good because 'It's showtime at Pickersgill, of course!'

And they all whooped in the living room.

Peter closed the fridge. He didn't want to go back in there as they watched the weather. He didn't really want to be a part of their little world of shows and bingo nights. Not right now.

Gary rabbited away on the television. 'Right, so let's go through the numbers!'

Numbers. Yes that would do. Peter picked up his work bag and headed back outside and down the stairs to the shed.

•

He had always been a tidy man, Ken Kennedy, and his shed at the back of the garden was what you might have expected from someone who liked to know where things were. Very orderly. Not overly neat and clean, but orderly. He was a man who liked doing things and as he often said, 'A bloke who likes doing things will always know where things are, and the things he needs will always be ready to use. You don't want to live in a bottle of bleach or some laboratory, son; a bit of mess here and there is all right, as long as it's not chaos.'

Peter had stopped going into his father's shed for chats not long after the birthday party on the beach when he was told to stop arsing around after he had said he liked the Council Chambers building.

He knocked now, entered the shed and saw his father by his beer bench, cradling a long-neck of something as if it were an infant.

He looked at him. You're old, he thought, so old.

Maybe it was the harshness of the fluorescent lights that did it. He thought of Lisa Sykes.

His father smiled at him. His big smile. 'Hello there, son. What are you doing down here?'

'Thought I'd say hello.'

'Lovely.'

Ken coughed a little and sniffed. He wore a cardigan and grey tracksuit pants and his soft zip-up shoes.

'You said hello to Kate today?'

Peter nodded.

'Good, is she?'

He nodded again.

The two of them said nothing for a little moment and then Ken Kennedy slowly wiped down the bottle he was holding. 'Beer. I love beer. Making it. It's a living thing, you know.' And he smiled. 'One of the few remaining legacies from our medieval ancestors – a fine concoction of water, grain, hops, yeast and sugar, all brewed together to create a drink worthy of the highest accolade a man can ever hope to be given: "That's not bad!"'

And he smiled and Peter laughed.

'Let's have one, then.' And Ken moved slowly over to his beer fridge. It was covered in magnets and stickers but one that had always stood out was a big messy magnet by the handle. It had been given to him by the twins years ago; they had made it at kindy. 'The World's Greatest Grand Dud', written in spidery little kids' hand, complete with creative kindy spelling, 'Worthy of a position in editorial at the *Pickersgill Courier!*' Mary Kennedy had said when it had been unwrapped.

'You never really took a liking to the home brewing, did you, son?

'No.'

'Well, I suppose it was always my little thing down here. But you do like your beer, don't you?'

Peter Kennedy nodded. 'Sure do, Grand Dud.'

'Good. Never quite sure with you, son – you can be a hard one to pick.' And his father smiled. 'Your nanna always said that about you, even when you were little.'

Peter still stood near the door. His father beckoned him closer with a slow roll of his index finger.

'Now you know, of course, how to tell a good beer? You probably do but, you know, I don't think I've ever told you.' He paused and then nodded. 'So I'll tell you now. It should be a clear brew. Always a good sign that you've made a commitment to basic cleanliness and hygiene standards. Doesn't mean it'll be any good, but – could be like those awful clear beers you young blokes drink – Coronas or Cortinas or whatever – they're clear and they've got no taste.'

He opened a bottle. 'The other way to go is to sniff the bastard. If it smells like an egger then odds on it won't taste good. We've all had those, but this . . .' He sniffed the beer. 'This is a good 'un.'

He poured two glasses. 'It doesn't have to be clear all the way through – the last little bit there should be cloudy, just the sediment from the secondary fermentation. And you should drink it. It's bloody good for you. Got 'em through the Middle Ages, all those monks and whatnot. A meal in a glass.'

He held out a glass to his son. 'Here.'

Before they drank, Ken held his beer up. 'And a wash on the glass is a sign of a good brew – should be able to see a rind of foam left on the inside of the glass after each mouthful.'

His eyes moved to his glass then back to his son's. 'Well, let's see.'

And they drank.

Ken held up his glass again. 'There's the wash. And that's . . .' He trailed off.

'Not bad,' said Peter Kennedy quietly.

'The highest compliment.' Ken nodded at his son and walked a little closer to him. 'Good one, this beer. A living thing. Don't know how many more I'll be making, but I should do all right with this one at the show.'

He moved closer, and to Peter's slight unease, took hold of his hand. 'And Kate, she's well, is she?'

'Dad . . .' Peter looked at his father and then went on, 'Why are you holding my hand? And where are your old *Post* magazines?'

Ken gave his son a perfect example of the Pickersgill Tongue Roll, counting all of his remaining teeth with a sweep around the mouth and ending with a click of the tongue.

He let go of his son's hand. 'Oh, well now, I suppose the hand business is an old bloke's thing and as for the *Post*s, they're where they always have been, Peter, under the old creosote cans.'

Yes, Peter knew where they were; he used to creep down to sift through them when the mood took him, and of course he never really got past the cover.

'What are you wanting with them?'

'I bumped into Lisa Sykes today down at the land registry office; she's a planner there.'

'Oh, I see. It's the box to the left, near the top.'

'You know which one?'

'It always pays to have whatever you want to use waiting for you.'

Ken laughed and threw his hands up. 'Give me a break! Pickersgill's only ever had one *Post* girl. Anyway, your mother wanted me to get it out when we saw her after she first moved back a few years ago.'

'Was she riding a bike?'

'Yes, going like the clappers, but she stopped to say hello and your mother noticed right away there was something going on.'

Peter laughed.

'Oh, turn it up – with those clothes she was wearing it stood out a mile; look at the cover! A woman doesn't change much after she's eighteen, son.'

And there on the cover was a girl kneeling on a beach; Lisa Sykes in her awkward pose.

It was an old and musty copy, and he wondered if either of Lisa's parents had kept their framed cover when they separated. This one smelled and felt of the past.

He held it as his father stood next to him. They studied it for a good few moments.

'Yep,' said Peter Kennedy.

'Yep,' said his father. 'There's a lot more of her these days than there was then, and in places where she never had much to show.'

'Christ, Dad!'

'Well, I'm pointing out the obvious. She was always a lovely girl but you know.' And he gestured with his glass. 'Another-y?'

'Why not? Thanks.'

Peter looked at Lisa on the cover and remembered how today in the archive cellar she couldn't frown, even when she had clearly meant to. He put the magazine back in order and put the box back under the creosote cans.

'Wonder why she did it?'

'Well, lots of people renovate things, don't they?' said his father. 'Who's to say whether it's right or wrong?'

Peter sniffed.

'Of course it might have something to do with who she married; might have been a case of DIY.'

'What are you on about?'

'You remember Dr Langdon up at Hove?'

Peter nodded.

'They say if a doctor has any kids then one of them is bound to be a doctor. Or, in Greg Langdon's case, a surgeon. A plastic surgeon – or whatever they're called these days: a cosmetic surgeon.'

'She married Greg Langdon?'

'Yep and he's got clinics in town and down the coast. Worth a bomb, they reckon, so he must be good. Maybe he practised on old Lisa?'

Peter took a drink. Then he shook his head. 'That is bizarre.'

'Yeah, 'tis a bit, isn't it? I wonder whether he talked her into it?'

'No, not about her having whatever she had done, but it's bizarre I was thinking about Dr Langdon's house today.' He smiled. 'About his pool.'

'Now, that was an afternoon. Crumbed fish, chips, dim sims and Tristram's sars-and-lime. Lovely,' said his father in a whisper. He walked back to his bench. 'You know, I can remember how all the laughter and the noise you kids made echoed off those pool walls. A beautiful sound, Peter.'

Ken drained the last of the bottle and put it and his glass on the washing-up tray. 'What on earth made you think of that this afternoon?'

Peter drank his beer quickly then held up the glass. 'Yep, there's your wash.'

He put his glass next to his father's.

Ken Kennedy tilted his head to one side and peered at his son.

Peter stood and wondered what he should do. The two men stared at each other.

'Want another beer?' asked Ken.

Peter nodded.

'I'll make it a stout.'

Peter took the bottle and a new glass from his father.

'You'll know if you get that one wrong because you've got to drink it with a knife and fork.'

After his father gave it to him, Peter stood with his head to one side, as if he were sizing up a job he had to complete. He needn't tell him about the showgrounds. His look-see could have been about any of the other blocks and parcels of land; the Peninsula was constantly being scoured by developers.

'I was looking at a plan of the Langdon house today. A building plan.'

'Oh yeah?' And Ken straightened his head and folded his arms.

His son nodded. 'You see, I wanted to get a collection of your plans, your building plans. I photocopied all the plans of places where you were the sole contract builder. One hundred and twenty-four.'

Ken Kennedy nodded again and Peter took a mouthful of stout. He wondered if this was the same drop that had sent Orlendo silly as a wheel that Christmas. 'It's a good effort.'

'Why'd you do that?'

'I just wanted to.' And Peter shrugged his shoulders. He felt a golf club in his hands. He didn't like it.

Ken suddenly smiled and shook his head. 'You are a funny bastard, Peter.'

Peter took another pull of his stout. 'Yep.'

'Well, what do you reckon?'

'You loved a verandah, Dad.'

The old man rubbed his hands together. He seemed almost embarrassed. 'You could have asked me for them.'

Peter Kennedy stood still. 'Some of them were interesting.'

His father laughed. 'Oh, thanks, mate. Is that Architect for "Not bad"?'

Peter smiled. '*More* interesting.'

His father gently took hold of his hand again and, despite himself, Peter let him.

'You best get off to your dinner with that mate of yours upstairs.'

'Dad, what are the numbers for?'

'Hey?'

'The numbers on the plans for the Langdon house. And you've put them on thirty-seven other sets of plans too. You marked them in your own hand, on the official records, which means it's not just the Langdon house, it's legally known as "Langdon House SN 33986 Gurton, J". You've changed the dwelling name with the annotation.'

His father let go of his hand.

Peter bent down and picked up the photocopied plans from his bag and held them out to his father. 'So that's why they're interesting. Only thirty-eight out of the one hundred and twenty-four are marked like that.'

'You're a clever lad, Peter.'

It was the way his father suddenly shifted that made Peter Kennedy notice a change come over him. Normally, you wouldn't have seen it, but somehow the old man held himself straighter. And his hands held the plans even more gently than they had the long-neck of pale ale they'd held earlier when Peter had walked into the shed.

'Dad, they're only copies, they're not parchment.'

Ken looked up to his son and said very softly, 'Maybe.'

•

The two men were still standing in silence when Omar started to bark. Mary Kennedy shushed the old dog away and poked her head around the corner of the shed door. 'Come on, Peter, what are you hanging around for? You off to dinner or what?'

Ken put the papers down on the beer bench and smiled to Mary. 'My fault, my love, we had to give a few brews a taste test. And your son approves.'

Peter nodded.

'So you think you're in with a chance?' said Mary.

'Well, you know, all those young blokes have got all the gee-whiz gear, but we'll see. We were also having a little bit of a chat about Lisa Sykes and her husband.'

Mary threw back her head and laughed. 'Yes, the cover shows you.'

She took Peter by the hand and, stepping over the barking Omar, led him up the stairs to the big house. 'Your father tell you she married young Langdon?'

Peter nodded.

'What a pair. She's lovely, still says hello, and he's quite pleasant in a shiny sort of a way. But you do wonder what they get up to on their holidays, don't you?'

'What?'

'Well, other people clean the gutters or mow the lawn. They give themselves a cut and polish and a new nose.'

Peter laughed.

'He is annoying, though. He's won the Decorated Cake contest every year they've been back. Three on the trot!'

And then she turned to him at the top of the stairs and said softly, 'And Kate? She well?'

Peter nodded.

His mother gently touched his cheek and said, 'Good. Now, go off with Wayne. I think he wants to chat to you.'

She left him there on the verandah and he finished his stout. He could see his father through the shed windows.

Ken Kennedy stood very still and in his hands he held the building plans.

Chapter Thirteen

As Peter and Wayne walked down towards the jetty, Peter Kennedy went through his dot-point thoughts. One: he wasn't any clearer on what the numbers meant. Two: he couldn't think why he had stopped going for chats with his dad in his shed – it was sort of fun. Three: why had his father said he might not brew many more beers? And four: why did Wayne Dixon walk so quickly?

Maybe it was because he was in the police force. Or maybe it was because he was fit. Maybe he was one of those people who believed any form of movement was exercise.

Peter wasn't really listening to what Wayne was saying as he was pretty sure with the speed they were going that he was getting a stitch.

He added another dot point. Five: it must have been the stout that had knocked Orlendo sideways, because it had certainly given Peter a kick like a mule.

He started listening to what Wayne Dixon was saying.

'Don't you reckon?' said Wayne.

Obviously, Peter realised, I should have started paying attention a little earlier. He could have asked what had been said, but that would mean having to listen so instead he just nodded.

'Yeah I suppose you're right. Still, he does move beautifully,' Wayne continued.

What in God's name was he talking about? Peter Kennedy decided he should say something. 'We should take a couple of beers out on the jetty, for old time's sake.' He was trying to take some sort of control of the conversation.

When they were in their late teens Peter and Wayne would get six-packs and walk to the end of the jetty and sit on the mooring platform, and drink them. They would chat about girls, football and what they wanted to do with their lives. And look out across the bay, past the flashing channel markers to the lights of Brisbane.

Peter smiled to himself. They had started out with Brisbane Bitter because that was the cheapest beer around, gone through to XXXX and then started to buy mixed sixes as the first imported beers crept onto the market. San Miguel from the Philippines, Heineken and South Pacific lager from New Guinea and the deeply exotic Southwark – from Adelaide. Wayne had bought that. He thought it had come from South Africa. Peter laughed as he remembered.

'I know what you're thinking: Southwark. Will I ever live it down?' Wayne laughed his nice laugh. 'All right, that'd be good, but we should try this Japanese place, too, you'll like it.'

So maybe he had been talking about the Japanese restaurant before, Peter wondered. But *who* had moved beautifully? Best not to worry, just let it be.

•

The restaurant was very modern. Very 'new Pickersgill', with tiny sunken booths and staff in Japanese dress.

The servings were agonisingly small for Peter, especially as he hadn't eaten since that morning; no wonder the beer had gone to his head. It didn't help that for old time's sake Wayne insisted on asking for something more to drink.

Their waiter, a pretty young woman with a lovely smile, brought over two bottles of Corona.

'Ah, Cortinas!' said Peter and knocked back his beer far too quickly. His dad was right; there wasn't much of a taste.

'I think I know that girl.'

'The waiter?'

Wayne nodded. 'From somewhere . . .'

'Maybe you gave her a ticket?'

'Up yours! No, I'll work it out.'

'She's probably still at school.'

'Yeah, that's it! School visit. Police week. Out at Living Waters Lutheran; she's a house captain.'

When the food had come Wayne and the waiter, whose name was Ruby, chatted about his visit to her school.

Ruby was very friendly and quite delightful. The sort of girl who makes a middle-aged man reassured about being the father of a daughter, thought Peter Kennedy. A nice, pleasant, normal young girl.

He felt a pang about Ellie; her swimming carnival. He considered ringing Kate to see how she went but realised that he'd left his phone in his work bag. Then he considered borrowing Wayne's, thought better of it when he remembered Kate's voice, and so ordered another beer from Ruby.

Wayne described the food as 'exquisite'.

Peter Kennedy found that word a bit odd, most un-Dixon-like. And he really could not believe how small the servings were, most un-Kennedy-like.

'You come here often?' he said to Wayne.

'Yeah, it's one of my haunts.'

Peter nodded.

'Gives you a little idea of how this area is going to change.'

'You think?'

'What, you don't think it's changed?'

'Well, population density will change anything and the more affluent the people who move in, the more the make up of the place will change, I suppose, but I've got to tell you, Wayne, there's still a lot of the old-school Pickers about.'

Wayne laughed. 'Yes, I know what you mean, but this place is opening up. I've got an apartment.'

'Where?'

'One up at Hove, by the harbour. Designed by some hack called Kennedy, apparently.'

They both laughed.

Ruby came back after they had finished their meals and asked if they would like anything else. Peter felt like ordering the whole menu twice over but Wayne said they were 'as full as a butcher's.'

Now, Peter decided, that is more like the old Wayne Dixon. 'Full as a butcher's.' Where did the 'exquisite' Dixon come from?

'Ruby, my friend Peter, here, thinks that Pickersgill hasn't changed that much.'

'Yeah?' said Ruby, smiling.

'Yeah, but take your school. When we were at Pickers high, Living Waters was just a primary school near where we played rugby. But today it's got – what, nearly a thousand students?'

'Yeah, I guess. There are five houses so it's pretty big.' Peter nodded and wondered about ordering another beer.

'Peter, here, left Pickers high in Year Ten to go off to school in Brisbane. Now, he'd only have to go out to Living Waters to go to a private school.'

Peter looked at Wayne Dixon. Mate, he thought, You don't get it; that wasn't the point of me going to Terrace.

'Did you guys both go to Pickers?'

'Yeah,' said Wayne. 'Me all the way through and Peter till Year Ten.'

'Did you know Darryl Barber?'

Both men blanched. Darryl Barber.

'Yes,' said Wayne, as if he had just heard the name of a dangerous criminal.

Oh, they knew Darryl Barber. He was to Peter *uber* Pickersgill. Pickersgill Man. A subspecies of a subspecies.

Darryl Barber was a nightmare, a bully who stalked the grounds of Pickersgill High like some awful beast. The first boy with facial hair like a grown man, the first with a tattoo, the boy who brazenly paraded a packet of Winfield Reds in his breast pocket like war ribbons on a US Marine's chest.

Ruby smiled her lovely smile. 'He's my dad!'

Neither man said anything for a while.

'Oh,' said Ruby Barber, 'there's lots of stories.'

And it was only because Ruby seemed so nice that Peter spoke, 'Your father . . . Your father . . .' He paused. He shouldn't say anything but he was tired, the food had been tiny and after the beer . . . So he decided he would say what actually happened.

'Your father . . . spat on my arm. A huge golly; heard him bringing it up from the bottom of his toes as I was walking into a Citizenship Education class. Yeah, they had a subject called Citizenship Education in those days and they let your father sit that class. And he spat on my arm and he said, "If you wipe that off I'm gonna punch ya."'

Wayne looked at Ruby and then to Peter.

'Yeah?' Ruby said. She was still smiling.

Peter nodded. 'I was going to wipe it on the weird kid with glasses – Pat Smee – you know, like it was an accident, but your dad said, "You touch Smee with my slag and I'll punch ya."'

Ruby nodded.

'So I sat there while we were taught how to fill out deposit slips at a bank with this grotesque piece of your father's sputum on my arm, trying to balance your dad's spit so it wouldn't drip off my arm. I sat there for the whole lesson.'

'Wow,' said Ruby.

Wayne took a deep breath. 'Your father burned a hole in my school shirt, above the pocket, with a cigarette, a lit cigarette that he was smoking at little lunch.'

Peter Kennedy remembered that. Wayne had been a library monitor and Darryl Barber had been smoking in the library garden. He could never understand why Wayne actually tried to say anything about the cigarette to Darryl. But then Wayne took his library monitor role very seriously, and off he marched with his grey Stubbie school shorts pulled high and his 'Monitor' badge glinting in the sunlight.

'He burned a hole in my shirt.'

'Wasn't he just trying to burn your badge, Wayne?'

Wayne snapped back, 'No, he wasn't! My monitor badge was in the middle of my pocket, that's where we had been told to place them and he did not go for the badge, he burned directly above it, above the pocket. I've still got a scar.'

There was a pause.

'Well, Ruby, I guess you could say we know your dad,' said Peter Kennedy.

Ruby looked at the two men and broke into her friendliest smile yet. 'I just love Pickersgill – everybody knows each other! It's so cute. I'll say hello to him from you.'

Both men looked at her in amazement.

'And since he found the love of Jesus Christ I am sure he will say hello back in his prayers.'

Poor old Jesus, thought Peter, all the crap he had to go through and he still had to front Darryl Barber.

Both men kept looking at Ruby.

She smiled. 'Would you like the bill?'

'Yes please, Ruby,' said Peter Kennedy.

•

Peter and Wayne settled down on the mooring pontoon below the jetty, laughing.

'Darryl Barber got Jesus,' said Peter.

'Scary thought. I say bully for God.'

'Mate, it's so Pickersgill.'

They sipped their beers and listened to the water.

'He was trying to get your monitor's badge.'

'Piss off.'

They watched a plane come in to land at Brisbane airport. Peter gave a little wave.

'You like your apartment?'

'Yeah. It's good. Really good. Good design by that hack Kennedy.'

'Well, he doesn't design any more.'

'Yeah, that's what Gary told me.' There was a little pause and then Wayne went on. 'Why doesn't he?'

'He just doesn't.' Peter looked at the water around the pylons, the lights throwing a shimmering pattern on it like little floating stars. A seagull sailed past, squawking in the dark.

'The sound of water and its smell is quite beautiful.'

'Oh, Peter.'

'What?'

'Why'd you stop? Designing.'

'Got tired, that's all. Needed a break. I was always sure I'd go back, but I don't know . . .'

'Things change.'

'Yeah. Look at Darryl Barber!'

'Maybe he has.'

Peter said nothing.

'People do change, mate.'

Peter had some more to drink.

'People change.'

'Yep.'

Wayne took a very deep breath. 'Except you.'

Peter said nothing.

'You're doing that thing you always used to do.'

Peter took another drink.

'You're doing it. Not saying anything until the conversation comes around to something you feel comfortable with.'

Peter did do this; he knew he did. This was not the Wayne Dixon he remembered. That Wayne wasn't so . . . acute

'Wayne . . . Oh, don't worry about it.'

Wayne laughed. 'That is exactly how you sounded when you told me you weren't going to Pickers high any more: "Wayne," pause, pause, pause, "Oh," pause, "Don't worry a –" pause – "'bout it."'

They both laughed.

'I can remember that, man. I was so upset. I got really upset.'

'Yes, you did,' said Peter.

'I'd tried not to cry but, fuck.'

'Why did you get so upset?'

'You were leaving.'

'Yeah, but I still lived here, we still came down here and drank Southwark –'

'Up yours.'

'We still played footy together.'

'You were leaving.' That came out louder than Wayne meant it to. Then the men were silent for a moment.

'People change, Peter. Sometimes, they're happy where they are. You know you work out what you are and what your bag is. You guys were like that.'

Peter said nothing.

'You know – you and Gary. That's what I was saying when we were coming down from your parents' place.'

Shit, thought Peter Kennedy, I really should have listened.

'You know what I was saying, about Gary?'

'That he moved beautifully.'

'Fuck off.'

'That's what you said.'

'Yeah, that was just about the way he moved when he played rugby.'

'Well, he could move, that's why he was on the wing. But you know . . .'

'What?'

'If you're going to be gay and you play rugby, you're bound to end up on the wing.'

'That's his joke.'

Yes it was. Gary Kennedy. The youngest child of Ken and Mary Kennedy had been gay for as long as anyone could remember and nobody had ever really minded. It had helped that he had been an exceptionally courageous footy player, even if he was a winger. A dual international, an Origin great.

It also helped that he was handsome and unfailingly pleasant and remarkably likeable. And was quite comfortable with being a homosexual male.

And Wayne was right, it was his joke. He'd use it at the sportsman's talk he'd give to schoolkids.

Peter sighed. 'Yeah,' he said, 'it's Gary's joke.'

'You know,' said Wayne, 'he was always certain of what he was and that's why I said he's pretty inspirational. You always seemed so sure of yourself, too. Some of us aren't as lucky; we have to find out about ourselves.'

Peter heard a fish jump. Then another and another. The mullet were on the run. You couldn't see them from the mooring jetty but they were there, in the dark.

'Yes,' he said.

'What?'

'You were saying, Wayne?'

'Well, I got upset. When you said you were leaving. I know why I got upset but I could never tell you.'

Peter said nothing.

'I mean, I've been a copper for thirty years and seen things. You see people lie – almost every day in traffic. Always bullshitting, thinking they won't get in trouble. And the number of people who just bugger themselves because they lie or try to hide. They nearly always get found out and even if they don't they know they're living a lie.'

Peter Kennedy said nothing.

'I . . . Well, maybe if you deal with people lying so much – and it doesn't mean they are bad people; there's all sorts of reasons why people lie. And they're not always bad reasons, but they're lies and if you deal with that amount of bullshit, it's only a matter of time before you say to yourself, "Fuck it. I am what I am." I learnt what I was.'

More fish jumped and Peter sat there trying to count; he'd got up to thirty-eight mullet before Wayne Dixon took a deep breath. Thirty-eight. Peter remembered how his father had just stood there, holding the copies of the building plans.

'Have you heard anything of what I've just said, Peter?'

There was something about Wayne's tone that made Peter think of the sound of Kate's voice on the phone. It had a resigned quality to it.

'You cried when I said I was going to school in Brisbane.'

It was the best thing that could have happened for me, thought Peter Kennedy, to get away from the Peninsula, to cross the bridge and see there was something other than old Picker high that life had to offer.

'Didn't know why I got upset then, but I know now,' continued Wayne.

'Yep.'

'I'm gay.'

Peter didn't say anything.

'I'm gay, mate.'

He had heard the first time, but Peter thought 'Gaymate' sounded like some kind of kitchen utensil. *Gaymate chops, dices, slices and cleans!*

'I'm gay. It took me a while but I worked out that's what I am.'

Another fish jumped but Peter didn't bother counting. He just took a deep breath.

'Well?' said Wayne Dixon.

Peter let out a long sigh. Well, he thought, I suppose that explains 'exquisite' and maybe even thinking that the restaurant was good, and it definitely gives a hint as to why he's gone for the Bucks Fizz look with his jumper sleeves knotted around his neck.

'Are you shocked?'

'No! I mean Darryl Barber finds God and you work out you're gay. Very Pickersgill.'

Wayne half laughed. 'Peter, that's why I cried that night. Don't you understand?'

Peter looked at Wayne and his knotted jumper and then gazed out to the flashing green channel marker.

'I realised I had such a crush on you.'

'Oh, give me a break!' Peter said in time to the flashing light.

'I'm sorry. I thought I should tell you. It didn't mean anything. I didn't know what I was, you know? We were only fifteen. But you were smart. And you had a lovely smile and I'm sorry, but you were kind.'

'Wayne, why are you telling me this now?'

'I thought you should know.'

'What, I'm here for a couple of days so you think you should tell me? "Oh, hi Peter. Hey, I'm gay and I had a crush on you thirty-three years ago. I'll see you around." I mean, mate, what do I do with that?'

'There are other things. Sort of.' Wayne Dixon stopped. 'Peter, I've got a partner and we're really happy. My life is pretty good. I reckoned I should tell you, that's all.'

Peter nodded. 'Well,' he said, and after a pause declared, 'There's no more beer.'

And that was that.

They walked back up from the pontoon to the jetty.

Wayne wanted to say something more but Peter put his hand on his shoulder. 'Mate, I am happy for you that your life is good. But it's time for me to get something to eat – I'm afraid your exquisite restaurant didn't do it for me.'

'All right. See you tomorrow at Pearl's bingo night, maybe? My partner will be there,' said Wayne as Peter turned away.

'Be good.' Peter said it in that way of his. A tone that committed nothing but gave an answer that could be interpreted any number of ways.

Chapter Fourteen

As Peter walked along the wooden planks he looked back once more down the jetty. Wayne stood at the end facing the channel marker and the darkness of the bay. The green light flashing; his jumper still knotted around his neck.

There was only one place Peter knew to get some food to soak up all the beer in his belly.

He saw the sign as soon as he stepped off the jetty, blazing there, not far from the entrance to Pickersgill. The World of Hot Dogs. He told himself he didn't have to think about those numbers that made up the manufactured meat.

He reached the food store quicker than he ever imagined possible – he walked almost as fast as he had when he was trying to keep up with Wayne.

He shook his head at the thought; Wayne.

Well, good for him. But really why did he have to add the bit about his crush? Peter walked a little faster. Crushes. His first crush probably would have been one of the girls on the cover of an *Australasian Post*. Maybe that girl holding a pineapple with her head to one side. He couldn't remember her name, but he could remember that to the left of her breast was the headline 'John Wayne's secret fear'. And John Wayne was looking sideways towards the girl with the pineapple.

And suddenly he remembered those two men at the airport – giggling about eye candy. He felt a little odd.

The World of Hot Dogs neon sign shone even closer. He didn't like thinking about those men. Because they were just men. He didn't like thinking about the sound of Kate's voice, either. And to his surprise, he found himself actually running. Running towards the World of Hot Dogs. Running, and he felt his knees give the hint that perhaps this wasn't the best of things to be doing.

As he reached the car park of the World of Hot Dogs he thought of talcum jet powder and his nanna's farm at Caboolture. How it was a Kmart now. He felt a pang as he remembered Cider, that mad dog who had chased him and been buried out there by his nanna's chook shed. He imagined how his bones must have been dug up and spread and crushed by the landscaping of the car park.

He staggered to a halt, wheezing like Darth Vader.

Funny, he thought, you never see Darth Vader running anywhere.

He waddled over to the entrance and saw an illuminated sign: 'Drive thru service only.'

He grunted, headed straight to the fibreglass King, and, feeling completely out of breath, he leant on the jaunty arm of the manufactured meat monarch for support.

He breathed deeply into the hot dog's face.

'Welcome to World of Hot Dogs,' a deep rumbling voice said.

Peter was so surprised he stopped panting for a moment.

The fibreglass hot dog smiled back at him.

'Mate, you right?'

Peter Kennedy burst out laughing. 'Sorry, either your cold has got a lot worse or your balls have dropped through the cellar.'

'What do you want, mate?'

'Oh, I expected the kid who served me the other night,' Peter said to the hot dog. 'He had a cold and I thought that he was working tonight . . .'

'His cold did get worse. That's why I'm here.'

'Oh.'

'Can I help you?'

'Yeah, yes. Sorry, just used to having teenagers speak through these things.'

'Yeah, well, sometimes you can't find one when you want one. That's what happens when you own a business.'

'Right.' And then Peter remembered who it was who owned this particular World of Hot Dogs restaurant.

Perhaps he was feeling a little light-headed, because he pointed to the King of Hot Dogs and almost shouted, 'You're Bevan Krunt!'

Bevan Krunt, the old football hero who was the franchise holder, the man Edwyn Hume had called 'Tough as nails and as hard as rock.'

'Bevan Krunt!' Peter repeated, yelling.

'Yeah,' said Bevan Krunt, King of Hot Dogs. 'How can I help you?' He sounded for all the world like a peed-off small businessman who had been forced to get out on a winter's night to sit in his takeaway restaurant and deal with the likes of Peter Kennedy.

'Oh, Bevan, Bevan Krunt. I've had a bit of a night.'

'Yeah?'

'Yeah, I have.'

'You going to order anything to eat?'

'Yeah. Yeah.' He had stopped breathing so hard. 'Yes, um . . .' He studied the menu board. There was the Neptune Dog – a hot dog and fish; good mixture. There was a special State of Origin offer, the Lockyer Dog. And even, remarkably, a vegan dog and a vegie dog. So many hot dogs.

'I'll have, um . . . Can I ask you a question?'

There was no answer from the hot dog.

'I was looking at what's in some luncheon meat this evening. And you know, luncheon would have to be a pretty close cousin of the hot dog, I reckon . . .'

A noise like someone clearing his throat came out of the King of Hot Dogs.

Peter ploughed on. 'And on the wrapper, mate, there's a lot of numbers and words like "emulsifiers" and "starch" and . . . stuff.'

The hot dog said nothing.

'A lot of numbers.' Peter could see himself reflected in the eyes of the King of Hot Dogs.

'Well, numbers can mean anything,' said King Bevan, finally.

'Numbers . . .' said Peter.

'If you want something, mate, then ask for it. If you don't, you'd best be getting home.'

'Do you eat hot dogs, Bevan? *Your* hot dogs?' asked Peter Kennedy.

There was a pause.

'No.'

'Why not?'

'Because they're filled with shit, mate.'

Peter stared at the smiling sausage.

'They won't kill you, but they're filled with shit. Like lots of things today. Do you want one or not?'

Peter laughed. 'Good sales pitch . . .' He went silent. 'I'll have . . .' And from his past he remembered something. 'Can I ask another question? Not about hot dogs . . .'

A car drove past with its radio blaring.

'About footy? You were a great footy player. Really.'

'Oh, Jesus,' whispered the King of Hot Dogs under his breath.

'No, listen – the best game: do you remember a game in, in about, about – it was 1974. I was ten. At Corbett Park against Brothers and it was pelting down with rain. It was the third of July – my birthday. The next day we were going to have a party in the park, but on my actual birthday I wanted to go to the footy to see you play. It was pissing down and it was so awful we were getting absolutely towelled. It was like thirty-two–nil. Do you remember?'

'Maybe,' said the King of Hot Dogs.

'And the game was almost over. Everyone had given up. My dad went back to the car. But I stayed – you were the one only still trying. And I was in that funny little scaffolding stand there all by myself and Brothers were going to score.'

'Were they?'

'You, you chased them right along the backs and . . . it was Wayne Bennett; he was going to score and you still bloody chased him!'

'Did I?'

'Yes. Yes, you did. And you sort of seemed like you were going to give up and I yelled out. I yelled.'

Peter was going to repeat what he screamed as a little boy on his tenth birthday in the pouring rain. He took a breath.

He was going to but instead a deep rumbling voice from that fibreglass King of Hot Dogs said it for him. '"Come on, Bevan! You can do it." That's what you said.'

Peter stood with two hands on the Hot Dog King's shoulders.

'Yeah,' Peter Kennedy said. 'That's what I yelled out. And you seemed to run faster and you dived for him and . . .'

'And I got him. Got the lanky bugger just out from the line.'

'I was so proud of you. It was a bloody great tackle.'

There was a pause. And then the hot dog spoke again. 'I had given up. I thought, Bugger it, let him go. Then I heard this squeaky little shriek and, I dunno, I decided that if a kid can care that much then I might as well have a go. It's a funny thing, what you remember.'

'You remember that?'

'Yeah. I can tell you – what's your name?'

'Peter.'

'Well, I can tell you, Peter, that I've been down a few dud alleys in my life but I'll never forget the sound of that silly bloody kid screaming in the rain, "Come on, Bevan, you can do it!"'

The hot dog took a breath. 'So Peter, thanks for that.'

Peter didn't say anything for a while. He took his hands off the King of Hot Dogs' arms and stood up straight.

'I've had a funny old night.'

'Yeah?'

'Yeah.'

'Then you don't need to eat this crap. Go home. Go home and go to sleep. Things might sort themselves out in the morning; give it a bit of time.'

'You reckon?'

'Mate, I'm the King of the Hot Dogs; would I lie to you?'

He nodded and gave a thumbs up to the fibreglass hot dog and walked back along the beach to his parents' home.

The jetty was bare. The green channel marker was still flashing. He walked up the crown of the hill and down the side of the house. Then he stopped near the stairs, bent down to scrape off a piece of the *Monstera deliciosa* fruit and held it in his hands.

'I know they were just pretending,' he said softly to himself.

But he walked up the stairs carrying the fruit, went into his old room and lay in the dark staring at the floor-like ceiling.

Just before he fell asleep, he managed to hold up the fruit pellets and drop them in his mouth. Before they hit his tongue he said, 'Luncheon meat!'

And he went to sleep.

•

When he opened his eyes Peter knew he wasn't supposed to be awake. It didn't feel right, so he closed them again and then felt a gentle slap on his face. He opened his eyes and saw his father.

'Come on, hurry up, son, we haven't got much time.'

Peter sank back into his bed. 'What's the time?'

His father pulled at his shoulder. 'Come on, you great lummox. Get up! There's a coffee for you on the table. Get your keys.'

'What do you want?'

'It's what *you* want, son. You want to know what those numbers are? You come with me.'

•

'Jesus, where did you learn to drive?'

It was early in the morning – the sun hadn't even risen – and it was completely obvious to Peter that wrangling Red Getz wasn't going to be easy.

'Sorry, Dad. Bit dusty and I'm not used to a manual.'

He stalled it again.

'Yes, there's a hint of that in the way you're going about things. Helps if you take the handbrake off.'

Peter turned to his father. 'What are we doing?'

Ken Kennedy took a deep breath and he held up a manila envelope. 'These are the building plans.'

'Yes? And . . .'

'You know how I was in the army?'

'Yes.'

'Served in a place called Korea.'

'Yeah, Dad, I know. You got a medal.'

'Yes. I got a medal. Son, I don't want to be a nuisance, but I suppose it's like the beer. You know, I never really told you much about it.'

Peter looked at his father.

'Well, I got a medal – a pretty reasonable one as medals go, I suppose. The bit of paper it came with said it was for conspicuous and sustained courage at the battle of Papoyong. Basically I got it for shitting meself and pulling a trigger. But there you go. It was a balls-up, really. Nobody saw it coming. The Chinese army hopped right in and we got caught up in it. There was a lot of rot about waves and waves of them charging, but there was a bloody lot of them, heaps more than us. But, uh, we had the high ground.' He glanced down at his watch.

'Yep,' said Peter.

'Anyway, a lot of people died. And I . . .' He stopped and rolled his tongue around his mouth and then gave a soft little click. 'I killed a lot of men.'

He cleared his throat and kept talking as if he were going on about brewing. 'And, as you do, you come home and you try to find your way about. It takes a bit of time. Time to land yourself . . .'

He smiled at his son and gently touched his hand. 'You'd better move the car, Peter – ease out the clutch and turn her down there at the shops.

'Your mother was very good to me, Peter. Go into second, son.'

'Dad, just let me drive.'

'All right then. Yes, your mother was very good to me, waiting a while before I . . . Well, before I landed. She could have looked elsewhere – you know, moved on – but she didn't. I told her I wouldn't have minded, but she didn't, and that was the making of me.'

He laughed and then he smiled. 'Now, we haven't got much time, and blokes have been through worse than me so we won't go down there; we don't want too much sugar in the brew because then that's no good for anything.'

It was when the twins were born, Ken explained to Peter, that he had decided to do it.

'We'd tried a while to have kids and, well, you know, we couldn't have been happier when we knew it was twins.

'And anyway it was the morning you were both born. I was having me brekky and your mother . . . She was off doing what

241

she did at the hospital; different world back then, I suppose. But at breakfast I was flipping through the *Courier-Mail* and I saw this ad. Some bloody thing about memories. Third of July 1964. Funny thing. But I worked out, well, people do forget things. They do. They live and die and people forget. So that's when I started it. Did it without really thinking.'

'Started what?'

Ken gently patted the folder. Then he opened it. 'I was working here, building this little shop. 1964. It was a butcher's.'

As they drove past he pointed to a freestanding shop in between a cafe and a chemist. It was a scrapbook shop now, a place where people could come and make cards and stationery.

'He was a butcher too. It made sense. I had just become a father and I remembered him. What a top little bloke. Norman Barsby. He always said that you'd be hard pressed to find an unhappy butcher. And it's true. You'll always be able to have a chat and a laugh in a butcher's. He came from Victoria. Died in the first hour of the attack. I remember him calling out to me as it started, "See you on the other side." Service number 337685 Barsby, N. Private.'

He turned to his son. 'Do you see, Peter? Why leave them just to be names on a stone wall in some place? Why leave them to be a photo in an album somewhere? I didn't want to forget them and so when I found a place that sort of suited them I'd mark these official records, like you said. Then I'd put their numbers on a load-bearing wall or major support so if the place was renovated or changed then the numbers would be left there, a little bit of these blokes.'

Peter read the serial number below the plan in his father's lap. His big hands, gnarled and broken, resting there lightly.

'Norman, ta ta, old son,' said Ken Kennedy. And then he held up the next plan.

'Now, go down past that servo by the croquet club, will you, Peter. Come on, mate, we haven't that much time.'

When they stopped outside a house with a wraparound verandah overlooking a little inlet, Ken explained that this was the house he'd marked for the big West Australian. He was a quiet man but once he had said to Ken when they were on picket duty how he missed the sea and if you closed your eyes, the wind that rustled through the branches and leaves of the funny little trees near where they were camped sounded like the waves softly rolling in.

'Do you see the big cotton trees above the house, son? As soon as I heard the wind blow through them one arvo I knew this place would be old Bisho's. SN 339743 Bishop, T. Cpl.'

Through the streets of Pickersgill father and son drove for nearly forty minutes. They stopped at the little weatherboard house that was the red-headed bloke's from Sydney. His because it overlooked the trotting track and because he had been a strapper at Harold Park.

The big Victorian's house by the tennis courts, because he had loved the game so much. Even the nasty man from Warwick, who was a bully and a bad bit of work. He was a sergeant and as Ken Kennedy said, 'Gave everybody the bloody shits. I was tempted to give him the bloody sewerage substation pump, but all of a sudden, when I was buying your mother some flowers once, I remembered how this fellow liked picking petals off flowers occasionally and saying "She loves me, she loves me not."'

Ken laughed a little. 'You can never tell what blokes will let you see when they don't think anybody's watching.'

The nasty man from Warwick got the pretty cottage by the Rotary gardens.

'Nobody can be all bad, you know, Peter.' Ken was quiet, then said, 'I wonder who he picked those petals for?'

They drove on past the houses of a man who loved to whistle 'Ave Maria' while he shaved in the morning, the Melburnian who was going to enter politics when he got home, the big strong lad from Bondi who was a lifeguard. On and on.

Peter stalled and crunched the gears of Red Getz, barely understanding what he was being given.

'Now come on, son. Quick, up to the showgrounds.'

The gates were open because the sideshow alley carnies had set up their rides and stalls and would come and go now over the three days of the show.

In past the caravans they kangaroo-hopped Red Getz.

'By Holy Mary, you are a shit-house driver, Peter Kennedy!' said his father, laughing.

The showgrounds were the site of the last buildings Ken had worked on for the men who had died in the battle.

There were three farmers, who of course had been honoured by the Horticultural Pavilion. 'They'd always bitch about where the best land was, how rich the yields were, and then they'd swing back the other way and say how tough you had to be to work the land they had,' Ken explained. 'Funny buggers.'

The Administration Block was for the handsome lieutenant from Adelaide who had postponed his wedding. 'He had the best manners, Peter, a real gent. A kind, lovely boy. SN 337549 Clarke, Adrian. Lt.'

The Schools Hall had been divided between the two teachers, one Catholic, one Protestant. The pair had shaken hands the night before the attack and wished each other luck.

And that was it; the thirty-eight names from the two companies.

'Come on, quick, up to the other end of the grounds, Peter.'

On foot now, they made their way past the eventing oval and the wood-chop area to the farthermost point of the Peninsula, to the Produce Pavilion.

Ken Kennedy smiled at his eldest son. 'Now, when you found this plan, when you saw where it was – so far away from the other buildings, how it's got the funny raised dog-leg to it – I bet you thought it was the worst piece of building you've ever seen?'

Peter didn't know what he had thought; he was just here now, listening to a man who, he realised, in some ways he barely knew. A man whose life was such a mystery to him. So he simply stared at his father and his father nodded.

'Oh, I know that look. But you see, I realised that old Pickers would change one day, so I thought to myself, if I build one place where they could all belong, then that'd be a bit of all right.' He looked at the odd-shaped Besser-brick building in front of them.

'This is it; all of them are in this one. It's the Produce Hall. Happiest place on the showgrounds, where the littlies come to buy the show bags, where all the rubbish is flogged and where the home brew is judged; the perfect place. The entire support beam's marked with their names. And I think they'd like the noise, you know.'

The two men stared at the building for a long moment.

'Why thirty-eight, Dad? Who was the thirty-eighth?'

Ken waited a while to answer. 'You been to China, Peter?'

'Yep, many times.'

'What are they like, the Chinese?'

Peter didn't understand what his father meant.

'What are they like?'

'Well, they get things done . . .'

Ken Kennedy nodded. 'I knew a Chinese bloke once.' And he walked down to the end of the Produce Hall with his son following.

The two men stood looking past the mangroves that grew at the bottom of the rise, to the bridge that led from the Peninsula, stretching off towards Brisbane.

'The second night of the attack was the worst. There was so much noise, so much fire. The bullets going past when they were fired so close . . . They break the sound barrier, you know. They don't whizz or ping, they crack like whips. Standing there, it was like you were standing against a gale. That was the night they came. Kept on coming. We had the high ground. And they came. By Christ, they were brave bastards. We all fought for something but, Jesus, Peter, you've never seen anything like it. They even tried bayonet charges.

'And that's when he got it. Just a young bloke, I suppose, it was hard to tell. I gave it to him as he came over the lip of our trench; was sure he was dead.' The old man stopped for a moment, then said, 'Won't be much longer.'

He turned to his son and stared at him with his head on one side, as if he was looking again at some problem he couldn't quite solve. The look he would give Mr Wisdom's Whopper, the crossword from the *Post*, sitting there on the verandah with Mary, the woman who was the making of him.

And then the old man spoke again. 'He wasn't dead, Peter. He was dying. I worked that out after a bit, about twenty minutes after the last attack. They didn't come back, but we could hear them. And this fellow just lay there. It's a thing to see a man die, know you killed him. He was frightened for a while. And then he went all quiet. Then he held out his hand to me. About this time of day, it was. On sunrise. Didn't know what he was up to. He opened his eyes. He was frightened. No, he wasn't that much older than me, son, and he held out his hand. Then he said, "*Wo zuihou de ri chou*", over and over again.

'Just looked at him, Peter, I did. Didn't know what he was up to. But his eyes . . . There was something . . . Crawled over to him, had the bayonet out in case. And he . . .'

The old man stopped. Then he stood tall and made a funny sound in his throat.

He's going to cry, thought Peter.

'And this bastard, he smiled at me and shook his head. "*Wo zuihou de ri chou.*"'

The sun began to break open the sky and the water birds down in the mangroves started to call.

'Peter, look – this is why this building is here. This is the first place on Pickers that you see the sun rise; it's the high ground.'

His father turned to him. 'You see, son, I grabbed that bloke's hand and he nodded his head, like he wanted me to pull him up. So I decided, bugger it, I will. And me and him stood, son, his hand in mine, him staring at the sunrise.'

Father and son stood now, staring at the morning sky.

'He died not long after. Later on, one of the intelligence officers told me what he was saying. "My last sunrise."

'"My last sunrise." There are times, Peter, when I'm sitting doing not much, when I can feel his hand in mine.'

The old man turned back to his son and a beautiful smile spread across his face. 'It's not a bad thing at all, my boy. I'm so happy you came up here. So happy it was you that saw the numbers. You're a funny one to work out but by Christ, I love you.'

Ken Kennedy held out his hand and his son Peter walked over slowly and took it, and the two stood there together and watched the day dawn.

Chapter Fifteen

Ken and Peter had driven back to the Kennedys' home on the crown of the hill and hadn't really said much, except when Peter had stalled Red on the final stretch.

'Peter, use the bloody clutch! The clutch – it's the one on the left.'

It felt a little like when his father had taken him out for his first driving lesson. They'd come back that day and Ken had declared to Mary, 'I can't bloody teach him a thing.' Then, 'I'll pay for your lessons, son. Christ, you're nothing like your sister.'

Peter hadn't really minded. But now he thought he would like to have spent that time with his father.

They walked up the stairs together and as they reached

the door, Peter stopped his father. 'Dad, are you. Are you all right? I mean, you're not, are you?'

His father tilted his head to one side.

'I mean . . .' Peter Kennedy stopped. He stopped because he felt an awful feeling of emotion bubbling inside.

'Peter, I'm just getting old; we've all got a use-by date. Mine hasn't been stamped, son, but well, I'm getting old, that's all.' He slowly shook his head. 'For such a genuinely clever man, you can be remarkably dense at times, son. You've got to notice things a bit more. Now, go have a lie-down – I want a cuppa with your mum.'

He walked off into the kitchen and Peter could hear them both begin their banter.

'Well, you were up at the baker's hours!'

'Just popped up to watch the sunrise with your eldest, love.'

'How did you get him out bed?'

'I can tell you, he's going back there now, he was out late last night. And he's the worst bloody driver, I can tell you that.'

'We always knew that. Now come here, old man, and sit with me.'

And he heard them kiss.

My old man.

Peter walked towards his room, but not before stopping in front of the wall of photos.

He had to notice things a bit more. That's what his father had said.

He stood and looked past the little Darren Lockyer doll with his arms raised in victory to the photos and he saw something that he hadn't noticed before. It was true that his sister Pearl took a shocking photo, but what he hadn't seen before was that she was almost always either beginning a smile or a laugh in the photos. She never really bothered to pose and when she did, she was the same as most people – awkward. But as Peter scanned the half-closed eyes and mouth-open shots, he remembered what had happened just before or after each one had been taken. He heard her laughter; heard the laughter of the people she had been with, the voices of his parents and his brother. He heard the laughter of his children, his wife. But standing there now, he couldn't hear his own.

He saw himself in the photos on the wall and maybe, he thought, that was the way other people saw him. There, but not really. Always thinking about something else, something beyond the photo.

He went to his bed and lay down. He thought of the laughter, of the men his father had told him about and the buildings at the showgrounds. And, just before he dropped off to sleep, he thought, there is no reason why development couldn't take place there, on the high ground of the Peninsula.

•

When he woke a few hours later, it was with a feeling of relief; now he could get on with the day.

He stared up at the floor-ceiling and thought of his father's buildings. No, don't do that, Peter, he told himself, just get on with the day.

Looking down at his watch, he realised it was well after noon, closer to one; he'd slept like a log.

'Shit!' he said, before hurrying to get ready.

•

Finally emerging, Peter realised the house was empty except for the two dogs. He went into the kitchen and felt the stove top, still vaguely warm. His mother must have cooked something that morning for the show.

He went to the fridge and there, on the big note pad stuck to the door was a message, *On the table, Peter!* in bright green Texta. Turning to the table he saw a piece of notepaper on top of a large envelope with *Check your phone – message from Kate!* written in bright red Texta.

He picked up the note and said to himself, 'Oh yeah.'

Downstairs the dogs barked and then he saw on the envelope itself, in bright purple Texta, *For you, Peter. If you've got the time to look. Dad.*

Green, red and purple exclamation marks everywhere.

He picked up the envelope, put it in his work bag and checked his phone.

There was a text message from Kate; never good, they were the electronic version of her thinking hard and were invariably written in capital letters. If she had *really* been thinking hard about him then they would usually read like an old telegram, all staccato phrases.

He took a deep breath and opened the message. It was old-telegram time; everything in upper case: PETER – SPOKE

TO YOUR MUM. STAY FOR PEARL'S NIGHT, BUT
SEND SOMETHING FOR FATHER–DAUGHTER
NIGHT. SEND IT! SEND IT!!

Great. Thanks, Mum.

He rang up Kate, got her voicemail, waited till he heard
the beep and hung up without leaving a message.

What, he thought, was the point of that?

He picked up his bag and headed for the door, then
reconsidered and went back to the wall of photos.

He looked at the ones of Pearl again. He wasn't quite sure
why, but he could still hear the laughter.

'Yep,' he said to himself. 'Yep.'

The dogs barked some more at him as he squeezed into his
car to head for the library. He assumed his mother and father
had gone off to the showgrounds to prepare the exhibits and
help set up the area of the Produce Hall where Pearl's Big
Valley Bingo Night was to be held.

'Christ almighty,' he said as he thought about it.

•

He shook his head as he walked towards the library. This was
where the historical and regional archives were housed and
where any gazettes or documents of historical significance
relating to the showgrounds would be found.

Not wanting to think about what his father had shown
him, Peter focused instead on the Big Valley Bingo. Nobody
had any idea why the night had first been given that name,
but it had been accepted by all.

Whatever anyone said about Pickersgill, it was safe to say that a bingo night to raise money for, among other things, a foster-parent charity was a unique form of communal fundraising. An event that Pearl had been organising for years.

Somehow the bingo night had evolved into an event where people decked themselves out in fancy dress and played the odd game of Housie and occasionally mimed pop songs to each other.

They dined on an array of culinary delights including cubed Coon cheese and green stuffed olives skewered by a toothpick or cubed Coon cheese and kabana skewered by a toothpick or, for even more variety, cubed Coon cheese alone skewered by a toothpick. Other staples of the menu were party pies and sausage rolls, as well as a selection of cask wines.

Every year there was a different theme but Peter Kennedy had only ever been to one; that was the World War Two Big Valley Bingo. It was not long after he and Kate were married.

He remembered it had been excruciating because it had been so haphazard. Some people had gone to a lot of effort while others not at all and just sat there, nibbling on the Coon-and-kabana, staring at the bingo sheets. Pearl, of course, always went to trouble. That night she had gone as a Dam Buster, wearing a funny leather aviator's hat and two long wings extending from her shoulders with two little propellers on each one and a large beach ball, painted black, stuck to her stomach.

It was the night when a large woman called Elma Durkin, who Peter remembered had been an incredibly officious and snooty tuck-shop lady at Pickersgill Primary, had dressed up in a suit and bald cap, and proceeded to smoke a huge cigar and mime while the speeches of Winston Churchill played over the sound system. She sat opening and closing her mouth like a freshly landed cod, all the while smoking her cigar as the great Churchillian phrases rang around the audience in the Produce Hall.

At first it was vaguely interesting, like a student's show-and-tell history project, and then even fascinating as Peter wondered what it might have been like to actually have Winston Churchill behind the tuck-shop counter serving salad rolls with luncheon meat and processed cheese, and custard tarts. But after a while there was no discernible synching between Mrs Durkin's cod fishing and the great man's oration.

Unfortunately, this lack of synching became even more noticeable after Winston Durkin, having inhaled more than she had puffed, became quite giddy and light-headed, and decided to move about on stage to liven up the speech. Agitated and nauseous from another lungful of smoke and in an attempt to relocate to her suitably period plastic outdoor furniture, she staggered about, all the while gamely opening and closing her mouth as Churchill spoke of his finest hours, before crashing spectacularly into a front-row table full of Joseph Stalin, some American GIs and somebody who was supposed to be Vera Lynn.

'This was their finest hour,' boomed Winston Churchill.

Peter shook his head at the memory and headed into the Archives and Regional History section of Pickersgill Library.

Two hours' digging produced five vice-regal gazettes and proclamations, one dating back to 1885, all confirming that the high ground of Pickersgill Peninsula belonged to the Crown and its people.

After another hour and a half, Peter had checked the Indigenous Heritage Gradings of the land and three archived reports that attached no cultural significance whatsoever to the showgrounds area. It was definitive: the place was free to be developed.

He sat there for a moment then reached into his bag and found the envelope his father had left him. Inside was a hastily written note suggesting he might like to check out an item that was in a compartment box in the history storage section of the library. There was another note, authorising Peter to view the historical item.

Sitting there, he read the note over again. Then he studied the writing; it was very neat, very definite. Even though his father's hands were old, they were still firm and strong.

Peter looked at his own hands. Big hands, his wedding ring locked beneath a big knuckle. Hands that had been pushed and broken by footy and cricket, but not hard hands, not hands that had seen a lot of manual work.

Not like his father's hands.

Peter went to the service desk and requested the item and then, without really thinking, asked if a copy of the *Pickersgill Courier* from the third of July 1964 was available.

The librarian returned not long after with a small archive box and pointed Peter towards the microfiche machines at the farthest corner of the library; the genealogical section.

'That's where you'll find all the old *Courier*s, in the microfiche records. And you can't leave the library with the box.'

He signed for the archive box and gathered his belongings, and as he walked along he realised how many people still used this library. He was surprised.

There seemed to be a cross-section of old and new Pickers here. A bloke who looked as rough as guts sifted through the cookery section, old women, young families and old men and a few people who spoke to themselves and had obviously come in to get out of the cooler weather.

And there were schoolkids, everywhere. Most were from Pickersgill High, his old school. There was a diversity to the kids that hadn't really existed when Peter had worn the uniform.

Maybe, he wondered, maybe things *are* changing.

He thought of Wayne Dixon, standing out on the jetty by himself, facing the bay, the green channel markers flashing. And then he remembered the words of Bevan Krunt: 'I had given up and then . . . if a kid can care that much . . .' and his father: 'You just don't see what's in front of you sometimes.'

He had slowed his pace as these things ran through his mind, until he stood stock still above the desks of the genealogical section.

'Hello,' said a girl's voice.

Peter glanced about and saw a girl in a Pickersgill High uniform sitting at a terminal.

He nodded. He knew her. It was Elenore, the girl who was staying with Pearl. Elanor. 'Oh shit,' he said and the girl blanched.

Peter looked at his watch. He swore again and threw his gear onto the desk. 'I'm sorry, Elenore, I just remembered I had to get something off to somebody.'

Somebody. His daughter Ellie. *His* Eleanor.

He took a deep breath and grabbed his laptop out of his bag. He could whip something up and send it off to the school now for the father–daughter night.

He looked across at the girl and smiled. 'Sorry about that; I just remembered, it's my daughter – Ellie, her name is Eleanor too but we call her Ellie – anyway, I'll . . .'

He stopped talking and concentrated on finding the school's email address. There was a dot-point list, a phone number, an email address and a Skype account number in case you wanted to speak face to face. No thanks, he thought.

'Nobody calls me Ellie.'

Peter grunted back.

'Pearl did once – but then she said that was because she has this niece, Eleanor, and she's always called Ellie. So she asked me if I minded being called Ellie. Pearl's the only one, but.'

Peter nodded and found the page he was looking for. 'Yep,' he said and started writing. Anything would do, really; he knew the format was almost the same every year, and being there in person really wouldn't make much difference. Fathers at these nights always said the same things: how proud they were of their daughter, how they had felt at her birth, how much she was loved and how they wanted her to be happy, and how whatever she ended up choosing to do with her life they'd always be proud of her.

Yeah, he could do this. Just don't mention anything too embarrassing.

He saw the girl looking at him across the desk. 'You doing some homework?' he asked.

The girl said nothing.

Say something nice about Kate, about 'your mother', he decided.

'Sort of,' said the girl.

'Eh?'

'It's a school project about your family. Your family tree thing, but done in a story. We've got half an hour each to use this thing.' She pointed to the genealogical database terminal.

Peter Kennedy nodded. He was up to almost half a page; that should do. Always run the spell check before sending, otherwise that could lead to a bit of explaining. We don't want the Ellie equivalent of the Little Twin's Hummer between the legs, he thought.

'Yep?' he said. 'That sounds like fun.'

The girl said nothing and he looked up. 'What's wrong?' He quickly scanned through what he had written. *Really believe in you . . . confident that you will be able to make the right decisions when you're faced with a problem . . . Remember what you've learnt at school and what you've learnt from your family . . .* Yeah, he thought, yeah, that's fine.

He pressed *send*, waited a few moments, and off it went to Our Lady's School.

'Yep,' he said. One thing to mark off the list. 'Not much fun?' He turned back to the girl.

She was sitting quite still, blushing.

'You right?'

He waited for a moment and then went over to the micro-fiche drawers and rummaged through the rolls to find the ones from 1964. This library, he thought, is extraordinarily well-organised.

'It's hard,' said the girl.

'Pardon?'

'Hard to write about your family when you don't . . .' She trailed off.

Peter looked over to her.

She looked back.

She seemed very young, all of a sudden.

'How did Ellie go in swimming?' she asked.

Peter found the rolls from 1964. 'Um, I don't know. Haven't got round to ringing her, but I guess she did okay. They always seem to have a good team.'

He tried to remember the last time he had been to a school swimming carnival.

'She likes swimming?'

'Yep.'

'Why?'

'Uh, well, she's sort of good at it. And her mum really likes swimming.'

'I like swimming, too. Because . . .' She didn't say anything else so he thought that was all she was going to offer, then, 'Because sometimes I can yell in the water and nobody can hear me. And because when I cry nobody can see the tears. Or if they do I say it's the chlorine. I only . . . it's only sometimes.'

Peter stopped rummaging through the microfiche spools but didn't look at the girl.

There was a little pause.

'My mum was good at roller skating.'

'Yeah?'

The girl went quiet.

'What about your dad?'

'My dad. My dad is dead. He wasn't that good to Mum, even though he loved her. She said he was good but that he got mixed up in stuff and that. That the bad stuff he did was the drink and the drugs and the good stuff, well, Mum said that was his heart, that was really him.'

This was panning out to be different from what he had expected, Peter thought, but she was only a kid. He sighed. And she blushed again.

'I'm sorry. I didn't meant to say anything. It's just that I know . . . I thought. Well, 'cause I heard Pearl say that you were the one that was kind.'

Peter Kennedy stared.

'She said you were always the one that was kind. Like the

other night when you stopped and talked about swimming. So I hope you don't mind me saying about my mum.'

'Your mum sounds like she's all right.'

Peter didn't want to waste too much time with the paper, but it was only one issue. He'd just find the ad or whatever it was that had prompted Ken to do whatever he had done with the houses. Then he supposed it was time to write the report to Greer.

'I know a lot about Ellie,' said Elenore.

Peter stopped fitting the microfiche film to the spool of the viewing machine. 'I beg your pardon?'

'This is what I wrote for my family history. It's hard when you don't really have one – I mean a family history. So I . . . I talked to Pearl. I mean, it didn't have to be *my* family history. Just *a* family history. Didn't have to be mine.'

Peter waited for the girl to go on.

'My name is Elenore, but people call me Ellie. I like swimming. A lot. I have two brothers, they're twins. They are both big. But one is slightly taller than the other so he is called the Big Twin and the other is called the Little Twin. They are loud and funny and laugh at my dad a lot.

'My mum is Kate. She is a teacher. She is from Melbourne. She has a smile that lights up the room. And she laughs at Dad, too. My dad is called Peter. He works very hard and likes to eat. He stares a lot and can frighten people because they always think he is watching them. But, if you know him, he is very kind.

'We live in a big house, but that's not important. My aunty Pearl says the best thing is that a house is just where people live. A home is where you live with the people you love. Like my dad. He grew up in the same sort of place with his mum and dad. I like his mum and dad. They are fun; my Nanna Mary and Pop Ken. She was very good at tennis and he brews beer and does crosswords.

'I have an uncle, Gary, who is the younger brother of my dad and Aunty Pearl; he is on the television. He does the weather. He was a real good football player and Pop Ken said he is one of the bravest men he knows. Not only because of the football or because he is gay and isn't afraid to let people know about it, but because he is honest. He has a new boyfriend who he really loves. My dad laughs at Gary because he's going bald.

'Then there is Aunty Pearl, who is the best. She doesn't have any kids but in a way she has heaps. She is married to a man called Orlendo Lane. He sells leaf-blowers. And that's about it for him, but he makes Aunty happy and so that means he is pretty good. This is not all my family but it's more than enough for me.'

There are many things Peter could have done after hearing this. Unfortunately, he did the one thing that people would have expected him to do. He held his face in that particular frozen way and stared straight at Elenore. She was right, he thought, it does frighten people. It frightened her – she was about to cry.

'I'm sorry. I'm sorry. I wasn't going to read it; I would have thrown it away. I would have. I wouldn't have handed it in. But . . . I don't know . . . The teachers say you have to sit here for half an hour and then write down an oral presentation of your family. And I don't have one so . . .' She stopped.

Peter carried on staring and as the girl looked back he did something that took even him by surprise: he smiled.

He actually felt it in himself. Felt himself smiling.

'Don't throw it away, Elenore. Because I would love to have it. I think . . . I think it's something I need to have. And I'm incredibly proud that you would think that . . .' He stopped and felt that funny bubbling feeling again. 'That you would think that I would be good enough to be your father. Sort of. Um, but you know I think your mum sounds very interesting. Where is she?'

'She . . . She's working in the mines. Up north.'

'Yep.'

'She got sick too, with Dad. Drugs. But she got off them. She had to go away to get better; that's why I had to go and live with Pearl.'

'Yep.'

'Then she got a job and she saves almost everything now. Shows me and Pearl what she's putting away. She reckons it'll be enough to get something down round here soon maybe.'

'What does she do in the mines?'

'She drives buses for the miners.'

'I'll give you a tip, Elenore. I reckon crying in the pool is pretty smart. Pretty smart. Means you don't take up other people's time. If you can manage the crying, that is. But I've got to tell you that your mum sounds like . . .' He paused; he wasn't used to talking like this. 'She sounds like she's an exceptional person. Truly. She, uh, goes through all this stuff and is wise enough to be able to see the good in people and works so hard.'

The girl was not sure where he was going. And why would she? He didn't know where he was going, himself.

'And she works so hard for something pretty amazing. Something that means the world to her.'

'What?' asked the girl.

'Well, something that I think is pretty special. You. And as nice as those words you've just read are, I think you and your mum deserve some words of your own.'

And he smiled again.

'You won't tell anybody I wrote this?'

'No, I won't, but I'm not going to throw it away, because I think it's beautiful.'

A teacher walked across and said quietly, 'That's your thirty minutes, Elenore. Time to go.'

Elenore collected her papers, folded her page of written work and slid it over the table to Peter.

He picked it up and put it in his bag.

She was across the room when she turned back, and he gave a nod of his head and saw that she smiled.

Chapter Sixteen

Peter sat back in his chair, thinking of what Elenore had written. He remembered what he had 'whipped up' for *his* Ellie. How he had marked it off the list.

He sat there for a good while, not feeling as happy with himself as he might have been a few days earlier.

This trip up here, he thought, was turning into something he hadn't expected. He needed to think seriously about himself.

He didn't want to do that straight away so he turned his attention to the microfiche machine and scrolled to the third of July 1964, a Wednesday. The papers weren't that big really so whatever it was shouldn't be hard to find. And it wasn't. Below a photo of a woman in an outfit that even today was decidedly un-Pickersgill with the caption '*Miss Australia*

Comes to Town!' ran the headline 'Pickersgill Spastic Society welcomes glamorous guest.'

Peter read on: *'Looking chick'* – that good old Pickers *Courier* spelling creeping in again – *'in a tangerine winter suit with black hat and accessories is Miss Australia for 1964, Miss Jan Taylor, who was welcomed to the Peninsula by Mr Percival Sorenson, Secretary of Pickersgill RSL, and some local Pickersgill Miss Australia contestants.*

'Miss Taylor told seventy guests of her overseas tour and the nationwide work for spastics going on in other Australian states.'

Peter studied the photo again; there was Miss Taylor and a suitably grumpy looking Percy Sorenson and three rather sadly optimistic Pickersgill contestants.

Tales of her overseas trip. It must have seemed a different world to the people of Pickersgill, but maybe not; there were only about seventy people there – maybe everybody else had just been getting on with their lives?

Then below that story, there it was: an advertisement for, of all things, road safety.

'Remember 1924? Remember how it was a lifetime ago?'

And there was a drawing of an old man in a trilby and raincoat with his arms held up high and his mouth open in a cry of shock. He was lit up by an oncoming car, which was driven by a clean-cut and determined-looking young man in a black suit.

'Remember! Drivers cannot always see you. Take care when you cross the road. Cross only at safe places. Be sure you have plenty of time.

'Remember 1924? Your memories are your life and life is so precious. The friendships, the good times, the happiness, the sorrow – your memories are your most cherished possession. Safeguard them; protect them so you can pass them on. Remember road safety.'

Was that it? Was that what had made Ken Kennedy embark on his project?

Peter picked up the archive box and lifted the lid. Inside was a leather journal. He opened it.

On the first page, in his father's writing, were words from the road safety advertisement: 'Your memories are your life and life is so precious. The friendships, the good times, the happiness, the sorrow – your memories are your most cherished possession. Safeguard them; protect them so you can pass them on.'

When he read them in his father's hand, they didn't seem so silly.

He turned the page and saw a photo of the butcher's shop and a photo of a laughing man in uniform. He knew at once who it was: Norman Barsby.

And as he leafed through the pages of the journal he saw more photos of men and their buildings, little notes and memories written about each man.

On one of the last pages was a photo of a sunrise and of a house on the crown of a hill with a family sitting on its steps, everyone smiling. And another note in his father's hand: 'A house is a place where someone lives. A home is where you live with the people you love.'

The final page was the Produce Hall.

Peter Kennedy closed the journal.

He began to write his report for Greer Harvson and Titan Developments. It didn't take as long as he had expected, because the case of the showground's capacity for development was pretty cut and dried. Still, he sat there for a while longer than he should have, mulling it over. It was late-night closing at the library so that gave him more time to sit and stare at the *send* button because he wasn't sure whether he should forward it to Greer Harvson. But in the end he knew he owed it to Titan Developments. He pressed *send* and packed up his things.

He would have preferred to go home to Kate and the kids but there wasn't much point now; tomorrow would have to do. He tortured Red's gears some more and headed for the Produce Hall and Pearl's Big Valley Bingo.

•

It was one of the Beatles who told Peter he was late.

'You've missed two full houses and the first of the jackpots, but at least you're here.'

'Sorry, Mum, just finished work.'

'I'm John,' she said, pointing to her name tag. 'And it's lovely to see you, you haven't missed anything important yet. Come on, you're with us.'

She led him into the hall where the usual hundred or so people were gathered. He wandered past two Elvises who were talking about a new sewage plant that was being proposed and pointing cubed Coon-and-kabana skewers at each other.

He walked towards the table where the other three Beatles were sitting.

Paul waved as he sipped on a beer. 'Hello there, son! Been busy, have you?'

'Yep, and, uh, thanks for that tip about the archive box.'

Paul nodded and then gestured to Ringo and George. 'Do you remember Howard Whittaker? He's Ringo.'

Ringo, looking a bit the worse for wear, turned to Peter and waved a crooked couple of fingers. He had an eye patch and very thick glasses.

'Hello, Peter, lovely to see you again,' gurgled Howard Whittaker. 'This is George, my wife, Rosie.'

'Peter,' said Rosie, nodding as she dipped a party pie in a little plastic bowl of tomato sauce.

Peter stood looking down at the 'fab four'; old people with mop-top wigs, black skivvies, tracksuit pants and comfortable shoes.

His mother was holding his father's hand.

'It's nice,' Peter said, 'to see John and Paul holding hands.'

'Oh, it's just an old blokes' thing,' said Ken.

'I don't think so, Dad.'

'Oh, let it be.'

'Boom boom,' said Mary.

Peter was about to sit down when a beefy slap fell on his back.

'Peter Kennedy, you haven't dressed up!'

Peter turned and for the life of him couldn't recognise who it was. Someone who was very square – like a fridge – was wearing a bright blue gown, a huge beehive hairdo, false eyelashes, pink lipstick and a collection of beauty spots in the shape of the Southern Cross on his cheek.

'You-uh have-uh no idea-uh who I-uh am!' said the apparition. It was the voice.

'Mister Mayor!' exclaimed Peter Kennedy.

'Oh-uh, come on, Eddie! For tonight . . .' and he dropped his voice low, 'you can call me Dusty!'

'Slim or Springfield?' asked Ken Kennedy.

'Very-uh good, Ken, you-uh old mop-top. Cracking night.' And not-so-slim Dusty Springfield staggered off.

'You can tell it's not an election year, can't you?' said Howie.

'Too right,' agreed Mary.

'Gary here?' asked Peter.

'You'll catch him very soon, big fellow.'

Peter turned his head to the voice he already recognised, but still jumped at the sight. 'Jesus! Weren't you coming as Limahl!'

'No, big fellow, had second thoughts and I felt it was a little too esoteric for old Pickers so I've gone for the Alice Cooper look.'

Forked lightning flashed across Peter's mind's eye and he burst out laughing. 'What in Christ's name are you wearing, mate?'

'Well, if you must ask I've dyed the Limahl wig black, picked up a pair of extra-long pantyhose from Coles and popped on an old one-piece of Pearlie's. Hey presto, the Department of Youth – aka Alice Cooper. He does radio now, you know.'

Peter was still giggling.

'What are you, big fellow? Boz Scaggs?'

The fact that Orlendo was genuine made Peter laugh again. 'No, Orlendo, this is just me.'

'Oh, sorry, I was trying to make sense of the chinos. Never mind, I've got to pop up and do the intro for Gary.'

Peter nodded to Orlendo and then looked to see two women waving to him from the next table. He held up his hand rather uncertainly and suddenly realised who he was saying hello to. The turban gave it away; it was Joanna Whiles, the Coffee Snob he had met that morning, and Mrs Skyes, Lisa's mother. They hadn't really come as anybody. They were just there.

Mrs Sykes rose from her chair and came over. Peter could hardly hear what she was saying.

'Hello Peter.'

'Hello, Mrs Sykes.' He didn't even know if that's what she called herself any more.

'Well, not for a long while – just good old Maureen Prescott now. Lisa said she'd bumped into you.'

'Prescott.'

She nodded.

He nodded.

'Yes.'

'And you met my friend, my partner for tonight – Joanna . . .'

Peter Kennedy looked over at the turbaned woman smiling at him.

'Yes, I did. She loves her coffee.'

Mrs Sykes smiled. 'Yes she does.'

'How's Lance?'

'Oh, you know he's still working at the airport and still playing the organ.' And amazingly she gave a sly wink to Peter before turning to his mother.

'Hello, Muz.'

'Hello there to you too, Maureen,' said Mary Kennedy.

'Lovely for you to have all the kids back.'

His mother nodded. 'It is.'

'Especially this one . . .' And Mrs Sykes put her hand gently down on top of Peter's head. 'This one.'

He looked up and he saw Mrs Sykes do something with her face that made him feel slightly odd, as if he was embarrassed by praise he didn't feel was warranted.

'Well, have a good night.'

He watched as Mrs Sykes walked back to her table.

'Mum?' he said.

'Yes, dear?'

'Why did you call her the Dutch woman? Prescott isn't a Dutch name.'

'I know that, you dill!'

Peter Kennedy looked at his mother.

She shook her Beatles wig. 'She just had big teeth. That's why I called her the Dutch woman.'

Ken Kennedy shook his head slowly and mouthed something to Peter that looked like 'Just let it go.'

Peter nodded. Then he burst out laughing. His mother just looked at him, shook her head again and smiled at someone over his shoulder. Howie Whittaker's face lit up too.

'Hello, Pearlie,' said Howie, as Gene Simmons from Kiss sat down next to her brother and gave him a massive Cassandra Denim.

'Now tell me, what did you say to Elenore at the library?'

Peter stared back at his sister.

She let out a peal of laughter and punched her brother on the arm. 'She came home and got me to ring up her mum and lucky for me she was on a break. Anyway, Elenore was asking her all these questions, and then ran off and wrote like crazy. Her mum . . . well, both of them, were so happy. What did you say?'

Peter shrugged.

'She told me you talked to her.'

He shrugged again.

'Oh, you're a funny one, Peter.'

Orlendo's voice boomed out around the hall. 'I'd like to introduce two charming people who have recently fallen in love and are pretty happy about it. And if they both look familiar to you, it's because they are. One you'll probably recognise from the telly and the other because he's probably booked you for speeding! Whamo!'

Peter Kennedy saw that his father had placed his arm around his wife's shoulder and pulled her close to him. Mary held her husband's hand very tightly.

There was the sound of someone hitting a button, the beginning of the national anthem, some laughter from behind the screen and Orlendo swearing under his breath and then Ray Warren-ing, 'Sorry, a slight gremlin here. Whamo!'

He'd meant Wham! And the couple burst out onto the stage holding hands and doing an incredibly energetic but slightly chaotic reenactment of an old music video of a song called 'Wake Me Up Before You Go-Go'.

Gary Kennedy and Wayne Dixon. Leaping about, laughing themselves silly.

They got a few onlookers singing along and giving the odd clap and at the end a pretty good cheer that rose to a fair old roar when Gary gave Wayne a gentle kiss on the lips. They made their way over to the Kennedys' table.

Peter sat there while his family looked at him.

He realised that Wayne Dixon had tried to tell him about this last night, and in fact that's why they had all been waiting there in his parents' living room when he had come back from the Council Chambers. They had all been there, even Orlendo, probably to give Wayne some support.

Peter sat quite still and looked at his family: his parents, his sister and her great stalking Alice Cooper, then his brother Gary and his old friend Wayne Dixon.

He saw it in Wayne's eyes. That uncertainty.

Peter breathed out a long sigh and Gary's face tightened. Pearl, he supposed, was Cassandra Denim-ing.

'What I would like to know is which one of you is George Michael and which one is the other guy? Andrew Ridgeley,' he said, finally breaking the silence.

'We take turns,' said Gary, laughing.

Peter stood up and grabbed his brother in a hug. 'You're a very lucky man, little brother.'

He heard his mother make a soft sound and his father whisper, 'I knew he'd be right about it all.'

His brother held his hand out to Wayne Dixon. 'Do you know . . . ?'

'Your boyfriend? Your partner?' finished Peter for Gary, staring at Wayne. 'Yes I do and I can tell you he's as lucky a man as you.' And Peter Kennedy smiled.

'Now that's the smile, Peter,' said Wayne Dixon.

Twice in one day, Peter thought. This was all very odd. But very Pickersgill.

Peter sat back down and this time it was Gary Kennedy, back on stage, speaking into the microphone.

'Ladies and gents, tonight is the twentieth Big Valley Bingo charity night and because of that we've got a little something special. Made possible by the technical gifts of the Leaf Blower King of the Northern Suburbs, Mr Orlendo Lane.

'Now Peral, as my elder brother was wont to call you, there's a couple of people who'd like to say a few things.'

Peter watched as Gary and Orlendo walked to various tables with hand-held mikes. Gary moved very smoothly while Orlendo stalked about and Peter noticed that he was wearing rather unusual footwear for a glam-rock god from the seventies.

'Pearl,' he asked his sister. 'Why is he wearing slippers?'

'Bunions. Even rocks stars get them.'

He smiled and then recognised the young woman who was now standing beside Gary.

'Pearl. I want to thank you tonight,' she said. 'Because I don't know if you remember, but I'm Mandy Higgs, who you fostered nearly six years ago. Now I'm Mandy Park and with a beautiful daughter of my own, Charade, and I want to thank you so much for the care you gave me when I needed it. Thank you.'

It was the mother of the little girl from the supermarket.

Then a big man spoke awkwardly and Peter remembered him as the kid with the crew-cut from the photo wall. 'Pearl, Dion Smyth. You gave a kid a lot of love when he needed a place and also a lot of care and good tucker and thank you so much. This is what I grew into. And Mr Kennedy, I'm sorry about them windows I broke, but any time you need a glazier, just give me a bell and I'll give you a window, gratis!'

One by one they stood, adults who had stayed with Pearl Kennedy. Some speaking easily and clearly, others barely audible, but all saying thank you to her. Even Dusty Springfield said a few words.

'Pearl-uh, we-uh here-uh in Pickers think that-uh nobody has a name that better sums up-uh how we-uh think of you-uh. You are and always will be our Pearl.'

Then Gary took over again. 'Now, Pearlie, not everybody who you lent a hand to was able to be here tonight, but thanks to Orlendo we've got somebody to say hello to you.'

The screen on the little stage flickered and on it appeared a smiling, energetic woman with messy dark hair, who bit her lower lip as she waved to Pearl. It was the girl who drew on everything.

'Hi, Pearl, Elizabeth Pearson here. Stayed with you for nearly a year in 1992. I'm over here working on a project in China but when I heard what was happening tonight I wanted to Skype a hello and thank you. Besides being someone who gave a lot of love to a kid you hardly knew, I also wanted to say thank you for those talks you gave me about going for what you dream about. I don't think I'd have been working as an architect if it weren't for you. Those stories of your brother, of how proud you were of him – that day you showed me some of his drawings and said that I could do stuff like that, too. Well, here I am. Just wanted to say thank you to you and, I guess, your brother. Have a great night.'

Peter Kennedy sat very still, feeling very uncomfortable. There was a huge round of applause.

He joined in, clapping his sister like everyone else.

He heard his father's voice in his ear: 'You right, son?'

He didn't know what he felt. Then on his shoulder he felt a hand and he looked over at a teary Gene Simmons, whose make-up was running, and heard his twin sister say, 'I like Swipe, Peter, but I love you.'

He nodded, then glanced up and saw the support beams in the roof of the hall. *Your memories are your life.*

He stood as the applause finished and walked quickly to where Orlendo had disappeared into the office.

Chapter Seventeen

Kate Kennedy had sat with Ellie for about forty minutes in the vestibule at Our Lady's School waiting for her father–daughter session to begin. There was always a delay but this time it seemed to stretch on for longer than imaginable.

Kate thought it was very sweet when the Twins had said they'd come along to support Ellie, but when the Head of Faith had come and informed her that there was a little technical problem that they were trying to work out with the message from Ellie's father, Kate could have throttled both her sons.

'Go, Dad!' said the Big Twin.

'What an effort to stuff it up,' said the Little Twin.

'He's such a spud,' and they both laughed. Ellie went bright red.

Ms Carmel Mound, a kind and well-modulated teacher and head of Student Relations, eventually collected the Kennedys.

'Now then, I believe we've sorted out our little glitches. Ellie, this way.'

They were led across the hall to a computer where four seats were placed in a row.

'It was quite a last-minute Skype hook-up so it took a bit of managing, but here we are. We'll go to speaker, shall we?'

There on the screen in front of Ellie Kennedy was her father. He was looking away and speaking to someone behind his computer, then a long thin man with bad make-up and funny hair tried to call her father and pressed a button on the keypad.

'There you go, big fellow. Helloo?'

'Yes, hello there,' said Ms Mound, uncertainly.

'All yours,' said Orlendo.

Kate Kennedy felt sick in her stomach.

Her husband stared out of the screen. 'Hi, Ellie.'

Ellie sat there, silent.

'Ellie?'

'Hi. Hello, Dad.'

Peter Kennedy could see his daughter and sitting beside her, his sons and Kate. He took a deep breath, sighed, then breathed again. He had no idea what to say. And so he said anything.

'Dot points. Always a useful way to construct a conference call, but this isn't a conference call, this is . . . Ellie, it's been a very odd couple of days up here. I sent an email off with some guff that . . . That wasn't guff, but it was stuff that people like me say when they have to say things.' He paused. 'What does that mean? Right, well, it means, maybe dot points are good. One . . .'

He couldn't think, he sat there.

Ellie turned to her mother. Peter heard his daughter sounding so uncertain, 'Mum?'

'Ellie,' he said, and his voice made her turn straight back to the screen. 'Ellie Kennedy, I am your father. And these few days up here, away from you, I've learnt. I've learnt how hard it is to say stuff you really mean. I really mean.'

He closed his eyes tightly for a few seconds.

Kate Kennedy looked at her husband, and she felt quite odd. Not bad odd, but odd.

He opened his eyes. 'I wrote a page of words to you for your father–daughter night and they were words that I meant. I *am* proud of you and I *do* love you and they're words that are true, but they aren't my best words. I wrote them to tick something off a list. *These* are my words.'

Ms Mound gasped slightly in the background. Behind Peter Kennedy's shoulder she could see six people standing in a doorway. Two old people with funny black hair, a tall man in women's bathers, someone who was dressed like they were from Kiss and two very fit-looking men in fluorescent legionnaire caps and shorts.

Ellie saw them and waved, and the group waved back.

'Ellie Kennedy, a man said to me recently that you'll never believe what a few words can do when you need them most. "Come on, you can do it." That's what this man had heard and I've remembered those words. "You can do it." And I can do it. I love you, Ellie Kennedy. I love you because I held you when you were newborn and I hadn't seen anything as lovely as you since I held your great silly brothers. And I saw you take your first steps. And sometimes I can still feel your little hand in mine. Life, Ellie, life is so precious and it goes by so quickly. The friendships, the good times, the happiness, the sorrows. It's all so precious and you know your memories are the greatest possessions you'll hold in your heart and when you share them, especially with people you love, then they glow.'

'Oh, my boy,' whispered Ken Kennedy.

'Life really glows. People can turn bits of bricks and mortar into a living thing; they can turn a house into a home.

'They make you remember people who have gone. Well, they still live somewhere inside of you.

'Ellie Kennedy, I learnt a trick where you just wait. And say nothing, and sooner or later the conversation will come around to something that you can control. It's a good trick. But that's all it is.

'You have your dreams or a secret and sometimes you don't think you can share them because you think people will laugh. Or worse still, you ignore something and wait till the conversation comes around to something that's more comfortable.

'Ellie, if you ever have the privilege of someone giving you their heart, be gentle because it's a part of them they'll be giving you. And if you ever, *ever* have a love that you share with someone, don't waste it. Oh, you know sometimes love ends and things go south, but don't take things for granted, don't let them drift. If there's someone you love then let them know you love them. Your mother . . .'

Peter knew he was running out of time. That awful emotional bubble wasn't going away. Take a deep breath, he thought.

'Your mother . . . I love her more . . . I love her.'

Ellie heard one of her brothers try to stop a little sob. And she smiled. She smiled just like her mother. She lit up the room.

'That,' she said to Ms Mound. 'That's my dad.'

Ms Mound sat very still and said quietly, 'Does he have a brother?'

'Yep,' said the little twin, 'and he's gay.'

'Trust my luck.'

Kate Kennedy sat there and saw Gene Simmons and someone in a baggy one-piece, two old people in Beatles wigs and two men in orange-and-lime shorts move towards a man who had been trying very hard to say what he actually meant.

Her husband.

Chapter Eighteen

It was just after he'd asked his father how he'd gone in the beer section that Greer rang.

'Highly commended.'

'That good?'

'Best I've ever got.'

'Going to try for a place?'

Ken Kennedy tilted his head and smiled at his son. 'Yeah, I reckon I got a few more years left in me.' Then he shuffled away to sell some raffle tickets for the Red Cross with Howard Whittaker.

Peter Kennedy answered his phone.

'Peter.'

'Greer.'

'Got your report.'

'Yep.'

'Yep to you.'

'Well?'

There was a pause and he heard her laugh.

'Peter, you should really design something again.'

'Yep?'

'Yep to you. If we want the showgrounds, all the decrees and gazettes are in a form that we can navigate. The land quality is not great but given time and the right amount of expenditure it could prove a valuable asset. That's pretty clear.'

'Yep, it is.'

There was another pause.

'Did your father really do that for those men?'

'He did.'

'Does it run in the family? Or is it just the water up there in the place where Toranas go to die?'

'What do you mean?'

'The quality of the people. You, Peter, are a good man.'

'Yep?'

'I wanted to let you know we'll be keeping a close eye on the showgrounds. But there's no way we'll be looking seriously at any development for a long, long time. If ever.'

'Yep?'

She laughed. 'Yep to you.' And she hung up.

•

Peter saw his mother in the Cookery Hall; the building for the 'quiet man with a nice laugh, SN 337865 O'Neil, Peter. Pte'. She was furious. 'That bloody fellow has done it again: two firsts and the grand champion.'

Dr Langdon had stretched his winning streak to four in a row. Mary pointed to two cakes in the special decoration section: one in the shape of a rippling male torso in budgie smugglers that would have brought tears to the eyes of Tony Abbott; the other, the grand champion, a roast chicken with Gold Coast 'Meter Maid' bikini tan-marks, sunbaking on a beach complete with a surfboard emblazoned with the message, 'Happy Holidays'. It was, quite frankly, a piece of work that even Salvador Dali would have been keen to add to his K-tel greatest hits album.

'They should show *that* to his prospective clients, that's what they should do, you know!' And Mary went off to grab Pearl for a cup of tea.

Peter wandered around. It really wasn't much of a show, but maybe that wasn't the point; the people who came enjoyed it and it still had a little of that magic about it.

A group of old codgers from the Morse Code Club had set up a line from the entrance to the administration building, so you could send messages the old-fashioned way. They'd be delivered by some Pickersgill Primary students.

Peter had sent one to Pearl. 'I like Swipe, but I love you. That's my line.'

Now and then he could see people being given their messages and hear them laughing. He should go now; he wanted to go home but he hadn't heard from Kate. He decided he would walk down to sideshow alley to see them, the laughing clowns.

A rough-headed man with no teeth running the booth tried with a very loud voice to get him to play.

Peter smiled at him and then watched the turning faces of the clowns. He'd been so scared by them when he was a boy. And he had never told anybody. Like most fears, he supposed, they're worse when you keep them to yourself.

He heard a voice. A kid's voice, and he looked down to see a student dressed in a Pickersgill Primary uniform.

'Hello,' he said.

'You've got a message,' said the kid.

'Have I?'

'Here it is.'

'Thanks.' He opened it, expecting something from Pearl.

'Every player wins a prize,' it read.

He read it again and stood there, staring at the paper, then turned to ask the kid who had sent it. Instead he saw the twins. The big one and the little one. And he saw Ellie. And he saw Kate. They stood at the laughing clowns.

'Every player wins a prize,' said Ellie.

Kate walked up to him and took hold of his hand. She looked into his eyes. 'And you're ours.'

Introducing *The Birdwatcher*
by William McInnes

Chapter One

A group of strangers pushed together for a short time usually ignore each other. Think of a lift: even a happily chatting couple's conversation dwindles to silence in the confines of a shared space.

Most trams are filled with people doing just that: not connecting. But some seem actively to repel it – showing a grumpy face, headphones or intense concentration on a book or magazine. Others don't necessarily *want* to connect, but do show an interest – staring at someone's outfit, listening to phone conversations. Others still, though glancing through the window, seem to be more open, even willing their fellow travellers to connect with them in some way – meeting someone's eyes, offering a small smile, showing recognition of those getting on and off and whether they need a seat. And then there are those people who are neutral and seem to have almost no awareness of where they are or who they're with.

David, a tall Anglo forty-something, grips a hanging strap as he stands on the crowded tram. He scans the carriage and its occupants, noting people's movements and their subtle indications of their intentions. A gentle inclination of an elbow and shoulder from an older woman hints towards a preparation to stand; she moves her bag to her left hand so she can pull the stop buzzer.

Sometimes, he thinks, sometimes, the way a person holds themself really gives you a glimpse of the kind of person they might be – like the young man with the iPad. David regularly sees him on this tram; always dressed neatly in fitted suits, his hair styled and his beard as carefully-kept as his clothes. Always on his iPad, his thumb sweeping across the screen, skimming through whatever it is he usually reads. But today his behaviour isn't the same. He's looking at something on the device, yes, but David can see his thumb moving more slowly across the screen, scrolling back and forth, to and fro. An image or words? The way the man's head tilts slightly, almost imperceptibly, implies to David that it's probably an image. A photograph, he thinks. He watches as the man's hand stays still for a few seconds and then moves back and forth again. Every few minutes he looks away from the screen and sighs, turning to the window, and almost always his left hand comes close to his face, his thumb gently touching a gold band on his ring finger.

Another deep breath. He's upset.

If David cranes his neck and leans forward he'll be able to see the image on the screen. He holds his position, uncomfortably contorted but in an inconspicuous way. Good practice, David thinks to himself.

A shuffle of feet as the other passengers holding the hanging straps move, like birds adjusting their perches on a branch to make room for another, and David sees the iPad screen. It shows a photo of the man on the tram with another man, almost as neatly styled, embracing on a beach. Then an arm covers the screen and the neat young man on the tram sighs again, clearly upset. The passengers in the aisle revert to their original positions.

David resumes his relaxed stance and gently swings on the tram strap. I was right, he thinks. Well, I hope something good happens for you today, Neat Beard.

Then a flash as something passes by outside the window. David looks out; a seagull. His eyes dart, his attention drawn away from his fellow passengers. Two ravens sit on an electric power pole, before one drops swiftly onto the garbage bin below. Imported birds – sparrows and starlings and blackbirds – are everywhere, increasing in number with the density in housing.

A strip along the tramline has been planted with flowering eucalypts. David looks carefully as they pass; honeyeaters are raiding the gum-nut flowers, while red wattlebirds and galahs fly above them. David leans forward to look after them, not noticing his invasion of the seated passenger's space until it's too late; he pulls back clumsily.

'I'm sorry.'

The passenger shrugs. 'No worries.'

David explains. 'Galahs.'

The passenger looks back at his book. David hesitates, about to say something else, before being distracted by an Indian myna bird flying past the window.

The tram approaches its next stop. David lets go of his standing strap and pulls out a very small notebook with attached pencil. The tram comes to a standstill with the familiar jolt so many Melburnians no longer notice, but which can easily hurl an unsuspecting tourist to the floor or, perhaps worse, into one or more of the less approachable locals.

As he waits for the half-dozen people in front of him to get off, David has a last look through the windows and, seeing nothing, writes in his notebook.

Stepping down from the tram, his awareness of other commuters finally kicks in. Some people almost leap off, some take it one step at a time, looking around carefully for cars, while others are already mentally elsewhere, darting quickly across the road. One action, same intent, so much variation.

David joins the city workers on the footpath, taking his usual route. Though long-legged, he walks slowly; a country man's mooch – steady and deliberate. He sees a crested pigeon, four spotted doves, some blackbirds, a thrush, some white-naped honeyeaters and a seagull. He watches the seagull as it takes flight from a garbage bin, following its path against the blue- and ochre-tinted sky. He slows down even more as he walks through a small park, the lawn dappled as the sunlight filters down through the trees and bushes. The grevilleas are blooming, the orange, pink, yellow and red spikes beautiful against the blue–green foliage.

Hearing a sound, David veers away from the path and pauses below a tall tree. He looks up and checks a pair of tawny owls – frogmouths – their nest almost invisible. David smiles, as he does every morning that he sees them; a good day.

Catching a movement in the grevillea, David turns to see what it was: small birds – honeyeaters? No; too small. Silvereyes? He's never seen them here before. He moves to the side of the footpath, letting people go past him, but trying not to unsettle the birds. He watches them flit about. Even though they are only twenty feet or so away, he pulls out a pair of small binoculars, and focuses on the birds. Silvereyes. They are definitely silvereyes; apricot-sized in shades of green feathering into grey, with white rings around their eyes. David continues to watch them for a while, seeing what they are eating. Insects or seeds? Nectar?

Passers-by take notice; David's tall, relatively young and, though not wearing a suit, is clearly dressed for work, so his using binoculars seems out of place, making him look like a private detective, a spy or a creep, rather than a birdwatcher. But people walk on by anyway, as he pulls out a battered notebook. He turns to a page marked '30th Aug', where there is already a list of birds. David jots down the ones he has seen while walking from the tram stop, then adds *Silvereyes (5). East William St (park).*

•

Some time later, David walks upstairs and into an open-plan office. It has various desks – drafting tables – as well as computer stations. He heads to his own seat and dumps his coat, nodding to Rosie, working nearby. She smiles at him.

'Hi, David. There are a few messages for you on your desk.'

David lets his nod be his reply and sits down, turning on his computer. He looks at the screen and after a long moment of nothing happening, sighs.

Go on. Just die.

The computer finally flickers to life, like a fluorescent tube light when it's first switched on.

I don't hate my job, David thinks to himself. I don't. I am on the side of good.

'Have a nice weekend?' Rosie puts a pile of envelopes on his desk.

David shakes his head, shrugging. 'So-so.'

'Did you go away?'

'No, I went to the football. We lost.'

Rosie is ready to speak but David raises his hand in a stop signal.

'I don't want to talk about it. How was your weekend?'

Rosie smiles. 'Lovely. We saw that new movie on Friday night, on Saturday it was Stephanie's dance final plus Pete's step-mum's brother's fiftieth, which was actually a hoot, even though I was dreading it.'

David doodles on the paper in front of him: a bird, it has an amazing sense of character to it, though sketched in just a few lines.

Rosie watches as she continues, 'Then on Sunday Josh had football; of course he has to play in the under-thirteens *and* the under-fifteens so there goes half the day, but then we –' She pauses. David's vague attention has been completely diverted from her to the window, where a bird outside has flown into a tree.

Rosie follows his gaze then looks back to her colleague, waiting. After a full minute, David faces her again. Realising the list of weekend activities is over, he offers up what he knows is a completely inadequate reply.

'That's a lot. Pretty busy.'

Rosie smiles, nearly forgiving.

David adds, 'I don't know how you do it.'

Rosie looks back out the window. 'What bird was that?'

'A black-faced cuckoo-shrike.'

'How can you tell that from here?'

'The way it shuffles its wings when it lands.'

Rosie looks out at the grey-and-black bird and shrugs; unimpressed, dismissive. 'It's never just a blackbird with you, is it?'

David forms a small, apologetic smile until Rosie disappears behind their divider, then sighs and pulls the pile of envelopes towards him.

Then he says, very softly, as he looks out the window at the bird, 'It's a blackbird if it's a blackbird.'

And he smiles.

•

The phone rings and David picks it up.

'Vic Land Care, David Thomas speaking.'

There is no response for a few moments and then, just as he is about to hang up, he hears a call in the background: a crow call; a Torresian crow – *Corvus orru*, only found in the northern parts of Australia. The caller must be a birder.

David's heart leaps a little. Someone has seen something! The crow's call was sharp and harsh: *ar-ar-ar*; an aggressive call, probably defending food from a rival. If it were in a city it would have been picking at something dead by the road. But it sounded too close to the caller to be in a tree and there was traffic noise as well. He can hear the sound of a heavy truck in the background, and remembers when he last heard that particular bird call and type of engine at the same time; it was when he'd passed a troop carrier filled with young soldiers in camouflage uniforms, with short tight haircuts and wearing wraparound sunglasses. And guns. Army. Army town.

Townsville, David thinks. No, wait . . .

He hears another call, though this time not a bird's. It's a man, making a faux bird-call sound, like a mix between a ringing phone and an old ham actor rolling his 'r's as some form of voice warm-up exercise.

It's Noel Barrellon. And if anybody should have been a ham actor, it was Noel.

He ran birding boat trips out to the continental shelf off Wollongong and David had known him for nearly fifteen years. Even when they first met, Noel wasn't simply a large man with a large beard and a large personality; he had always been more than that. He was someone who played Falstaff while wearing an old Illawarra Steelers Rugby League jersey and track pants and who spoke with an accent as broad as his stomach.

But Noel wasn't only a character, he was also real and so was his love affair with birds and his knowledge of the creatures. He had taken to David, because David was very good at listening and if there was anything that Noel loved more than birds, eating, wine and the sound of his own voice, it was being listened to.

His bird call was a signal he gave when he had seen something he thought was special and wanted only a few of his favourites to know about it early.

The first time David had heard it was via a phone call from Noel when a wandering albatross had drifted in from the other side of the world. Even now, he thought it was odd that a living creature would fly from the other side of the world to come to Wollongong. Not that he would ever tell anybody that, though – least of all Noel. Just as he never told Noel that he had seen the wandering albatross a fair while before Noel had given David his bird-call signal.

David doesn't wait for Noel to speak now. 'Noel, what's that crow doing?'

There comes a chortle that sounds like the fat old actor who used to sell Heinz tomato soup in television commercials.

'Well, what do you think he's doing, Dave?'

'It's hopping about by the side of the road over . . . a dead possum.'

There's a pause, then a crow call and then an abrupt, 'Well, bugger me! It *is* a possum. I thought it was a cat. You're on form, Dave.'

'Noel! Long time; how've you been? What are you doing in Townsville?'

There's a disgruntled sigh from Noel before he speaks again. 'Well, now, nobody likes a smart-arse.' Then he laughs. 'On very good form. I've been good; good and busy. Listen, I'm just giving you the nod on a sighting of a pale pygmy magpie goose up here, north of Port; I'm driving up to see it now.'

'A *what*? *Really*? Sure it's not a green-freckled?'

'I dunno . . . Thought that at first, but it was Bill Matthews – he brings the minibus up every year. From Adelaide. Bunch of oldies, but they know what they're doing usually. They saw it this morning, halfway to Mossman. Jeanne Gallie was up there and she just called me. And David – they heard from Noel.'

'Noel?'

'Yeah. He left any messages for you?'

David pauses a moment. He reads the sticky notes before him. *David – PPMG here. Noel – call.* 'Shit.'

'I *thought* you didn't have a tick on it. 'S why I rang.'

'Shit,' he says again, incensed. 'Shit.'

There is a pause. Noel begins to sign off, 'Call me if you get up here.'

'Call me if you see it,' David gets in just before Noel gives his bird call again and hangs up.

David stares at nothing. 'Shit!' Louder this time.

Rosie tentatively pokes her head up over the divider. 'Are you all right?'

David doesn't hear her so she repeats the enquiry, louder. David hears.

'Fine,' he says dismissively, picking up a filled-in form, at first trying to decipher it, then just pretending to decipher it.

Shit, he thinks. Then shakes his head firmly. He brings up a graph system on his computer screen.

David looks at his watch then back to the form. At his watch. At the clock. At the screen.

He logs into his bank account online. It's a pretty sad sight, but there is *some* credit available. He looks up a travel-agency site and starts typing: *Origin: Melbourne. Destination: Cairns.*

There's a flight at eleven to Sydney and one at two to Cairns. He could be there before dark, or at least for first light tomorrow. Thinking, he looks up car hire for a four-wheel-drive. Bloody expensive; ridiculous.

He goes back to his envelopes and pulls out another form but, like a man with a persistent itch, he can't settle. He looks at the calendar and remembers something.

Shit, he thinks. He kicks the table in frustration. Quickly lowering his head before Rosie can respond, he picks up the telephone and dials.

'Hi, is Genevieve Forti there, please?' David swivels on his chair, keeping his back determinedly turned away, but he can almost feel Rosie's stare. He hunches closer to the phone receiver.

'Hello?'

'Hi, Genevieve. It's David. David Thomas.'

Genevieve laughs. 'Hi, David Thomas. And I *do* know which David. Didn't we sleep together last week?'

David winces. 'Well, yeah. Of course. And, um, yeah. It was lovely. You were lovely.'

'*Were?*'

'*Are*, of course. You are. Um . . . This thing on Thursday night, with your friends . . .'

'Yes . . .'

Genevieve doesn't give much away in her tone.

'Is it, um . . . ? I know it's important to you.'

'Yes.'

David struggles through the silence and the building tension. 'I just might have to go away. Only might.'

Another pause, then Genevieve says, 'Only might. So, is there a choice here? Have you got appendicitis or something? Not sure if it's going to perforate? Or is your mother on her deathbed somewhere?'

David pauses, a bit taken aback by the neutrality of the voice combined with the sharpness of the words. 'My mother's already dead,' he says, without thinking.

There is a pause. 'Oh. I'm sorry.' There is an apology in the tone, but one that only admits fault knowing the other is at greater fault. Then there is another pause. Genevieve breaks first. 'So?'

'So. It sounds like I should come.'

'No, you *shouldn't* come; it would have been nice if you had *wanted* to come. What is it you "might" have to do?'

David screws up his face as if knowing his mother will belt him, knowing he is immature, knowing he is wrong, already hating himself, but unable to stop. 'There's a bird I want to see.'

'A bird.'

'I haven't seen it before.'

'What — it only shows itself on a Thursday night?'

'It's in Cairns. Well, north of Cairns . . . I'll be back on Saturday.'

'Cairns? A bird?' Genevieve is incredulous.

David lets his words sit, still grimacing.

'God. The scary thing is I actually believe you!'

David waits, hopeful.

'Well, hey — don't come back on my account. There might be a possum you need to check out. Or an island resort. I mean, if you can just fly to Cairns for a weekend, why wouldn't you want to get out on the reef? Have a strawberry daiquiri or two, find Nemo. It's meant to be beautiful. I wouldn't know myself.'

'Nemo's a fish,' he responds, idiotically. 'Why would I want to go see a fish?' It sounded pretty ordinary to him as soon as he thought it and when he hears the tone of exasperation at the other end of the phone he tries to back-pedal. Or at least buy some time. 'I haven't decided whether to go or not.'

'So you rang me for what? To take me with you? That doesn't seem to have come up.'

David is silent.

'Then why? To give you what — permission? For me to say, "No, that's fine. I don't mind what you do, don't worry about my dinner and my friends," who I told about you because I thought I might have actually met someone halfway fucking decent and reliable?'

David lets her words wash over him, wincing and not unsympathetic. He's heard similar before.

·

David knocks on the thin divider meant to delineate boss from worker, private from public. Being slightly lower than David's height, it does neither.

'Yep?'

Maggie, a middle-aged woman, is going through a mass of papers on a table with a keen young intern, Daisy.

'Hi, Maggie. When does this job have to be finished again?'

Maggie looks at the papers all around her. 'This job is never going to be finished. What you mean is, "When are they going to stop paying us?"'

David offers her a vague apologetic gesture. 'Well, yes.'

'Maybe when everything is extinct, or everything is GM whether we like it or not, or when some sound bite or election bribery transforms our crap amount of money into something decent, or maybe even tonight when I have to submit this yearly funding application report I can't finish writing because my stupid computer that they said they'd "upgrade as soon as possible" three months ago crashed and the technical department has been outsourced and –' She glances at Daisy, all lipstick and eagerness, then stops, sighs and looks at David. 'Why, David?'

'I just need a couple of days off. If I leave now, I could be back on . . .' David mentally calculates, 'Friday. By lunchtime. Leave without pay.'

Maggie gestures towards the papers everywhere.

David pleads. 'It's barely two days . . . There's a bird I've got to see.'

Maggie sighs again, almost defeated already. Then she makes a little jutting movement with her chin.

David knows she'll turn to her laptop.

She turns to her laptop. 'A bird, huh?'

He nods.

'What's it called?'

'Pale pygmy magpie goose. PPMG.'

She nods. 'Sounds like an accounting firm. Wikipedia okay?'

'It should give you an idea.'

'So sure of yourself, David.' But she's smiling. It's a game and it's obvious she likes him – or something about him, something she's interested in trying to uncover. But she realises she hasn't got that much time and she juts her chin out a bit further. 'This thing better be special . . .'

David sits down. He gives her a look that says, *It is*.

'It *is* an accounting firm!' Maggie laughs. 'And some other silly bloody thing: a media management group in Beverley Hills and a . . .' She clicks onto something else and gives a hoot. 'A nice big blackfella with bad ears. Good suit, though. Oh, the joys of a browse on the web.'

David stares at her.

'He's a boxer and he's had his fiftieth birthday and your PPMG have hosted it for him. Na, they hosted the official after-party for his fiftieth. Wanker. Oh well. Evander Holyfield. And he's even got a foundation named after him. His ears – his ears really are bad.'

'One was bitten.'

'What?'

'One was bitten in a fight.'

Maggie stares at him.

'Another boxer called Mike Tyson bit his ear.'

'True?'

He nods.

'You blokes. A fella bit my ear once. Well, he nibbled it. On a date. Thought I should return the favour.'

David looks at her pen. She twirls it a bit. Not the whole way around. She's thinking.

'Thank God I had a bit of a look down his ear. Wasn't pretty – put me off custard for a while.'

David makes a face.

'Oh yeah, it's all right for you. You blokes want us girls to go all Star Trek on your bits and pieces. Boldly go where no girl should ever go. Here's your bird.'

They stare at each other.

Maggie twirls the pen between her fingers. Still not the whole way around.

'It's rare.'

'Very rare. Endangered.'

'Can see that. What makes it different from the pale pygmy goose?' She's looking at some other webpage.

'Well, it's pied. Predominantly black with white end markings and it's got the pale nape and bill. Iridescent green when it's mating season, but other times a pale green.'

Maggie nods. 'You still seeing that nice Italian girl? What was her name . . . Genny?'

'Genevieve.'

'Yeah. She ever bitten your ear?'

'No.' He suddenly felt something nearing shame. 'She's not likely to be biting anything of mine in the near future. Or ever, really.'

Maggie stops twirling the pen and looks at him. She shakes her head. 'She was really nice. What's a dabbling duck?'

'It's a water bird that feeds from the surface, or just below. It doesn't dive, but the PPMG isn't really a part of that group – it's got lineage from a Gondwanan waterfowl. And it sings.'

Maggie looks at him. 'You making this up?'

'You want that on Wikipedia. It sings, the only waterfowl that sings. It is a very special bird.'

'That girl Genevieve and her not biting you in the foreseeable future – or ever . . . That got anything to do with the singing goose?'

David just looks at her and repeats almost helplessly that it's a very special bird.

If she twirls her pen in her left hand all the way around in a circle, flipping it gently between her fingers like a marching girl leader flipping a baton, then he'll be okay.

She flips the pen – but not all the way.

'I'm not filling in one extra form for you. Not one word. Forge my signature if you have to.'

'I'll do it all.' David moves to the cupboard and finds the leave forms. He smiles at Maggie. 'Thanks Maggie. You're a brick,' he says, before starting to walk away.

'A brick. Great.' Maggie mutters after him, deadpan. Then, louder, 'Don't you get tired of just wanting to tick stuff off? You ever want to stop long enough to really get to know one thing?'

'Does anyone, Maggie? You can see things; know what someone or something will do. But does anyone ever really *know* one thing?'

Daisy looks between them both. 'Maggie jutted her jaw out,' she says, as if to disprove David's point.

'You know my dad travelled all over – never settled – for years. Until he ended up in a village in Thailand watching some old guy fishing. Then the old guy catches a big fish and he's suddenly happy.'

David stands with the leave forms in his hand.

'Sure, it's a big fish, but this old guy seems so happy. My father went and asked him how long he'd been waiting to catch the fish.'

There is a silence. Then Daisy says, 'How long?'

'Well,' says Maggie, 'the old guy thinks a little and takes the hook out of the fish and holds it up and then looks at my dad and says, "For a fish like this I waited sixty years." Then he looks at the fish and says almost to himself, "Sixty years." And then lets the fish go.'

'Why did he let the fish go?' asks Daisy.

'Because he said he suddenly understood the fish. And he understood that all he wanted to do was catch it, not eat it. The river was full of little fish he could eat almost any time. He got to know the big fish and himself, what he wanted. So he let it go.'

'What did your dad say?' asks David.

Maggie doesn't say anything and Daisy looks between her and David.

Maggie takes a deep breath. 'He said he didn't know whether the old guy was wise or a bloody fool but that he knew it was time to come home and stop wandering.'

'You keep moving, you keep learning . . .' David smiles softly.

'Isn't that just skimming the surface of knowing something?'

'It's only a few days.' He smiles. 'And it's a bird, not a fish.'

She does the thing with her jaw. 'You're just being a dabbling duck – just interested in the surface, not what's down below.'

David stares back.

'One day, David Thomas, Mr Bird Know-it-all, you're going to chase something and actually find it. And you're going to have to decide whether you really understand what finding it means. It's the old-guy-and-the-fish moment. Maybe this singing goose of yours is going to make you decide if you really want to learn.'

She looks at him and he sees something in her eyes that he has never seen before. She's looking right at him, as if she's trying to sense his essence. Like a birder. She stops jutting her chin and the pen makes a full circle in her hands. Then Maggie winks at Daisy. 'Bloody whitefellas. Always wanting to go walkabout. Bloody unreliable.'

•

Rosie is waiting back at the cubicle.

David smiles as he shuts down his computer and puts his jacket back on, tries a joke. 'Maggie's the only person I know who can panic in slow motion.'

'She's not letting you go . . . ? Just like that?'

David starts shoving things in a bag. 'Leave without pay. I'll be back on Friday.'

Rosie frowns, cross. 'We want them to renew this project. We have to meet the deadline. It's the best job I've had for ages. I feel like I'm doing something really worthwhile.'

'We're compiling reports that nobody's even going to look at. The only way they'll make a national park is if some stupid opinion poll tells them we have to.'

Rosie feels the blow, but stands firm. 'That's cynical.'

David feels the return blow, but shrugs and buttons his jacket.

'They still need the information. They still need people to try. Walking down the street with protest signs doesn't tell the real picture. The figures tell the real picture.'

David feels mean. 'I know. You know I care. And God – I need the job too. I'll be back on Friday.'

•

David walks home from work the same way he walked there – still clocking birds, but moving faster. The silvereyes have gone, but a willie wagtail is on the lawn, doing its signature dance, desperately trying to draw attention away from its partner's nest, to an oblivious audience of passers-by.

David sees a tram coming and, surprisingly for a usually slow mover, runs fast to board it.

•

David's flat is above a shop. The entrance is actually behind the shop, reached by a small lane off the side street, which adds a half-kilometre to the route from his flat to the tram stop, which is right outside the shopfront. But David has lived there for many years and seen shopkeepers come and go. When the system works, the shopkeepers are able to use David's downstairs kitchen and outside bathroom, and he uses their entrance.

When he first found the place, the shop and flat were both owned by the proprietors of Mahanis' Pet Supplies, a family-run pet shop. David had always hated the idea – and usually the reality – of caged birds, but the family was eccentrically endearing, and loved their pets so much they often adopted them when they couldn't face selling them, which meant that David could set aside his usual judgements. He had seen both Mr and Mrs Mahanis and their daughters refuse to sell pets to customers they thought weren't 'right' for an animal.

David had an unrequited crush on their eldest daughter Eirene for a time, and still smiles at a memory of her explaining falsely and at length why a particular customer just wasn't a good enough fit for her favourite hermit crab. The crab hadn't moved during its viewing for the potential sale, so Eirene had 'translated' its behaviour to the man and his daughter.

'Put your hand in again and we'll see if he's getting used to you . . . Oh no, oh, that's not good. Sorry, you've upset him . . . What's wrong with you today, Hermie?'

The little had girl removed her hand.

Eirene had carried on. 'He's very nervous, shy, but also, I have to confess, aggressive. He was treated badly as a little crab and now . . . Well, he finds it hard to like people. It's so sad. I think Hermie's incapable of love.'

The little girl had looked increasingly doubtful as she listened to Eirene wax lyrical about the joy the right pet can bring, before being sent away with a goldfish she didn't really like, but which Eirene had assured her was more capable of loving eight-year-old girls than any other fish, more capable in fact than any other marine creature she had ever known.

•

Eirene had married years ago and taken a position at the Werribee zoo, where she now managed its captive breeding programs, established to rescue endangered species from certain extinction. The Mahanises' second daughter, Zoe, was finishing a Law and Arts degree in between stints of volunteer work at refugee camps around the world, happily slaughtering chickens and goats to feed the hungry. David's friendship with the whole family had gradually enlightened him about the world of animal and human interaction.

The older generation of Mahanises had finally retired, worn down not so much by their age, but by the pointless battle against the proliferation of chain pet stores in shopping malls, and the couple's increasing inability to sell anything as they deemed more and more people unfit for pet ownership. They had packed up their menagerie and taken it home to Glenroy, where David still visited them from time to time. They had let David stay in the flat for as long as he wanted with low rent in exchange for his agreeing to share his bathroom and kitchen with the new tenants of the shop and the better rent they would get as a result. They also left him Mr Peachy.

During the Mahanises' occupancy, David had grown very fond of Mr Peachy, their tame and talkative cockatiel. It had its own cage, but the door was never closed and it treated

David's flat as part of its territory, too. It would follow him up the staircase behind the shop's back door and into the light and spacious multi-purpose room, or down the short hall to the kitchen, where an old, unusable wood-fired stove left just enough space for an electric cooker, narrow bench and a table with two chairs.

Today, the fridge still lives with the washing machine and the shower in the lean-to shed outside the back door. And leaning against the lean-to is the toilet, the plank door only big enough to cover the mid-section of a seated person. When David was seated, Mr Peachy would often perch on the top of the door and offer him words of encouragement, and equally pompous discouragement to any potential bird visitors.

•

David jumps off the tram and enters the shop, currently a gift shop selling mostly scented candles and recycled retro home wares. The business is owned by a stockbroker's wife, helping to ease her husband's tax problems, and staffed by a self-identifying interior decorator called Janice. David thinks of the Mahanises, missing them. He waves a brief hello to Janice, busy with a customer.

'I really think you'll love this collection of pillowcases with the elegant dancing-bear motif – because *I* love them and you seem to be very similar in your tastes to me.'

The customer, a woman with ironed blonde hair and a face graced with a surgeon's refinements, nods back.

'You know –' says Janice. 'Eclectic everyday quirky.'

'Yes, yes, yes. The elegant dancing bear,' says the customer.

David shivers a little and heads out the back and upstairs. He opens his front door and feels a pang for Mr Peachy, even though two years have passed since he died. He can still remember the morning he found Mr Peachy on the sofa, motionless and hunched, as if playing, ready to bounce up and prattle.

He had held the tiny bird in his hand, felt its warmth; Mr Peachy must have only just died. He cupped the creature in his hands for a good while; he didn't know how long exactly, but long enough for the warmth to go and the body to stiffen.

No movement.

No life.

Mr Peachy.

He thought of what the Mahanises would have done. Probably weep. But David hadn't. He'd held the bird's body and looked at it. No, he wouldn't weep; he was too busy trying to understand something: it was just a bird, and a fairly common one at that. But it was also Mr Peachy. His conflicting feelings had unnerved him slightly and he couldn't quite explain why.

For some reason, remembering this made Genevieve Forti spring to mind. He knows something has passed and he tries to explain to himself why he feels a catch in his chest. He stands still for a moment, and then shakes his head and moves over to his desk.

•

David's big room is still full of birds, though non-living ones; fine drawings, loose sketches and beautifully rendered watercolours, one of which lies half-done on the table beneath the window, surrounded by coloured inks, crayons and pens.

Another, in a tea-tree wood frame, sits by a window. It's a painting of a cockatiel: Mr Peachy. David doesn't look but he knows it's there and he claps his hands like the pleasant-looking blonde actor from *I Dream of Jeannie*, to dispel the memory.

Then he thinks, She did it with arms folded and a nod of her head. So he does that, too, and laughs a little.

He also has a collection of prints of Australian birds; some look like the rescued items from the op shop they actually are, while others – gifts – are museum quality, signed and numbered. There are also various Gould League certificates, including one from his childhood; a brightly coloured detailed print on glossy paper, with 'Daffid Thomas' printed neatly in the space for the new junior member. Finally, there are collections of bird magazines, books on birds, plants and trees, as well as many maps.

•

David rushes about – experienced and quick at packing a suitable-for-air-travel swag – but still stops to insert the notebook containing his tram bird list, pulled from a large and neat pile of notebooks on the table. Next to that pile are other piles, neatly labelled with dates going back over the last twenty years. He packs three empty 'field' notebooks, a battered old ornithology guide, a small telescope and tripod, his larger set of binoculars and a watercolour set with paper in his swag. Finished, he does a mental then visual check of the room, pats his pocket to confirm he has his smaller binoculars and a pen, as well as his wallet, then locks the front door and leaves the flat.